Praise for

"Like McCarthy's Border Trilogy or Frazier's *Cold Mountain,* this is American literature at its best, full of art and beauty and the exploration of all that is good and bad in the human spirit." —*Kirkus Reviews* (starred review)

"This is a masterpiece that deserves a full serving of accolades." —*Booklist* (starred review)

"Brown's expressive language captures the harsh realities of the South at the time. A nail-biting journey from first page to last." —*Library Journal* (starred review)

"A Civil War odyssey in the tradition of Charles Frazier's *Cold Mountain* and Daniel Woodrell's *Woe to Live On,* written in a vernacular that resurrects the era and fully brings alive Callum and Ava's adventures on the road." —*Publishers Weekly*

"Like [Charles] Frazier, [Brown's] narrative often verges on the edge of poetry. . . . *Fallen Land* confirms Brown as a talent to watch." —*StarNews* (Wilmington)

"A story of love and loyalty set within the madness and chaos of war, *Fallen Land* is also a thrilling fugue, in both senses: of flight, and intricate composition. It is also the story of a revenge quest, the horrors of Sherman's March, a noble horse named Reiver, of sacrifice, endurance, and redemption. No one who reads *Fallen Land* will ever forget it. In this first novel Taylor Brown proves himself a fresh, authentic, and eloquent new voice in American fiction." —Robert Morgan, author of *Gap Creek, Boone,* and *The Road from Gap Creek*

"A shattering debut that puts one strongly in mind of the young Cormac McCarthy, and the best historical fiction I've read in ages." —Pinckney Benedict, author of *Town Smokes, The Wrecking Yard,* and *Dogs of God*

"It is rare thing for a writer to have the talent and scope to exhibit both the worst and best of humanity in one book, much less in one scene, but that's what Brown does here: he literally floods the page with violent beauty and devastating grace. Well-known and oft-praised writers will look back on long and storied careers only to wish they had written a debut novel as flawless as *Fallen Land*." —Wiley Cash, author of *A Land More Kind Than Home*

"Taylor Brown has given us the wonderful tale of Callum, who will make his way through his own private Civil War. His is not so much a war of grand battles and armies, but a real war of personal survival. Powerfully written, wonderfully told, *Fallen Land* needs to be part of every collection of great storytelling of the American Civil War."

—Robert Hicks, author of *The Widow of the South* and *A Separate Country*

"Harrowing and haunting, Brown's novel travels through the brutality of the Civil War, the desperate yearning of young love, and the glint of hope that can illuminate tragedy. Thanks to Brown's genius, you don't just read this book—you inhabit it." —Caroline Leavitt, *New York Times* bestselling author of *Is This Tomorrow* and *Pictures of You*

"A literary gem . . . If you liked Charles Frazier's *Cold Mountain,* you probably will enjoy *Fallen Land.*"

—*Star Tribune* (Minneapolis)

"Taylor Brown reminds us that the written word is both alive and well here in the American South."

—SouthernLiving.com

"Filled with metaphor, poetic imagery, and rich descriptions, *Fallen Land* is a beautifully written chronicle of love and hardship."

—*BookPage*

Fallen Land

Fallen Land

Taylor Brown

St. Martin's Griffin New York

This is a work of fiction. All of the characters, organizations, and events portrayed in this novel are either products of the author's imagination or are used fictitiously.

FALLEN LAND. Copyright © 2015 by Taylor Brown. All rights reserved.
Printed in the United States of America.
For information, address St. Martin's Press, 175 Fifth Avenue, New York, N.Y. 10010.

www.stmartins.com

Designed by Molly Rose Murphy

The Library of Congress has cataloged the hardcover edition as follows:

Names: Brown, Taylor, 1982– author.
Title: Fallen land : a novel / Taylor Brown.
Description: First edition. | New York : St. Martin's Press, 2016.
Identifiers: LCCN 2015037367| ISBN 9781250077974 (hardcover) | ISBN 9781466893078 (e-book)
Subjects: LCSH: Survival—Fiction. | Brigands and robbers—Fiction. | United States—History—Civil War, 1861–1865—Fiction. | Historical fiction. | Love stories. | BISAC: FICTION / Literary. | FICTION / Historical.
Classification: LCC PS3602.R722894 F35 2016 | DDC 813/.6—dc23
LC record available at http://lccn.loc.gov/2015037367

ISBN 978-1-250-11684-0 (trade paperback)

Our books may be purchased in bulk for promotional, educational, or business use. Please contact your local bookseller or the Macmillan Corporate and Premium Sales Department at 1-800-221-7945, extension 5442, or by e-mail at MacmillanSpecialMarkets@macmillan.com.

First St. Martin's Griffin Edition: January 2017

10 9 8 7 6 5 4 3 2 1

This book owes much to the traditional ballads of Ireland and Appalachia. To the musicians who keep alive those old songs of horse thieves and highwaymen, lovers and lonesome pines—thank you.

Author's Note

Though Ava and Callum are creations of my imagination, and *Fallen Land* is by no means a history book, I endeavored to interweave my characters' story with the world as it was at the time. Many of the episodes in the book are drawn from first-person accounts and historical record, and I would be remiss not to mention the authors and scholars whose work helped me in this process: Virgil Carrington Jones, *Gray Ghosts and Rebel Raiders: The Daring Exploits of the Confederate Guerillas* (Promontory Press, 2004); Noah Andre Trudeau, *Southern Storm: Sherman's March to the Sea* (Harper Perennial, 2009); David Power Conyngham, *Sherman's March Through the South: With Sketches and Incidents of the Campaign* (HardPress Publishing, 2012); Joseph H. Ewing, *Sherman at War* (Morningside Bookshop, 1992); and Major John Scott, *Partisan Life with Colonel John S. Mosby* (Harper & Brothers, 1867).

Fallen Land

Chapter 1

Pale light crept into the black stanchions of pine, the ashen ground, the red center of dying coals. The camped men rose, silent, and broke the bread of old pillage between blackened fingers. One of their number looked at his own. Soot and powder, ash and dirt. Neat crescents accrued underneath the nails, trim and black, like he'd tried to dig himself out of a hole in the ground. Or into one.

Some of the others chewed loudly, bread dry in dry mouths. No tins rattled. There was no coffee, not for some days. He always wanted to talk in this quiet of early morning, to speak something into the silence that assembled them into the crooked line of horsemen. No colors among the trees. No badges, no uniforms. He wanted to ask what peace might be gained if they hovered here longer in the mist, did not mount and ride. But they always did.

So he sprang up first. He shoved the last crust down his

gullet and kicked old Swinney where his britches failed him, an inordinance of cloven white flesh.

"Goddamn katydid," said Swinney, second in command.

"Least I ain't a old ash-shitter."

"You be lucky to get this old, son. Right lucky this day and age."

The boy set his cap on bold.

"Lucky as you?"

Old Swinney hawked and spat a heavy clot of himself into the coals.

"Luckier."

They rode horses of all colors, all bloods. "Strays," they called them, tongue in cheek. Horses that offered themselves for the good of the country, under no lock and key. The quality of a man's mount was no measure of rank, a measure instead of luck and cunning and sometimes, oftentimes, cruelty.

The boy went to mount his own, a fly-bitten nag with a yellow-blond coat in some places, gray patches of hairless skin in others. She'd been a woman's horse once, most likely. The men used to joke about this. Then one of their favorites, an informal company jester, had been blown right from her back. The mare had stood there unmoved, flicking her ears, biting grass from the trampled soil. No one save the Colonel enjoyed a horse so steady. They left off joking.

The boy stuck one cracked boot into the stirrup, an ill-formed shape clanged from glowing iron by an idiot smithy. Or so the men had told him. They told him many such things, their faces fire-bitten and demonic over the cookfire, the embers circling them like burning flies. The boy believed them all. Never the facts, the names, the settings. But what they were getting at, this he believed. There was faith in their eyes, so black and silvered—like the move of steel in darkness.

Rays of dawn shot now through the black overhang of trees, spotting the ground with halos of warped design. The rest of the men slung themselves into their saddles, a cadre of stiff-jointed grunts, and some of them stepped their horses into the light unawares. The boy saw them go luminous among the black woods, specterlike. Like men elected to sainthood. Faces skull-gone, mouths hidden in the gnarled bush of their beards, showing only their teeth. The equipage of war hung by leather belts, pistols and knives and back-slung scatterguns of all gauges. This hardened miscellany jolted and clanked as their horses tapered into the long, irregular file of their occupation.

They rode the forest until the white face of the sun hung right above them and the insects clouded so thickly that men soiled their cheeks and foreheads with dirt or ash from the previous night's fire. The horses flicked the mosquitoes from their rumps with their tails, the skin of man and animal growing spattered with spots of blood. They came finally to the verge of a small green valley of sparse trees. There was a farmhouse down there, a barn. Out of habit they stopped for lunch, though there was little to drink and less to eat. They stopped within the cover of the trees so as not to be seen from the valley below.

When the boy dismounted his horse, old Swinney slapped him on the shoulder.

"Welcome to Virginny," said the old man.

"Virginia?" said the boy, his eyes going wide with wonder.

"That's right. Colonel wants you to see if they got anything to eat down there."

The boy nodded. He crept toward the edge of the trees, his face dark amid the shadows. He could feel the older men's eyes upon him, their ears attuned to the snap of stick or shrub.

They listened because he made no sound, this boy, the lightest of foot among them. Their scout. A former horse thief whose skills translated readily to their pursuits. At last he stared down upon the rough-planked barn, the once-white house, the single white pig mired in a sagging pen of mud. He stared down upon Virginia for a long time, a stranger unto this country. Then he turned his head and made a whip-poor-will's whistle over his shoulder.

When he returned, the men of the troop, thirty-odd strong, were tightening their holsters and sighting their rifles, sliding their knives back and forth in their sheaths, back and forth, making sure no catches might slow the draw. The boy carried a French dueling pistol of uncommon caliber. He mounted up and pulled the heavy J-shaped weapon from his belt and thumbed the hammer back. The filigreed metal of the action spun and clicked into place. The rich wood frame was scarred by countless run-ins with his belt buckle, tree branches, roots where he'd dropped the thing practicing his pistoleer skills.

Swinney stood below him.

"You got any bullets left for that thing, boy?"

The boy held the pistol toward him butt-first.

"She's a firecracker," he warned, smiling.

When the older man reached for the pistol, the boy dropped it sideways from his hand and hooked it upside down by the trigger guard and spun the gun upon its axis, catching it by the backstrap, the trigger fingered, the barrel at Swinney's chest, the older man's eyes wide with fright.

"Let them sons of bitches learn the hard way," said the boy.

In fact, he did not have any bullets. He was out.

Swinney's eyes narrowed and he shook his head.

"What you need is a good ass-whooping, boy. Not them parlor tricks."

The boy spun the gun and stuck it in his belt.

"Now don't you go getting jealous on me, Swinney."

The older man, his keeper of sorts, made a derisive gesture and waddled down the line.

The provenance of the pistol was known—one of a pair from the vast arms collection of a Union sympathizer whose home they'd raided. The boy's first of such prizes. He'd been promptly swindled of one of the guns in a bet over the estimated height of a sycamore that was fated for firewood. That left him one pistol and five balls for the smoothbore barrel. Two went to target practice, one to drunken roistering, one to a duel with a blue jay on a fence post (lost), and the last plumb lost along the way.

He could only wait now for another of his comrades to fall. Be first to scavenge.

"Hey, Swinney," he called. "You think they're down there? Any villains?"

"Somebody is," said the fat man, turning back down the line.

The boy sat astride his horse and made ready to maraud. When their leader rode past, the boy could smell him. The Colonel was riding the line with words of exhortation, of courage and duty and triumph. He had long curly locks, dark as crow feathers, flying loose under a plumed hat. He wore four Colt revolvers on his belt, butt-forward, and carried two dragoon pistols in saddle holsters, and he wore fine riding boots that went up to his knees. He was the man who had once poled across the foggy Potomac in the dead of night to ambush the Maryland Guards in their sleep. The man who had kidnapped a Northern general from a hotel room in West Virginia, pulling him from the bed he shared with a purchased negress. He was the man who had blown more Baltimore & Ohio Railroad bridges than anyone, and captured at least one of those B&O trains for his own profit, keeping the gold, and been stripped of his commission for it. His battalion of Partisan Rangers had been disbanded, some said by order of Lee himself, but for these few who remained. He led them through the hills on missions their own.

The Colonel rode out into the light and struck his saber heavenward, no gleam upon the corroded blade. The band spurred their horses' bellies at the slashed order of charge, dropping down into the valley upon a thunder of hooves. The cavalcade fanned out as they descended, tearing divots from the soft turf. The boy, so scant of weight, pulled ahead of many in the onrush. He was not first to the house but first onto the porch, his horse needing no dally to stay her. The porch planks gave beneath his boots, sodden or thin-cut or both. The door was standing wide and he ducked into the sudden dark. Pistol first, knife second. The ceilings were low, the furniture neat. No roaches scattered before him. No people. Other men clamored through the door behind him. Outside, war whoops and the squeal of the slaughtered pig.

No one in the front rooms, the rear, the kitchen. He found the stairs and shot upward into the blue dark of the second floor, the balls of his feet hardly touching the steps, the point of his blade plumbing the gloom like a blind man's stick. The curtains were all drawn, the floor dark. He stepped from one room into another. Quilted beds neatly made, wardrobe of cheap wood. Then he crossed the threshold into still another room, this the darkest.

He swung the pistol toward her white back, the dark hair all upon its contours like a black eddy of stream water. She had not heard him, was watching the other door. Her thin shift was open at the back, skin and cloth pale as bone. He swallowed, suddenly nervous, and realized how hungry he was, his stomach drawn up empty inside him. Heart, heart, heart again. It sounded in the cavity of his chest. The pistol began to quiver like a pistol should, whelmed with power.

His voice a whisper: "Ma'am?"

She spun on bare feet, kitchen knife clutched to chest, face silly-hard with courage, fear.

"Which side?" she asked him.

"It don't matter which."

She was not looking at him, not listening, either, staring instead into the black tunnel of the barrel like she might jam the pike by willpower alone.

He looked at her and then at the gun, kinking his wrist to better see the thing. An object foreign to him. He lowered it to his side and sheathed the knife as well, and the two of them stood staring at each other, unspeaking.

"What's your name?" he asked finally, dry-mouthed, his words hardly crossing the six feet of space that separated them.

She pointed the kitchen knife at him.

"Ava. Any closer and I kill you."

The floorboards jolted, steps upon the stairs. He shot across to her, past the blade.

"You got to hide."

"Nowhere to," she said. "I'll take my chances."

"They ain't good."

A bearded sharecropper with tobacco-juiced lips, black-gritted, clopped into the room. The boy knew him but not his name, not at this moment. A Walker Colt hung loosely in the man's hand. He saw the girl and smiled.

"Christmas come early," he said.

The boy stood beside the girl, his mouth agape. She spoke to him without looking.

"You a man, or I got to protect my own self?"

His mouth closed. Slowly he raised the dueling pistol, ornate and empty, at the older man's heart.

"I don't reckon it's Christmas yet," he said.

The man spat a black knot on the floor and leveled his pistol at the boy, casual-like.

"Now Mr. Colt here, he beg to differ."

The boy went to thumb back the hammer of his weapon, but back it was.

"Where them pistol tricks, boy?"

"Don't reckon I need them."

Black caulking divided the man's teeth.

"You killed yet?"

"Plenty."

"No. I knowed you was a virgin the day we took you on. I knowed by plain sight and I know it still. You want to be a man? Tell you what, I'll let you watch."

The fingers of his free hand began to unbutton his britches as he walked slowly across the room, legs straddled.

The boy put the palm of his hand against the girl's belly to push her behind him, and her waist was as tiny and delicate as his idea of what was fragile in the world.

"No," said the boy to the sharecropper. "No."

The man kept coming.

"No."

At last the boy lunged, unsheathing his knife, and a white crack exploded inside his head, and dreaming or dying he felt his blade plunge into the liquid underbelly of all that might have happened. All that would have. He saw her eyes come over him, blue rimmed, the pupils deep and black and wide as wells. All for him. Then darkness.

Hands upon his face, his brow. Palms smooth. Tough but smooth, callus-shaven. No scratching, no frictive grit. A voice like running water. The layers that bound him were cut away, piece by piece, until he was naked, unwooled, committed to dark.

In and out for hours, days. Drifting. Sometimes there were voices over him, whispers and orders he could not decipher. He floated in a world his own, dark with nightmare. Dreams of his past, fevered, like the night of the wreck. The men he pushed under, the men who pushed him. Ladders of them, limb-conjoined, wanting for air. The spouts of exhalation, gargle-mouthed. The groan of the ship sinking beneath them, sucking them under. The white jet of expelled air, last of the pockets that saved him, shooting him to the surface, white-birthed.

Then and now black-whirled. Nightmare and memory.

The ship gone, the waves high. The pale slit of coast, like snow. The beach underneath his feet, his knees, his face. Then the lopsided shack, the man called Swinney who nursed him on fish and whiskey, who took him in as a father might, and then the Colonel, who took them all. After that the land grown mountainous, and meaner, and scarecrow men who haunted the ridges, and rib-boned horses beneath them, and always the hunger, insatiable, and the wagons raided, and the barns and the farmhouses, and never so much blood.

With these fever dreams came the vomiting. Hot on his

chest, aprons of himself expelled. Sickness and sweat and instruments on his skin, metal-cold.

One day he could hear the words of the men over his sickbed:

"How long's he been like this?"

"Couple days. Took that long to find you."

"How old is he?"

"Couldn't really say, Doc."

"He's hardly even whiskered."

"Well."

"Well, where did he come from?"

"Shipwreck off the coast, blockade-runner."

"Immigrant? Another Irish, with sympathies?"

"Could be. What's that matter to you?"

"Niggers turned inside out is what they are. They don't fight for us."

"This one does."

"Well, he won't be fighting for anything, this swelling doesn't diminish."

"You best hope it do, Doc."

"Shall I, Mr. Swinney?"

"Otherwise you might find yourself there beside him. Untongued."

"Where is your commanding officer?"

"Don't you worry your head about it."

"Where is he?"

"With the girl. And you, Doc. You with me."

Days later the sickbed gone, the house, too, his world beginning to sway and totter beneath him, uncertain of step. It expanded and collapsed and sweated and snorted, a ribbed joinery articulating beneath him as though the surface of the world had sprung from engines hot and deep beneath the soil and rock.

Sometimes he could not sit the horse, too dizzy, so they laid him belly-down across the torso of a horse with no saddle, his head lying against one of the flaring sides. In daylight, the sun leered sickeningly above him, the trees all warped and gnarled, the world ugly and pale and mean. He shut his eyes against the light. Nightfall, he was led stumbling to void himself in the trees, liquid and quaking. A round man, gone strange to him, leading him by a length of rope.

Swinney, he realized.

He came back into the world but slowly. The ground growing more certain, the light less painful. The dreams shorter. The pain duller. Then he was back in it, all at once, and it was hunger that brought him. He awoke on the back of the horse. The light was slanted, late afternoon, and he had never been so hungry. He tried to wrestle loose and found himself rope-bound to the animal like a sack of feed or beans or other provision.

He called out when someone walked past, his voice strange with disuse. Before long another man stood beside him, unhitching the ropes with thick fingers. He slid to the ground and leaned against the horse. The blood receded from his vision, leaving old Swinney standing there before him, loose loops of rope in his hand. The boy rubbed the chafed skin at his wrists. He touched his head lightly, the bandage, the long crust of blood.

"I a prisoner, Swinney?"

Swinney shook his head.

"No, boy."

"Should I be?"

"Colonel said you done him a favor puncturing that son of a bitch. Said he never did like him."

"So is he . . ."

Swinney nodded.

"Bled out. Colonel's orders."

"And the girl?"

Swinney turned from him.

"Come with me, boy. You need to eat."

They walked toward the light of the fire. The boy staggered along behind, finding his legs. He was still disoriented, his boots tripping along the ground.

"Where are we?" he asked.

Swinney was to the left of him. He said something, but the boy didn't quite hear him. He stepped closer.

"What?"

Swinney answered again. Again the boy didn't catch his words, not fully. He stopped and clamped his nostrils and blew to clear out his ear canals.

Swinney came around to the front of him.

"Your ear?"

The boy tapped his left one, just underneath the bandage. Swinney came around to that side of him and leaned forward to whisper into the ear. The boy heard only strange mufflings, like the whisper of a foreign language.

"I can't hear," he told Swinney.

The older man came around to his good ear and patted him on the shoulder.

"I said, a few days north of that farmhouse. It's been near a fortnight. Doctor said you was bad concussed. Ear ain't much to lose, considering what you could of."

The boy nodded. "North," he said, mostly to himself.

Swinney looked at him a long moment. His belly shook.

"Lucky dog," he said. He turned.

The boy thought to say something, but nothing came.

He followed the old man the rest of the way to the fire, the men and horses glazed with flame. The boy sat on the white heart of a hickory stump, and the others showed him their smiles, yellow-toothed, dark-gummed. He cocked his good ear toward the fire. They handed him a tin of stewed pork and he slurped down its contents in a single go.

When he handed back the empty tin, he saw the sleeve of his coat.

One of the men leaned into the fire, showing his face.

"She sewn it for you," he said.

"We had to cut away your old," said Swinney. "We was going to give you Oldham's."

"Oldham?" said the boy.

"Man you killed," said somebody. "Probably you ought to know his name."

"You know all their names?" the boy asked him.

A chuckle rose multilunged from men's chests, choral.

"She wasn't wanting you to wear Oldham's," said Swinney. "She sewn you that one out of old what-have-you."

"Rags and quilts and such."

"Bedsheets, too."

"I heard scraps of old Oldham hisself."

"A coat of many colors."

"Yea," said another man. "Like Joseph's of old."

The boy held the sleeves toward the fire's orbit. Ribbons and patches of cloth cross-laced the coat, thick-stitched. He stood among the men and worked his arms inside the coat and found the cut of it closer than any he'd ever worn, his small frame normally swallowed in volumes of wool. This one hugged him like a second skin. He thought of who'd stitched it, of how she must know the contours that shaped him.

"How is she?" he asked them.

They rustled. No one spoke.

"What the hell y'all done to her?"

The boy looked around, his face darkened.

"Should I of stuck every last one of you? That it?"

One man, then another, put a hand to his knife.

Swinney stepped forward. He cleared his throat.

"We left her," he said. "She ain't none of your concern."

"Says who?"

"Says the Colonel."

The boy looked to where the Colonel's fire flickered a good ways off. He knew he should lower his voice but didn't.

"What does he care?"

Swinney let his hands fall open, silent.

The boy looked at him, his eyes slowly widening.

"The Colonel is married," he said.

The men shifted on their blankets and stumps. The boy looked at them a long moment. His voice was low. "He's had his way, then."

It wasn't a question.

The men said nothing. Their assent.

Then he whispered it, the question that remained: "Against her will?"

None of the men looked at him. They looked at the fire or their hands or their boots but not at him. The boy swallowed thickly and thumbed the bandage on his head.

"So be it," he said. He sat back on the stump and stared into the fire.

Sometime later he discovered a giant pocket sewn into the

inner flap of the coat, on the left-hand side, as if made for something specific.

"Say," he said, "I get something out of all this?"

Swinney stood and pulled an object from beneath his bedroll. The men handed it one to the next, circling the firelight until a woolen sock, heavy as a giant's foot, arrived in the boy's hand. He slipped off the sock, and the Walker Colt sat in his lap. It was a giant of a pistol, twice the weight of a newer Colt, built to kill not just men but the horses they rode, this one outfitted with trick grips that glowed like a moon in his hand. It looked made for a man twice his size, a frontier treasure for which men would surely kill. For which they had.

"You earned it," said Swinney.

"Yeah, you did," said somebody else.

The boy pointed the pistol into the dark of the man's voice.

"Five shots left," he said. "One through my head."

Nobody spoke, and he knew they wondered what spirits might have snuck through that wound of his. Into his head. What meanness. He did not feel like a boy anymore. He felt old as any of them. Older even.

He rode for three days among them, quiet. Alien.

Waiting.

One night, Swinney pulled him aside.

"What the hell is wrong with you?" he asked.

"Tell me how to get back."

"You got to be shitting me."

"Tell me," said the boy.

The third night, he lay down to rest early. The cold was coming down out of the north and the ground could keep a man from sleeping if he didn't get to sleep early enough, with some sunlight still left in the dirt, the rock. He pulled the bandage from his head and felt the scabby place where the ball had passed along his skull, an inch from ending him.

After a time he rose from his pallet of old sacks amid the snoring of his compatriots and moved toward the far-off embers of the Colonel's fire, silent as a wraith, one hand on the grip of his pistol to mask its glow. When he passed Swinney, he saw two white orbs look at him. Just as quickly they disappeared, closed, and whatever they saw prompted no movement.

The boy kept on picking his way among the stones, the heads, making no shadow, no sound. The coals of the Colonel's fire glowed red, the flames low. His black thoroughbred stood seventeen hands tall, thick-muscled, big haunches twitching in its sleep. A stallion. The boy did not see the saddle sitting in the shadows, but he saw the Colonel's slouch hat lying there beside him, the twin tassels still gold even for all they'd ridden above.

The boy pulled back the sleeve of his new coat and crouched, slow to lessen the crackling of his boots, and took the hat by the hand indentions over the crown. It would cover the scar. As he turned to the horse, the shadow of the round brim crossed the Colonel's face. The boy saw him shift, his hand groping for the butt of the pistol under his bedroll. By the time the Colonel sat upright, he must have found himself all alone, his gun pointed toward empty space. Leaves, fire-spangled, quivering where the horse had been, hoofprints welled with firelight.

The boy laid his cheek low against the horse's neck as they crashed through underbrush and low-hanging limbs. He hit upon an old wagon road whose dust shone white and crooked down the mountain switchbacks. The company shunned such roads, where spies could estimate the size of their force, where they could be detected at all. They took horse trails or even game trails instead, or they cut their own where the brush grew thick. The boy had the strongest horse underneath him and he was the lightest rider to boot and he believed he might outrun on the open road whomever they sent to catch him.

He dropped down, down out of the mountains in darkness, his breath and the breath of the horse pluming together, their dust hounding them as they rode. He thought of the men pursuing them, riders with plumes of dead birds in their hats, guns of many hands come to rest finally in their black-creased palms. He knew they fashioned themselves the most devoted Yankee-killers in all the land, and there were but two things that sated them: blood and money. He didn't have any money.

First light rose colorless over hills crumpled and creased into one another, a sheet enameled over a miscellany of untold items, of corpses and rock and whatever else gave the earth its shape. Sparse trees bristled from the hillsides gold-leafed, a touch of red. The season was turning, and fast. He had been out of the world for what seemed an eternity, and if he could just see her, he thought she might embrace him surely as the coat she'd made him. Their courtship so short, seconds alone, but the true shape of him displayed forevermore in the event that split them. He thought this would count above all else.

At a high outcropping of rock, he tethered the horse and climbed to the flat top to surveil the terrain behind him, the terrain ahead. Dust rose from the road far behind him. Whether of riders in pursuit, he could not say. Plenty of others traveled these roads. Couriers, runaways, men of uniformed war. Militia and home guard, too. Enemies all for a boy of his position and exploits.

He let the horse drink at a rock-strewn stream and drank

some himself and set off again. In daylight he left the main road and traveled parallel, rounding into and out of sight of its commerce, his path much slowed over the closed ground. When darkness fell, he returned to the road.

Day and night he rode to see her. His Ava. Dusk of the third day he rode out onto a ridge and saw farmhouses of the sort he sought, houses like hers in the valley bottoms. Swaddling them were forests richer with autumn than the forests out of which he rode, more abrupt spurts of red and yellow against the green. Whether by time or altitude, he could not say, the land of his past mainly evergreen, few colors to mark the seasons. His heart swelled upon the vista below him until he saw the black kink of river that lay in his path, no bridge in sight.

He rode down the ridges until he reached the riverbank, where the road attenuated into a long white spear under the shallows and disappeared. A wooden barge sat beached on the bank, a ferryman dozing on the afterdeck.

The boy hauled the horse to a stop alongside and kicked the hull.

"Hey there."

The ferryman opened one eye beneath the shadow of his cap. He eyed the boy and the horse he rode and the hat he wore.

"Ten bits to cross," he said. "No bartering 'less you got something to drink."

The boy looked out at the flat river, the black surface vented here and there with hidden currents. Then he looked behind him at the road. Then back again to the river, deep as the nightmares that plagued him. The shipwreck.

"Two bits," said the man again.

"Where's the nearest bridge?" the boy asked him.

"Bridge? Two bits is cheap, son. Specially for a man with a horse like that one. Course, if you got you a drop of whiskey—"

"I need a bridge, sir. No ferries."

The man looked hurt.

"Well, if you're extra partial to bridges, the nearest is ten miles yonder. Them sons a bitches blown her last month. Dynamite. But she's still operable, least tolerably. Don't you go telling nobody, though. That's in confidence."

He winked.

The boy looked upriver in the direction indicated. Then he tipped his cavalryman's hat at the ferryman.

"I'm much obliged, sir."

As he hauled the horse down to the soft flats of the riverbank, the boy knew his pursuers would learn all they needed to know from this man. They would know what condition he was in, what condition his horse. They would know what direction he was headed, how much ground they could gain on him by taking the ferry. And, most of all, they would know he was not a boy without fear.

He stopped the horse a ways down the bank and looked back over his shoulder at the dozing ferryman. The boy knew how he could remove all of that knowledge from the man's head. All that might betray him. And he could prove to them what kind of a man he was. A kind better left alone. His fingers touched the butt of the Colt. A moment later he gripped great fistfuls of the horse's mane and shot away toward the bridge.

He began to catch shapes quivering upon ridges he'd crossed, dust rising from paths he'd taken just hours before. They were gaining. He stopped for nothing, and still they gained.

They overtook him two days later in the valley of the

farmhouse. It was the Colonel and two of his fastest riders, the Colonel riding hatless on a big blood bay, the other two flanking him. The trio broke from the trees diagonal to the boy in a flying wedge, the Colonel leading with his horse pistol drawn, the others with Spencer repeaters already shouldered like buffalo hunters of the plains. It was just the three of them, riding light for speed, and it was plenty.

They came on not firing at first to save the horse he rode. They headed him off right before the porch of the house. He called out to her over them, and they smiled from behind the long barrels of their weapons, pointing him down. Ava appeared in the window of the room where he had first and last seen her, where she had perhaps sewn the coat he wore with those white and slender fingers that spread now flat upon the windowpane like a prisoner's.

"Off the horse," said the Colonel.

He had his horse turned broadside to the porch steps, the front door.

"Didn't hear you," said the boy, cocking his ear toward him.

A blow landed across his back and he fell forward. His hands streaked across the sweat-slick musculature of the horse, helpless. It was too lean to grip. Too hard. He landed shoulder-first in the yard and his wind left him, thumped out of his lungs. He rolled onto his back and looked bleary-eyed at the men and horses, their shapes warped and wavering as those seen from below the surface of a well. He could not get enough air.

The Colonel shucked his near foot from the stirrup and brought his other leg over the pommel and dropped from his horse without ever turning his back. The gaunt hollows of his face, his cheeks, looked down into the boy's. The upturned points of his mustache sat upon his face like a black smile. He reached out of sight and his hand came back, placing the slouch hat on his head, pulling the brim into place.

"I give a boy a chance, and look what it gets me. All for a goddamn woman."

"Her name is Ava," said the boy. "I saved her."

The Colonel pulled him off the ground by the coat.

"But can you save yourself?"

The boy heard the patchwork of colors strain against the stitches that bound them, begin to tear faintly but not to give.

"I saved her," he said.

The butt of the horse pistol came hard across his temple, his jaw, his nose. Bone and cartilage succumbing to harder matter. The Colonel dropped him, broken, to the ground.

"Get her, then," he said. "Go in and get her."

Faintly the boy saw a hand against the sky, a finger pointed heavenward. Wayward from the house, the window. The boy could not see if the Colonel was wearing gloves or if his hand was just that black with gunpowder and soot.

"Go get her."

The corners of the boy's vision were darkening. He looked up at the Colonel, tall above him, his chest pushed out. Pleased. He was standing that way when his heart exploded from his chest. Only after seeing it did the boy hear the shot. More followed in quick succession, long plumes of smoke bursting from the trees, the Colonel's two riders shot from their mounts. One of the horses screamed, struck too, the others thundering in flight. Their hooves shook the ground. Then silence.

Soon he found other men around him, strangers, these in uniform. Gray or blue, he could not tell. They asked him who he fought for and what company and what name. Their breath was rancid, their words quick. He could not answer them.

They asked him how he came by such a horse and was it not stolen. They asked him whether he was a deserter or a bounty jumper or a coward or a foreigner, and he could not tell them. They told him the men they'd just killed had died trying to kill him, and they could only honor the dead by carrying out their final wishes.

They said they did not want to waste another bullet.

They rode him up onto the ridge where he'd first looked down upon this valley, this state. They slung a rope over a heavy limb and sat him on the horse he'd stolen and slid the noose over his bare neck. There were three of them. He did not fight.

Below him the forests glimmered firelike in the last rays of sun, colors as brightly variegated as the coat he wore. He could hardly swallow for the snugness of the rope. He looked down at his Ava, a white cutout in the black upper window, and he was sorry she would remember him this way. He looked down upon that whole country so pretty in the fall, in the season of blood and gold, and he was no longer a stranger unto the land.

A man stepped forward to bind his hands. He was wearing the Colonel's slouch hat slanted rakishly over his brow like some kind of joke. Another had a repeating rifle propped over his shoulder. The third was scratching his groin, smiling, his long sharpshooting rifle cradled across his chest. The boy put his hand into his coat. Slowly, to provoke no alarm. They watched him. He pulled the pistol butt-first from where it hung hidden in the folds and offered the bone-white grip of it to his captors, one finger on the trigger guard.

"She's a firecracker," he warned, his smile broken in the gathering dusk.

Chapter 2

The hills were welling with darkness, the high and fiery treetops here or there extinguished into shadow. The gun smoke had risen at first in billows and now it descended again in a fine ash. The boy removed the noose. He climbed down from the horse and took the repeating rifle from the grip of one man, shocked by how stark white the emptied hands looked against the blueing ground. One of the men was still alive. He'd begun to moan, gut-shot. It could take him a long time to die.

The boy shouldered the rifle. Aimed. The man raised a hand, shielding his face. As if that might stop what was coming. The rifle began to shake in the boy's hands. He lowered it and got back on the black horse. It was the only animal that hadn't bolted.

He descended the path down again into the valley. He didn't look over his shoulder. He looked only to the window where Ava stood, still there. The house, so sorry in daytime, glowed in the dark. He propped the rifle on his knee, the barrel skyward. It rocked this way, that way as the horse descended into the shadows.

They reached the bottomland, where the black marks of marauding hooves still pockmarked the blue slope. The mud was hardened, the pig gone from its sty. The boy could still remember its squeal. He looked up at the window and saw Ava disappear like a ghost into darkness, dissolve. He waited for her to reappear through the front door, a pale and delicate creature in the black frame.

She didn't.

He stood before the empty doorway and leaned the rifle on the wall. He tried to call out but the words caught in his throat. He tried to say her name but couldn't. Behind him the Colonel and his men and one of the horses lay craze-limbed on the ground, wrecked, their bodies humped upon the blue swell of turf as upon an inland sea. The long guns of the sharpshooters had caught them unawares.

He stood there at the threshold and did not want to go inside uninvited, not again. He didn't want to be like them anymore, the ones behind him. Marauders, killers, thieves. He stood looking into the dim blue depths of the house, which seemed colder even and danker than the air outside. He could hear no movement.

He looked to one side of the porch, where a swing hung catawampus from a single chain, the other ripped from its hook by some member of the Colonel's troop. He looked up at the high ridge from which he'd come, up where the falling sun was still lighting up the tallest trees like bloodred spires, and he saw no silhouettes against the sky or trees, no slouch hats of men sky-lit like they must have been a half hour before. No, they were flat to the ground now, outspilled, and he was here, on the porch. He pulled the coat tighter around himself and palmed the Walker deeper through his belt, burying the blood-painted handle in furrows of cloth. It was very quiet and he could hear the air whistling through his busted nose.

He found her underneath the stairs, her knees huddled up against her belly. She who had been so brave before, now afraid, rocking slightly, her hair covering her shoulders in black streaks. When she looked up, he saw her cheeks were hollowed out and dark, her skin stretched thin and film-like over the bones in her face. It looked like something eating her from the inside out.

"You all right?" he asked her.

She quit rocking and looked him in the eye.

"The son of a bitch is dead, ain't he."

It was not a question.

The boy looked out the front door to the yard, the crumpled bodies.

"I reckon so," he said.

She took a breath, held it. "Well, I ought to be just dandy, then."

She nodded once, to herself. Then she stood, quickly, surprising him. He stepped back. They were standing close. She was taller than he remembered. Her eyes startled him, so blue, the rest of her body smooth and pale as poured milk. His eyes came only to the level of her lips, slim and white. He was staring at them. She placed her hands against the small of her back, arching to inhale.

"I suppose you should know about this baby, then," she said.

"Baby?" He was silent a long moment, his throat tight. "His?"

She twirled and began walking down the hall.

He watched her. "Are you sure? It hasn't been that long—"

She stopped and turned. She seemed steadier now than when he'd found her, steadier than him maybe. Certainly taller.

"You think I'm lying?"

"That's not what I said—"

"How many children has he got?"

The boy shifted on his feet. "Twelve."

"Right," she said. "Don't sound like he misses much, does it?" Her jaw ground sideways, and she turned back down the hall. "Told me I'd make him thirteen."

He followed a little behind her, toward the stairs. She spoke without looking back at him. "So don't give me no more shit about it. Week or two we'll know for sure. But me, I already know."

"I wouldn't give you shit."

"Big talker," she said, "like the rest of them."

He continued following her down the hall, watching the way her long shoulder blades lanced up and down under the shift.

"How old are you?" he asked her.

She paused on the first step. "Seventeen," she said.

"Me too," he said too quickly.

"Bullshit," she said. "You ain't a day over fifteen."

"I am too."

"I've seen you naked," she said, starting up the stairs.

The boy stayed at the bottom, one hand on the banister.

"So?" he said.

"So I can tell."

She kept on going up the stairs.

"Well, I just come in here to thank you for my coat."

"You're welcome," she said, still climbing the steps.

"Well, where you going?" he asked her.

She disappeared into the blue gloom of the second floor.

"I'm packing a bag," she said, "so you can take me and this baby the hell out of here. That a problem?"

The boy could feel his eyes like round white antler nubs in his face.

"No, ma'am," he said.

He stood stone-still a moment, and then he shook out of it like a man coming awake from ice. He thought of the bodies in the yard where she would see them. He went looking for a blanket. His boots clopped down the hall and he went into the nearest room, a study of some kind, the walls lined with glass jars. He started to step forward but stopped, a stench. He looked down and saw a gleaming wreckage of broken glass, a chemical smell overpowering the small room. He stopped, standing on one foot, taking in the sight of the room from one wall to another.

There were strange white shapes curled on the wrecked floor, their skin and bodies shriveled. Shrunken. Others on shelves, in jars or tanks. There were creatures he almost recognized but did not, like distant cousins of the animals he knew. Lizards with unknown markings written geometrically on their skin, tiny mammals curled fetal-like on broken glass, a snake with white scales. His stomach twisted up inside him like a worm on hot stone. It reminded him of a carnival show, like all that was strange or holy had been given no respect, been stuffed into a jar and drowned in chemicals, some kind of strange afterlife.

He turned his head away. The men of the troop had wrecked all this, he was sure. They wrecked everything, strange or beautiful no matter. He turned to go but saw a small square-cornered jar on a shelf just inside the door. The rest of the shelf had been swiped clean of specimens, but not this, left fully intact. Inside the jar floated a tiny white creature, unborn. It had four limbs, he saw, and thumbs, too, and closed eyes with creases at the lids like the crow's-feet of an old man. It had a tiny organ, male, like a white acorn, and a long veined tube protruding from the belly that swirled and swirled around the jar and ended with a tiny knot of twine to seal off the surgical cut. The creature was curled into itself, as if with a stomachache.

Slowly, as if not to wake the thing, the boy reached out and touched the lid of the jar. He rotated it in place until he could see the notched spine impressing the delicate skin, no terrain of muscle to protect the bone, just smooth flesh.

He heard a creak at the top of the stairs: Ava coming. Quickly he hid the jar in his coat and hurried out of the room and into the hallway, then outward into the yard, carrying the thing close to his chest. He went to the big bay the Colonel had been riding, dead now, and stuck the jar in one of the saddlebags. Then he undid the girth strap and dragged the saddle out from underneath the animal's belly. It was a cavalry McClellan from before the war, re-covered in rich russet, outfitted with hooded stirrups and brass moldings and a hair-padded seat. A fine saddle, fit for an officer to ride.

He threw it over the horse he'd been riding, the stolen black one which had been so steady beneath him. He looped the mohair cinch underneath the enormous belly and secured the strap to the quarter ring, snugging it. He took the bridle and placed the snaffle bit in the horse's mouth and fitted the noseband and browband and throatlatch, the rosettes glinting like stained coins in the darkness. He slid the rifle into the bootleg scabbard, the pistol into one of the two holsters that hung across the pommel. He left the Colonel's bedroll pack strapped to its cantle grommets. The leather tube held a heavy buffalo blanket that many had lusted after on a cold night.

Above him, stars had begun to prick through the darkened sky, no moon. He heard Ava coming down the hall. He looked down at the Colonel, the man's heart spilled into the grass. Dead, dead, dead. But even now the man scared him. He whipped the coat off his shoulders and snapped it flat above the body. It hovered a moment, winglike, then began to drift down to cover the details of the killing from the girl's eyes.

"Callum," she said. "Don't do that."

He pulled the coat back just before it touched the body.

"You know my name?"

"Course I do."

She stepped off the porch and came walking through the yard, her thin body swaddled in a bed quilt, her long legs covered to the knee in men's riding boots. He could see she had tied a bedroll of things slantwise across her chest and shoulder like an infantryman. She also had a larger bundle tucked under one arm. She stood over the Colonel. Callum watched her look down into the ruined chest, the hollow where the man's heart had been.

"It's a sorry sight," he said.

Ava looked up at him. "Sorry ain't a thing to do with it," she said.

But he saw she was a little uncertain of step when she walked up to the horse. She put a hand against his haunch.

Callum took the bundle from under her other arm, gently, and fit it into a saddlebag. Then he boosted her onto the back of the horse, careful where he placed his hands, and slung himself into the saddle from the other side. She put her hands on his hips to steady herself. He turned the horse toward the high ridge from which he'd come, the way south. They both looked a last time over their shoulders at the house white in the valley, the bodies dark in the grass.

Callum expected she might say a few last words over this scene, blessing or curse, but she said nothing. She just turned back around and put her chin on his shoulder, just beside his good ear.

"Let's go," she said.

Callum nodded and urged the horse onward, south, the only direction they could go. Winter would come quickly from the north, and so might warring men, leaderless now, who loved blood, and how much better it was with vengeance to sweeten the glut.

They rode up the same path he and the horse had descended hardly an hour before. He knew no other. He was glad that it was full dark now, and no moon. He didn't want to see again what he'd done. When they passed the spot, the noose swung slowly over the path. The two men were there. Dead. The third was gone. He'd dragged himself into the woods, thought Callum. To die. He said nothing to Ava. They kept on riding into the night, higher and darker as the hours wore on.

In the spare hour before dawn, they stopped to rest. Time and again during the night's ride, Callum had heard a snap of twig, a crackle of brush, like the sound ambushing men would make, and he'd ridden all night with his good ear cocked and his shooting hand on the revolver, afraid. Ava set to building a neat tepee of twigs over a small ball of dry wood shavings. Up here in the mountains, everything seemed wet. Not soaking, but moist to the bone. She had her own knife she'd brought, a folding one, and together they flayed the bigger sticks and branches to get to the drier wood.

Ava had thought to bring a brass match safe. Callum watched her light the doomed little structure she'd made. The kindling crackled, took light. Before long the twigs glowed red and collapsed to greater flame. They piled on the bigger fuel piece by piece, squatting close to the fire, both on the same side to avoid the smoke.

Ava got out the salted meat she'd brought and gave them each a thin shred.

Callum held his by one end, watching how easily the wind made it quiver.

"What wc supposed to do with this? Strum 'Dixie'?"

"You got something better?"

Callum put his piece in his mouth, eyeing the rest of the meat while he chewed.

"How'd you hide that from the men?" he asked her, chewing, his mouth open.

"I didn't. The Colonel gave it to me before they left. Had them steal it from Old Man Tatum one valley over."

"I bet they cleaned out the whole county like that."

"Seemed like," she said. "When you were on the sickbed, they came home nearly every evening with plunder of one kind or another. Old Man Tatum used to make that white 'shine. One night they got hold of a barrel he had hid in his cellar and drank themselves blind in the yard. They'd hauled in this buckboard from God knows where, and they burned it. Danced around the fire half-naked, screaming like little devils. One of them kept dousing his arm in whiskey and taking a match to it, lighting it right off his arm in this blue flame."

"Until he lit his whole self on fire."

"They told you."

"No," said Callum. "But somebody'd kill himself about once a month doing something like that."

She shook her head, her vision far off.

"Somebody threw more 'shine on him once he started burning," she said. "I think the person throwing thought it was water. I hope he did. Any case, the man ran off flaming into the night, running just this straight line, like he could get away."

Callum could see the reflection of the campfire dancing tiny-flamed in her eyes.

"How far he get?"

Ava shook her head, looking into the fire.

"Far," she said. "Near to the tree line. Lot farther than I'd of imagined."

He nodded. They both stared into the fire, the wood glowing red at the heart, the bark white with heat. He looked at the saddlebag, the square bulge of the jar.

"So what happened to your family?"

"Mama, she died when I was a baby. Daddy and my older brother, Jessup, they both joined the militia in '62."

She didn't add anything. Callum knew what that meant. They were gone. And her in that house all alone.

"I'm sorry."

She straightened. "You ain't sorry, not really. Nothing against you. Nobody is. You hear the same sad story so many times, that's all it is—a story."

They squatted there, silent awhile, palms open to the heat.

Callum eyed the saddlebag and bit the inside of his bottom lip.

"Say," he said, "was your daddy some kind of a—"

She sniffed. "He was a doctor," she said, "and a good one."

"Well—"

"And what about you, then? Where are you from?"

He wiggled his fingers in front of the flames. Shrugged.

"No place, really."

"Ain't that mysterious."

"I ain't big on talking about it is all."

"Fine," she said. "But I'll get it out of you, somehow."

He looked at her.

"Will you now."

"I have my ways."

"Uh-huh."

She sat back, her palms flat on the ground.

"You got to talk to somebody, you know. And I don't see nobody else round here to chat with."

He grinned. She, too. They looked around, bright-eyed a moment, but the smiles slowly died on their faces. The world was dark beyond the small ken of their fire, so dark, and the notion of somebody else out here, anybody else, struck them silent, as if the mere saying of the thing could call up something evil—men or demons or ghosts.

"Let's get on," said Callum.

She nodded. They threw dirt on the fire and spread the ashes and coals around to hide the heat, the fire's newness, and climbed back on the horse. Callum urged it back onto the trail. He looked up at the moon.

"Ireland," he said.

"What?"

"Ireland." He cleared his throat. "That's where I'm from, originally. Come over when I was eight."

Ava leaned closer.

"With your family?"

He shook his head.

"No, this family the priests had put me with." He paused. "One that took in orphans."

"Oh."

"We come over in steerage, into New Orleans. Trying to escape the workhouse. The famine. The men, they were supposed to help dig these canals down there."

He paused.

"Work wasn't there?" she asked.

"No, it was. Plenty of it. But so was that yellow fever."

"We heard about that."

He nodded. "I got kicked around for a while after that. This place, that place. What they called a 'double orphan.'" He shrugged. "Soon as I could, I ran away. Started to stealing horses, figuring I was too young to hang."

"You weren't."

He shrugged. "Turns out you ain't ever too young in Louisiana, long as you steal the wrong man's horse."

"Hell, I could of told you that."

"Well, somebody did. Little late." He sniffed. "They were hunting me hard. I had to get out of there, out of the state, really. So I went down to New Orleans and got on as a hand on this blockade-runner."

He paused again.

"Well, what happened then?"

He leaned and spat. "The blockade."

The trees murmured coldly with dawn, like they were waking from a long slumber. Callum did not know their names, most of them. Some of their trunks rose dark and straight from the earth, others gray-gnarled or twisted or green with lichen. So many of them in their ranks, as different as the forms of men. Some scorched by lightning, others uprooted as if by violent calamity. Chestnuts, he knew those. Red-gray, with twisting, furrowed trunks and sun-yellow leaves.

He took trail to trail, bearing southward whenever he could, the land rising higher and higher by slight degrees. The paths they rode were not well beaten, but traveled enough to worry him. The mires where falling streams crossed the path had hardened into the many hoofprints of loaded horses or mules. Here or there they passed the black scar of an old fire. Whoever took or needed to take such high and narrow roads through the mountains was no one he wanted to meet. Outlaws, fugitives, spies. Men jealous of such a horse and such a girl. Men like those he'd ridden with, men maybe like him.

The horse was strong, even with two riders, and its strength disguised the steepness of their ascent, so that by noon of this first day the trail broke onto a sparsely wooded ridgeline high above the bottomlands. They looked down upon whole valleys flushed red and yellow, white-housed, even a smattering of livestock to fill the pastures.

Callum stayed the horse. He was tired, and the hills were golden with sun. The fears of the night seemed no threat to him now, not in the sun, the shine, and he just wanted to sleep awhile. He got off the horse and dallied the rope to a nearby tree.

Ava looked down at him, awake.

"We going to stop here?" she asked. "In daylight?"

He had never known that sunshine could be so heavy. It pulled at him pleasantly, at his eyelids, the warmness good on his battered face.

"Just a little while," he said.

She licked her lips and made a small nod of her head, outward, toward the hills.

"Okay," she said. "But give me the pistol."

He looked down at the white grip of the Walker. He had it stuck in the front of his pants.

"Just gimme the goddamn thing," she said.

"All right," he said. He lifted it up to her. She hefted it, looked at one side, the other. She held it like she knew how to use it.

"Careful," he said.

"Just get some sleep," she said, and scooted forward into the front of the saddle. "I'll wake you when it's been long enough."

He nodded. He was light-headed, heavy-eyed. He sat back against a tree, in the sun, and did not think of anything. He let his eyes close, his mind drift.

"So where you reckon we're gonna go?" asked Ava.

He lolled his head against the back of the tree and opened one eye.

"South," he said.

"That's not a place. It's a direction."

The sun was warm on Callum's face, despite the season. He closed his eyes.

"They got sunshine there," he said, "and winter's coming."

"I got a good feeling we're gonna need more than sunshine to keep alive."

Callum opened his eyes just to the thinnest slit. The hills glowed, the tiny houses white as the dream of a house, a valley.

"There's more," he said.

He didn't mean to say this, not yet. But the hills were gold, the sun warm, and he could not seem to help himself.

"I got a elbow cousin," he said. "Down on the coast. Georgia. Second cousin to my grandmother—some such—on my mother's side. Her husband's a planter. Got himself a plantation, a big house, everything. Grows rice down there, maybe citrus. Has him like fifty slaves or something."

Ava was quiet a moment.

"What's their name?"

"Gosling."

"Not very Irish."

Callum shrugged. "Well, *he* ain't. She come over as a house servant. Man's wife kicked the old bucket."

"You better not be lying to me," she said.

Callum had closed his eyes. He opened them just barely, again to the hills, the valleys, everything storybook from such height.

"No, ma'am," he said. "I wouldn't lie to you."

He closed his eyes and let himself swoon on this dream, heavy and warm, like eating a pie of some kind, apple or pear or peach. He did not hear anything from Ava. Just the steady breathing of the horse, an animal needing no dream to make it strong.

Chapter 3

He was there beside that great swollen river, chocolate dark under the sun, and he was thirteen years old again. He was hiding amid the bony knees of a great cypress, hidden in shore reeds. Out in the river, a tramp steamer blew its horn, as if to alert the people of Vacherie, Louisiana, that a horse thief lay in wait.

No one seemed to hear.

It was a sugar plantation. The manor house was built high off the ground, its cypress bones fleshed with fired brick. The Acadian trappers he'd met coming south from Plaquemine said it was owned by a former French naval officer. They said he owned a great cremello stallion, cream-white with crystal blue eyes, that would fetch a handsome price in the back alleys of New Orleans or Baton Rouge. They spat and winked.

He waited the day long, in the reeds, and watched. Clouds wheeled over him like big tufts of cotton in the blue sky. He thanked them when they shrouded the sun. He was a year out of that last orphanage, the one in Alexandria, and he was ready for a horse that would change his place in the world. He'd been stealing coldbloods—draft and plow horses that kept his belly full a week when he sold them. He was ready for a hotblood. A thoroughbred. Something that could keep him full for months, maybe a year.

Come dark, the windows of the big house flickered golden, and no one was about. He could move like a whisper and did, floating across to the barn. There was a pinch-faced attendant with narrow black mustaches, sharp at the ends, as if to impress somebody. He was sitting in a ladder-back chair alongside the barn, scraping his supper from a tin plate. A single-shot scattergun sat propped on the wall beside him. In an hour, he was asleep.

The stallion, they said, was called Le Magnifique. He stood more than sixteen hands tall, and he glowed like the ghost of a horse in the cavernous darkness of the barn. He came right to Callum's hand, and his nose bloomed pink beneath the hair of his muzzle. Callum took no saddle. He rode him bareback out of the barn, across the manor grounds, and onto the river road. Slave cabins lined both its sides, built low-roofed at the foot of the levee, and when the great white horse trotted past, carrying its strange rider, everyone in their dirt yards looked away.

So easy.

That night, miles distant, he slept in an untended field before an abandoned sharecropper's cabin. The stars were bright and many, like some gift, and they gathered all around him on every side, as if to comfort him. The horse stood tall against them, like a thing made for night, and seemed happy out of his barn. Callum had tied him off on a single dead locust in the middle of the field, its crown all jagged, and he himself made a pillow of his coat against its trunk. He had come a long way from the workhouse in Tipperary. He could still remember when they'd installed the triple bunks to accommodate the flood of new inmates, and they'd put him on the top because of his size. The ceiling was so close against his face, like someone had mortared him into a stone coffin, and it had been like a scream in his chest to get out. And here he was now, in the open night, and in just a few days, in New Orleans, he would be a man who could do as he would, his coat pockets heavied and sure.

He fell asleep to that, from a dream into a dream, and it was good until the ground began to shake, to thunder with hooves, and he knew they were coming for him.

"Callum!"

His eyes snapped wide. He felt it in the ground: *riders.*

"Up!" she said. "Come on!"

She had the horse on the edge of the trail. She leapt off with the reins in hand and he reached out and grabbed hold of the horse's tail and together they pitched over the ridge and headed nearly straight down, just missing all the trees grown twisted from the slope. The horse slid and pitched, scrambling on the loose ground, unhappy at the slant of its world, and Callum followed, his stomach in his throat. Ava, huge-quilted, led them, her boots skidding on the wet stones and roots. They went head-on into a bed of brambles and stopped. They crouched amid the thorns, hearts crashing in their chests, and tried not to breathe.

Riders appeared above them on the trail, riding hard, as if

in pursuit or flight. Three of them, black-coated, and the last looked hard at the ground as he passed. Nevertheless, they rode on. Callum did not know them, not specifically, but they struck him as something he knew. White men, desperate, their cheeks hollowed, nothing but viciousness to keep them alive. He knew some of that. And he knew there was real danger in these highlands, and no one could help you.

They waited a long time, silent, maybe a quarter of an hour. Callum knew they could be outriders of a larger force, even his old troop pursuing them, and so they waited long enough to make sure the fast riders were long gone and no one behind them.

Finally they ascended the slope together. Callum boosted Ava into the saddle, then mounted up.

Ava broke the silence. Her words, hardly a whisper, seemed loud and dangerous, like they might drown the sound of danger coming down the path.

"Those riders—you think they're fleeing somebody, or chasing them?"

Callum squinted down the path before them, behind them, too crooked to see very far in either direction.

"I don't rightly know," he said.

"You reckon it's us they're after?"

Callum wiped his nose on the sleeve of his coat.

"They're liable to be after anything they can get their hands on, I reckon."

She reached around him with the pistol.

"Thank you," she said.

He nodded and took it back. He lowered the hammer and double-checked that it rested over an empty chamber for riding. Chances were in his favor for that. All but two were empty. They had the repeating rifle as well, a Spencer carbine.

Good to have but unwieldy in an ambush. He'd left the Colonel with one of his big dragoon pistols still gripped in one hand. He hadn't wanted to prize it free, nor take any of the blood-soaked revolvers from his belt. He wished he had.

Maybe the men of the troop were after them, maybe not. They had loved the Colonel as a father almost, a man of great cruelty who nevertheless protected them, led them, eclipsed any guilt of theirs with his own. At his behest they had razed and butchered, no reason but hunger and the Colonel's orders. Without him, Callum worried what they might do, how viciously they might grab for a new purpose, a new mission, and what better motive than love and vengeance neatly twinned. They had long ago forsaken the war of newspapers for the one they carried everywhere with them, and which had no colors, no sides, and which could be fit neatly to any new opportunity that presented itself: ambush, pillage, torture.

Outside of Asheville, they had disemboweled a man for attempting to fornicate with a hog. They had bade him carry out the task by his own hand, his own knife into his own white belly, as the Colonel said the great Japanese warriors had done, sometimes thirty or fifty at a time, on their knees. All this for disgrace. For letting their master die. The Colonel had a word for this, something silly-sounding from a book, but no one had laughed. The hog man had been unable to accomplish the deed, hardly pricking his skin, so the men had strung him to a tree and slit him a wide gash just below the navel, like a mouth. The boy had swallowed the bile that scorched his throat when the man's tubing came spilling onto the ground, wet and blue.

He could not appear weak before them, only the boy he was. Their eyes ignited at weakness, sight or scent. And yet he had always felt protected by them. They had not made him do the things they did, not yet, and for that he'd felt them almost as brothers to him, elders, who rode as killers among the killed and would make him a man to be feared. And what more could a boy ask for in lands like these, in this cold and high place where such men commanded the roads?

They rode the same ridge for the rest of the day, no place else to go. The leaves were at their brightest now, curling and crackling on the black limbs of the trees. He had to wonder why the colors changed so brightly in this land, what made them turn so fire-colored and alive-looking just before they fell, just like a match struck on the thumb would flare terrifically in a dark room, moment-bright, then burn quickly down to a cinder, nothing but dark smudges between a man's fingers.

He looked through the slatted trees to the golden ridges beyond. Here and there a spurt of the brightest otherworldly red marked the hillside. The color explosive, lifting, like a hemorrhage from the earth. Callum looked hard for these sights, and they made him ache. He knew the falling land was telling him something, and the message yearned in his throat to be spoken. But he would not speak it. Could not. When Ava fell asleep on the back of the horse, he took her cool white hand in his own for a long moment. Her palm was calloused like a boy's, her finger bones delicate. He placed her hand back in the pocket of his coat, where she kept it warm.

They had originally planned to ride more in darkness than daytime, to keep themselves unseen on the roads should anyone come asking. But he had decided after the first night that he would rather be able to see what was coming on the roads or lurking in the brush.

So daylight.

They rode sunup to sundown in the following days. They

slept in their blankets, and their fires were small and hot-burning and a good ways from any known path or road or trail. The ground was cold. They curled themselves close to the embers for warmth, nearly encircling the heat head-to-head, boots-to-boots. Ava apportioned the meat in what the men of the company would have called "quarter rations," and there was good feed for the horse from the Colonel's provisions. At night he would hobble the horse's forelegs and stake it and loop a nosebag over its ears, letting it eat. It fed better than they did and probably deserved to.

One morning, Callum woke to a terrible retching. He turned over in his buffalo blanket and saw Ava huddled on her knees before a chestnut tree, her both hands planted on the trunk, her head hung between her arms, making sick. She'd cast off the quilt, and her rail-like body quaked beneath the muslin dress.

"You okay?"

She straightened and turned to him. She wiped her mouth with the back of her hand.

"It ain't nothing," she said. She stood. "Let's get moving."

Callum started to say more, but she walked past him, to the horse.

Day after day they climbed. The land grew colder, harder. Ava was sick sometimes in the mornings, but she never complained. Callum tried to eat less of what was rationed him, but she wouldn't take more.

The wind seemed to blow upward out of the valleys here, lifting the leaves from the trees. Somewhere near was the great thrust of rock where the snow was said to fall upside down, rising up out of the gorge below. Where an Indian brave, heartbroken, had leapt into the wilderness, only to be blown back into the arms of his lover. It was known now as an especially bad place for partisan war, for brother against brother, and cutthroat guerrilla bands that rode through the hollers with torch and sword and rope. He and Ava continued on south through the mountains, wary of every grove and deadfall where men could hide.

Before sundown after a long day on the trail, Callum started looking for a place to stop. Ava woke up and looked around them, sleepy-eyed. Rock on one side, a sheer drop on the other.

"I don't see a way off this trail," she said.

"We just got to keep on riding," said Callum. "We'll find someplace."

They rode on. Night fell. Moonlight licked down through the dark fingerlings of the trees that tunneled their path, slinking like quicksilver along the ground. Ava leaned forward, her mouth right over his shoulder, her breath tickling his ear.

"Know what they say about all this warring?" she whispered.

"No," said Callum. "Bet you're gonna tell me, though."

"They say too many of the dead are going unburied, rotting aboveground."

Callum straightened in the saddle. He thought of the men unburied, the Colonel and the men he himself had shot. He snorted loudly through his runny nose, as if to sniff at the danger of the trail, the story being told.

"That's just how animals die," he said. "Nobody to bury them."

"Exactly. Animals got nobody to do it. But we're supposed to be different. We're supposed to bury our dead. They say the spirits don't get home easy if they ain't buried. And pretty soon that could lead to real trouble. The land full of all these haunts, sorely displeased at the meager terms of their departure."

"Sounds awful vain to me. Seems like they should have themselves bigger issues to chew on, like being dead."

"People think the dead are somehow enlightened, but I don't think so. I think they're just like us: petty and mean-spirited mainly, a few of them pleasant. Then, being dead, they got nothing to do but get sour and moan. Try to get somebody to listen to their bitching."

Callum watched tree-broken fragments of moonlight glimmer like blades in the black woods alongside the trail.

"This your idea of a joke, 'cause it ain't funny."

"I'm serious," said Ava, leaning well over his shoulder.

"Well, why didn't you tell me to bury the Colonel and all them back at the house?"

"Him? I wanted that son of a bitch to get his fill of eternal bellyaching. Rest of them, too. Let them moan. I won't be there to hear it."

Callum looked back at her like he would a two-headed woman.

"Girl, I'm starting to think you might be crazy."

She shrugged. "Big talk from you, stealing the Colonel's horse."

"That wasn't crazy. I needed the fastest horse, so I took it."

"Well—"

The underbrush crackled loudly of a sudden, followed by the high-pitched scream of something not human. Before Callum could even draw the pistol, a sleek shape bounded into the middle of their path, two almond eyes with slit-shaped pupils. Its white fangs caged a small animal, nearly limp, just the tiny paws clawing at the air. The horse shuddered and wrenched its head away, turning broadside to the big cat. Callum yanked at the pistol; it caught in the saddle holster. Behind him Ava rose out of her seat, shooting both arms over her head, outward, her fingers curled clawlike, her black hair haloing her head, and she shrieked at the creature. A shriek high and angry and full of blood, like the reputed shriek of the banshee.

The cat sank low to the ground and shot away into the woods, making only two or three diminishing sounds, like it flew downhill on great flying strides and hardly touched down its paws.

Callum got his pistol free and pointed it this way and that toward where the cat had disappeared. After a moment he lowered it and half-turned on the saddle to look at Ava. He was wide-eyed and slack-jawed when he did, like he was looking at a creature of some unplumbable species. The quilt made her seem huge and yoke-shouldered, and her blazing eyes and smooth face, ovate and hard-boned, struck him silent.

"Showed that son of a bitch," she said, half-smiling.

Callum nodded slowly, his mouth still agape, and turned back to the trail.

"Reckon you did," he said, his mouth dry, his chest thundering.

He decocked the Walker and slipped it back into the pommel holster, making sure the leather thong wouldn't catch again.

They rode on until a midnight fog crept into the valleys below them. It rose and rose, like a coming flood, until it seeped silver-backed and ghostlike through the woods, the canted trees on every side. Callum prayed for a place to leave the trail and make a fire. They needed light, warmth. An ally in the dark.

The trail started descending, and the big shoulders of the horse rippled and bulged, the trail steep at times. They happened across a muddy wash where a stream crossed the trail, black-mired, and the horse stepped lightly, unhappy, his hooves disappearing to the fetlocks in muck. He snorted his discontent in dual streams from his huge nostrils, and Callum just coaxed him forward, whispering words of strength in a sweet voice he rarely used. The horse only shook his head and snorted more, as if to say he was the wrong creature for that language. They got through, black mud glistening on the horse's black legs, and then a shack appeared on the side of the trail. It was dark-windowed, the porch warped and slanted, the stone-masoned chimney crumbling into the yard.

Callum did not like how close to the trail the shack was. He gave the reins a slight slap to keep them going. The horse eyed the house and snorted.

"You ain't gonna stop?" asked Ava.

"I don't like it," said Callum.

"Me, neither," said Ava, "but I ain't seen a better idea in the last two hours. You?"

"That chimney's no good for a fire."

"Then we won't have one."

Callum looked up the trail, down. Nothing. He hadn't heard anything suspicious in hours, not since the big mountain cat. He was tired. His eyes were wide open, alert, but his head and arms felt full of lead.

He rode them off the trail, toward the shack. He was almost in front of it before he realized there could be men in there, asleep already, or not sleeping. Waiting. He halted the horse and stepped down from the saddle, silent. He pulled the rifle from its scabbard and handed it to Ava. She nodded and shouldered the weapon.

He had the pistol out. He walked toward the front door,

which was half-agape to a darkness deeper than the surrounding night. He went silent-footed—his talent. He got just to the door and leaned his back against the wall to one side. He had a two-handed grip on the pistol, its inordinate heft hanging pendulumlike between his knees as he listened for breath inside the cabin, or the click and lock of a hammer. Nothing. He looked at Ava. She had one eye squinted, the other lined down the rifle's barrel. The horse stood motionless as a sculpture of black stone, no movement save the steady spume of his breath.

Callum turned and kicked his boot through the door, leveling the big pistol into darkness. He hurdled forward, tripping over something, maybe a chair, and crashed onto a wood-framed bed, a straw mattress. Empty. He whirled and reeled forward again, probing the barrel into the black. His foot clanged a metal bucket across the floor, and his opposite knee struck a table or desk. He swung the pistol this way, that way. Nothing. He lowered the gun and stood there, silent, the long barrel of the weapon hanging down past his knee. He turned and saw behind him the lighter dark of the front door, and he walked back outside.

"Empty," he said.

Ava lowered the rifle.

"Goddamn," she said.

She got off the horse and led him to the front of the house. "We can't just tie him up out here. Anybody comes along this trail will see him, know we're here."

"Let's tie him up behind."

But the ground rose steeply behind the shack, little place for the horse to stand.

"Inside?" asked Ava.

They got the big horse through the door and stood him inside. He was not afraid, as if accustomed to being quartered inside. Callum looped his reins over a bedpost.

The air in the cabin was thick and heavy, full of mold, but they were too tired to care. The floor was covered with an assortment of untold items, mostly broken or crushed. Ava collapsed onto the bed, enveloped in her quilt. Callum stood by himself in the middle of the one room, turning slowly, shards of glass crackling underfoot.

"All right," said Ava. "You can sleep in the bed with me, but no foolishness."

"Don't kid yourself," said Callum, collapsing next to her on the bed.

His heart beat at the prospect, but he didn't care. He was too tired, too cold. Exhaustion swaddled him like a bed quilt. Within minutes he was drifting, and drifting turned quickly to falling, as if the bed itself had fallen right through the floor. It seemed that way for minutes, hours, and then the falling stopped. He opened his eyes to stillness, shut-throated by noose, no horse underneath him, and he saw them coming for him, the men he'd killed or helped to kill. The ones he'd been unable to save. The unburied. They were shot or slashed or burned. Gutted or drowned. They were after him. He found the pistol in his hand, the Walker, butt-first like before. He tried to whip it around like his trick of old. It didn't work, not this time. The pistol dropped at his feet. The dead men were close, leering, hungry for still-warm blood. He tried to scream but couldn't, his voice caught dead in the noose.

He convulsed awake from the dream and found himself entangled with the nearest body, clinging, and then she moved against him, coming awake in the quilt they shared. Her body was warm, as he'd imagined it would be, and so smooth, and before long she moved over him, belly to belly, grooving him, her place slick with heat, and he could remember nothing save the hot dream of himself expulsed into darkness.

Afterward she told him not to get used to nothing and rolled to her side. He watched his breath cloud over him like some kind of ghost, his mind blank, and then he slept.

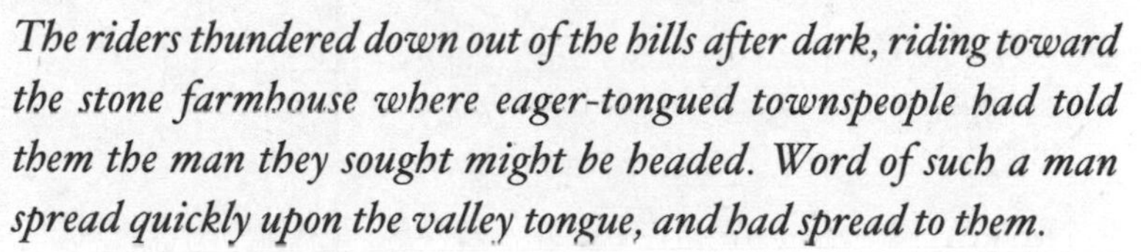

The riders thundered down out of the hills after dark, riding toward the stone farmhouse where eager-tongued townspeople had told them the man they sought might be headed. Word of such a man spread quickly upon the valley tongue, and had spread to them.

The riders fanned out into a ragged phalanx as they crossed the pastureland before the house. They half-surrounded the two-story structure of limestone just as an open wagon pulled by big draft horses came to a halt before the front steps, the animals' shoulders rippling and twitching with inaction. A white man drove the wagon and another emerged onto the porch, both of them with uncut beards shaved only at the upper lip.

"Got them Lincoln beards on 'em," said one of the riders.

"Quakers," said another. He spat in the grass.

In the bed of the wagon lay a hexagonal pinewood box.

The bearded men looked at the riders, their eyes unshaken.

"May we help you?" asked the one on the porch. He had a steaming mug of something held both-handed against his chest. His gold wedding band tapped the porcelain three even times, loud. Behind him, the yellow-lit windows of the house began to wink out one after another.

The men looked at Swinney. His manner was softest and kindest, likeliest to elicit cooperation from the populace before resorting to fiercer means. Swinney rode forward a step, his carriage slumped, his breath ragged and audible.

"We're looking for the slave hunter."

The man on the porch lifted the cup two-handed to his mouth and took a sip.

"I'm sorry, sir, but I believe you men have come to the wrong place. We have no slave hunters here."

Swinney nodded, satisfied, and began to back up his horse, but another of the riders rode forward. "What you got in the box?"

The man on the porch rotated the mug in his hand, his eyes alight and unquivering.

"The body of my aged mother come home to lay aground."

"Well, God rest her," said the rider, smirking.

Swinney held up his hand to quiet him, then turned toward the other riders. "Obvious we come to the wrong place—"

Just then a horseman debouched from the trees, riding hard upon the wheel-tracked road the wagon had taken. He was tall upon a gray horse and hatless, only one hand upon the reins despite his speed.

"That's him," said one of the men, a Georgia slaveholder who'd had dealings with him in the past.

The Quaker men stood stone-faced, watching the rider come. When he arrived before them, they stood between him and the coffin, unarmed and unmoving, gazing into his sunken eyes. Looking for the inward light, perhaps. No sign of any affinity whatsoever crossed the divide between them. No words. Neither they nor the rider paid any mind to the men sitting their horses around them, as if they were entranced.

When the slave hunter finally announced himself, his name, the pine box began to thump and jolt, the dead come awake, the coffin lid hammered at from the inside. The slave hunter watched, no surprise on his wasted face.

"You are required by the Fugitive Slave Law of 1850 to hand him over to me," he said. He nodded at the box.

The Quaker stiffened. "That Bloodhound Law no longer applies." He paused a long moment. Inhaled. "Not since the Emancipation."

A smile twisted the slave hunter's face. "Tell you what," he said. He leaned forward, his one arm resting on the saddle horn. "You hand him over, I might forget your cellar. Might forget to bar the door and torch the rest them runaways you got hiding in there."

The Quaker on the steps looked a long moment down into his coffee mug, silent. Finally he nodded.

The pine box began to quake again, a scream reeling out of its hollows: "Lemme out! Please Lawd! Cut my throat fore that Clay-Born take me!"

The riders turned and smiled at one another, at what great fortune had befallen them.

Here was just the man they needed.

The slave hunter. The profiteer. The Colonel's brother.

Chapter 4

Callum awoke without opening his eyes. He listened. Just the sound of breath: his, hers, the horse's. He was back-to-back with Ava, curled up like that baby in the jar, knees to chest and cold. He opened one eye first. Pinpricks of light shone through the rough-sawn planking of the cabin. They were small lights of uniform caliber, violently constellated, a whole galaxy of them. He had not seen them the night previous.

He turned onto his back and sat up. Ava stirred, did the same. Narrow shoots of light crisscrossed the cabin interior on remnant trajectories. They looked down at themselves, then at each other. Callum looked past Ava to his shadow on the far wall. He shifted to one side and saw a shadow haunt where his had been, this one dark-painted upon the wall as if by a frenzied painter's brush.

Blood.

He crept across the bed, past Ava, toward the dark marking. There was a single glowing hole in the center. Slowly he looked over the edge of the bed frame and saw what he feared he would: Slumped on the floor below the patch of blood on the wall was the remainder of a man, dark-boned and slack-jawed, as though in final awe of the spirit that had evacuated him. He sat in a black pool of stain. He enjoyed no gloves nor boots, and Callum wondered if those items had been what got him killed. He still had his coat, a gray one that housed his rotting ribcage. Callum figured no one had stolen it for all the holes.

Ava looked over his shoulder at the thing and gripped his upper arm in both hands.

"I slept next to him," she said. "Jesus God, I slept next to him."

Callum looked at the horse. He was awake, regarding the body with his huge black eyes, no white in them, no concern. He flicked his tail and looked at Callum.

"Let's get on," said Callum. He got off the bed and stuffed the pistol into the front of his trousers and buttoned his coat and led the horse out the front door. Ava followed quickly behind him, glancing back at the body against the wall.

Callum had not unsaddled the horse the previous night, but the horse had not complained. The light in the east was pale through the trees that wickered the ridge, little color as yet. He got the small bag of feed and draped it over the horse's neck. He and Ava took turns drinking from a beef bladder of stream water, and it went down cold in the cold morning light. The dirt at their feet was gray, the rocks on the trail black.

"How 'bout some breakfast?" asked Callum.

"Ain't hungry," said Ava.

"I wasn't asking if it was just you that was hungry." He

paused a long moment and looked at his boots. "You seen dead men before?"

"I never slept next to one."

"Well—"

"Well, that man in there was sitting there staring at us all night, and I didn't even know it."

"I reckon he was looking a lot farther off than that."

"It ain't funny, Callum. Not to me."

Callum moved so he could see him in there, hollow-skulled, the goo of self dried up long ago. His vacant gaze had watched them move, sleep. He looked at Ava.

"You wanna bury him, don't you?"

She nodded.

He scratched his chest as if he had hair there to itch him.

"All right. I'll try and drag him out. Why don't you look for somewhere to dig the grave and something to dig it with."

She nodded.

Callum went back into the cabin and stood over the man. His bones had not gone bleach-white like those of old animal carcasses he'd seen, not yet. Dark strips and patches of tissue gummed the underpinnings like a rotten effigy. The hands and feet were webbed by old flesh or sinew, the flesh gradually disintegrating from the pale dome of the cranium, the skull itself rising openmouthed through the dead tissue that bound it. The teeth were yellow and complete save a gap where a musket ball had struck him in the mouth. Closer, he saw bone fragments stuck to the wall.

He took a breath and gripped the lapels of the gray coat and hauled the body across the floor, toward the door. It was lighter than he'd expected, and he was dragging well until one foot hooked a bedpost and the whole leg came loose at the hip.

"Shit."

He kept hauling, the head silly-necked and lolling like a drunkard's. The body started to come apart limb by limb, the connective tissue hardly more than dust, only the coat and trousers keeping them together. By the time he got him out the door he had little more than a woolen uniform of bones. Then the head caught a rock and cracked loose and rolled a couple of feet away. Callum looked around for Ava and didn't see her. The head stopped face-first against a large stone. It had a big hole blasted in the rear where the musket ball had exited. Callum turned the skull toward him with his boot and stared down into the black barrels of the eye sockets.

"You better not haunt my ass after all this."

"*Callum.*"

He straightened.

Ava had the blade of a shovel she'd found, no handle, and she slapped it in the palm of one hand.

"What are you doing to that body?"

"Nothing. He's coming apart on me."

"There's a trail out back. Goes to a small plot of pasture."

"I don't think he's gonna make it that far," said Callum, rolling the skull back toward the rest of the body with his foot.

"Then wrap him up in your coat."

Callum stiffened and pulled his coat closer around himself. "Don't sound sanitary."

"It'll be fine," said Ava. "He's all dried out."

"But you sewn me this coat."

"And now I'm asking you to put it to good use."

Callum snorted through his runny nose. Then he turned his head and pinched the bridge of his nose and blew a thick tail of snot onto the trail.

"Careful your brains don't go missing," said Ava.

"Nobody asked you."

Callum unbuttoned the coat and laid it out flat on the ground and piled in the slack-limbed carcass at odd angles of the joints and wrapped it all up like a picnic. Then he stuck his pistol through his belt and followed Ava up a steep trail behind the cabin, slipping on wet rocks, cussing under his breath. They came out into an old pasture just big enough to graze a few animals. Ava got on her bald knees and started digging two-handed with the naked shovel blade, as if it were a trowel. She dug and dug. Black-handed, dark-browed. Before long she'd carved a black scar of soil in the grass.

"Let me help," said Callum.

She shook her head at him.

"What about the horse?" he asked.

"He'll be fine."

Callum looked back toward the cabin. The understory was too dense to see anything. Beyond that the sun was just breaking the jagged line of the far-off ridges, igniting the hills like a west-moving fire. The bag of bones sat on the grass next to him, the bottom soaked with ground dew. He got closer to Ava and squatted down beside her and gently took the shovel from her hand. She let him. He tore into the earth with steady strokes, switching hands when one arm got tired. Ava squatted there beside him, watching, her breath captive, as if they were about to break through to a new world of some kind.

Some men said if you dug deep enough, you'd reach hell. Others said China. Callum thought of what hell might be like. He thought of a big dark place, like a great cavern, where the damned carried on whatever pursuits pleased them. Whatever outrages. Mobs of them down there, with long knives and sharp teeth. Men not very different from the Colonel's, perhaps.

The shovel struck rock. Callum challenged it, gently at first, then harder, quicker, scraping as if against some tomb in the earth. No use. The shovel made thin white streaks against the rock.

Ava touched his shoulder.

"It's deep enough."

Callum stopped himself. It was. He took up the coat and unrolled it. He slid the remains into their new home, endeavoring to position the various body parts into some semblance of anatomical correctness. It was the least he could do. They shoveled the earth back over the grave with their hands, careful to cover the body fully so that no gaps or vents could compromise the dead man's peace—or theirs.

Done, they found the sun upon them, the pasture flooded gold. The two of them followed the trail back to the cabin, solemn-faced and unspeaking. Callum carried his coat over one shoulder. He would shake out the bone dust and brave the wearing of it later, with a little more distance between him and the hole in the ground.

Ava led, the heels of her tall man's boots skidding on the wet rocks. The path terminated at the rear of the cabin. Callum saw the pile of junk where she'd found the shovel. He was just going to sift the pile for other items that could come in handy when he saw Ava round the front corner of the cabin and freeze. The shovel sparked on a stone beside her foot. She turned toward him, a silent scream distorting her face.

Chapter 5

The horse was gone, stolen. Too loyal to run off, too brave to flee. They were high in the mountains now with the cold coming, and they had no food, no water, no rifle, no matches—nothing. Everything gone, and the wind seemed colder, the rocks harder. The world meaner. They looked together at the cabin, the punctured walls, which whistled faintly when the wind blew. To stay would be to invite murder, a question only of specifics, of date and time. Callum put the coat back on, bone dust and all. They started walking.

Day and night they walked, their boots crackling on the leaves dead-curled on the path. A cold came out of the north, cruel and untimely. Twice they tried to stop and light a fire by striking the shovel against the right kind of stone. Once at dusk, once at midnight. Both times the right stone escaped them. No spark. They kept on, hardly talking, not bitter, knowing that any such sentiment was a luxury for the warm and well fed. Callum thought to take Ava's hand, but she had both of them hoveled deeply under her quilt for warmth. One hour, in weakness and cold, they huddled together amid the gnarled roots of some tree, close-clutched and hoping to warm.

Ava spoke up.

"What was their name again?"

"Who?"

"These relations of yours, on the coast."

"Gosling."

"How come they didn't send you over to them, when your parents died?"

Callum looked a little sideways at her. "Church don't pay for something like that. Doubt they'd even of tried anyhow, her husband being a Protestant. They put you with who'll take you."

"Oh," said Ava.

"Really they just want to get the children out the workhouse."

"Was it bad in there?"

Callum looked out through the trees and nodded. "People got to calling it *casan na marbh*—pathway of death—so many people didn't come out. Everybody crammed in close, worked to the bone, doing their unmentionables in the same tub. They did feed you twice a day. Stirabout and milk. Some potatoes. Problem was disease. Runs wild in those places. Each morning they wheeled out the dead in these special carts they had. There were pits for them out back. They had to cover the bodies all in lime, to help the smell."

"You were in there with your family, or after?"

Callum scratched his nose with the back of his hand. "Both," he said. "Went in with my mother and sister. I think it was typhus that got them."

"You don't know?"

"They were in a different block."

"And your father?"

"Hanged for a Fenian in '53. I don't hardly remember him."

"Fenian?"

"A rouser. A Irish Republican. One of them that rose up against the British."

"Catholic?"

Callum nodded.

Ava's hand tightened on his arm.

"I'm sorry," she said.

Callum shrugged and spat between his boots. "Wasn't you that killed him."

Day and night again. Once they heard horses and cleared from the path. They watched from the trees as a ragtag line of blue-coated cavalry riders passed them, heading north. They were shoddy-clothed and slumped in their saddles, their once-gold shoulder braids and trouser stripes moldered a sickly green. They pulled a string of riderless horses behind them, fitted with empty saddles.

Later, for decency, Callum took a narrow game trail into the woods. He was unbuttoning himself when he saw something on a rock near his foot: a smear. He followed the trail over a small rise and found an empty camp. Piled were the carcasses of two deer—one buck, one doe—both neatly knife-gutted, nothing but castoffs. In a second spot lay two men. They were wearing blue cavalryman's trousers but no gloves or boots or shirts. They'd been shot in the torso, the wounds ragged and erupted as if by scavenging knifepoint. He left them where they lay and returned to his spot by the blood-painted rock. He finished his intended business. Back in the road he could see faint markings where the bodies had been dragged. He said nothing to Ava. He didn't want to worry her.

That night, a few bivouac fires held small and flickering vigils on the far-off hills behind them. Fires like those the Colonel's men might make, or others like them. A riot of shots erupted once in the distance. The many-ridged echoes thwarted any estimation of their origin, what direction or distance or altitude. Several sporadic pops followed, men or horses finished off.

They walked through more days and nights, just how many becoming muddled. Callum's cold had worsened, his head distended with pressure, his upper lip mustachioed with snot. His thoughts were slow. His once-steady stride turned to shuffling. Ava's, too. Climbing hurt them in the lungs and thighs, descending in the joints and feet. Their stomachs had curled into angry knots. They zagged down the path before them, unmindful of things beyond their imaginings of biscuits and stew newly cooked. Now and then Callum felt eyes upon them, inhuman. He thought he saw the double-orbed gold of the lion's eyes once—perhaps the trick of an exhausted mind. Sometime later there were closer shots, two or three. Ahead of them maybe.

When scared enough, Callum pulled the Walker from his pants and held it low against his leg, the overlarge heft dropping his shoulder, the barrel hanging past his knee. Slivers of moonlight toyed at the edges of his vision, wraith-like and taunting. They had buried a man, and he felt some good in that, but there were too many unburied to worry his mind. Those he'd killed, those he might still have to. But slowly, slowly, those thoughts began to bleed out of his mind as if from a long-open wound, and he was empty, depleted.

"You smell that?"

A whisper from Ava, in the deep time of night. Callum sniffed, and even despite his congested nose, he could smell it: a cookfire.

Meat.

Ava looked at him, he at her. Their jaws tingling, their mouths wet.

When the smell grew strong, they left the path and circled a long way around, navigating by their noses. Ava was not as quiet as he was, but quiet enough. He glanced back with big eyes whenever she stepped on a stick or rustled a bush, and pretty soon she grew more aware of her own silence and the making of it. Callum found a narrow creek sluiced from higher up the mountain. Fallen leaves speckled its banks like wafer-thin coinage, bright in darkness. He had them walk its banks because the leaves were all wet and made little protest under their boots.

An orange glow in the woods ahead. They huddled behind a massive section of rock that must have fallen in some prehistoric epoch. Deep-set in the ground, trees grown twisted around its bulk. He jacked the hammer back on his double-loaded pistol and whispered for Ava to stay put. He gave her his slouch hat. He couldn't hazard the wide brim catching a branch or bramble. He told her to meet him at the road if she heard shots fired. She told him not to be a hero. He told her he didn't aim to be.

He moved forward to reconnoiter the terrain ahead. The Colonel had ordered him to do so many times before, the whole company waiting hungrily for what tidings this small and silent boy might bring them from the darknesses beyond their ken, houses and barns and bivouacked men. What provisions or livestock? What bulwarks or defenders?

He followed the creek upward, but it soon kinked sideways

along an upthrust of bare ridgeline, away from the source of the glow. He knelt at the bank and blacked his face with creek mud before taking to harder ground.

There could be pickets posted, men lying in wait for intruders. The fallen leaves could easily betray him, crackling like hearth fire under his boots. Still a good ways off, he began to toe himself leafless footprints before committing his full weight to each forward step. He could not sniff at his running nose. The snot ran freely onto his lips and chin. He ducked and twisted edgewise and contorted himself into strange positions to shape himself through the maze of gray and black branches. The leaves glimmered before him like tiny pennants. He moved slowly and with the patience of something not quite human, making no sound. His face was black, his hands, too, the bone-whiteness of the pistol grip hidden in his fist. He became the kind of thing he feared, mindless and hungry.

He saw the pond first, fire-mirrored, the source of the creek he'd followed. Beyond that the silhouettes of horses and men, black and one-dimensional against the flames of their fire. The fire was big and bright, licking the black sky with myriad tongues, shooting red-glowing cinders aloft like little rockets. He could make out three men and four horses. Something else, too, a dead animal of some species hanging by the hind legs from the overarching branch of a tree near the pond's edge.

The men had camped a good way from the road, but anyone with that outsized a blaze must be armed well enough to greet the uninvited. Callum knew that, and he knew also that one of the horses was the black one, the Colonel's, the physique evident even at such range.

He began to circle the pond toward them. He kept far

enough from the water's edge to remain hidden, close enough to keep watch. Whenever he did make a sound—any misstep at all—he would freeze in place, his good ear cocked, and wait for noise or movement, any sign he'd been heard. There was never any. No one knew what was haunting the edge of the woods.

He crouched behind a large-trunked tree as near to the men as he dared. Twenty paces. There were three of them: one man in a stovepipe hat with his back to him, one across and facing him, a third reclining off to the side in a plumed officer's hat devoid of insignia. All of them sunken-cheeked, with heavy dark beards. He thought they might be the trio of riders who had passed them their first day, or maybe others nearly interchangeable with them, long-faced men who had been living hard in these mountains for some time.

They were watching a pot boil on the flames. The horses were restless and shifty save for the Colonel's, nearest him. On the far side of the fire, he saw that it was a mountain lion hind-strung from the tree, its throat slashed, its forelegs reaching limply for the ground.

The reclining man sat up and pointed to the lion and said something, his words swallowed in the whoosh and crackle of the flames. The man closest to the lion stood up. He wore two pistols butt-forward and a twine-handled knife on the outside of his belt. He drew the knife and went to the animal. A section of the flesh had already been carved for meat and it seemed he was going to carve another. Instead, the man squinted and thumbed at the lion's side until he found the place he wanted. He pulled out his thumb and dug in with the point of his knife, working the blade as a doctor would a scalpel, his tongue jammed into the corner of his mouth.

After a while he called back over his shoulder and the top-hatted man put down the saber he'd been sharpening and tossed him something. It gleamed metallic when the firelight struck it, a ramrod fitted with a worm puller. An extractor. It looked like two tiny snakes coiled around each other, the heads sharp-pointed for drilling. Many of the Colonel's men carried such a one, a necessity for partisan warring where there were no hospital tents or aproned surgeons.

The man inserted the ramrod into the wound and began to twist, screwing the wormlike threads of the extractor into the softer lead of the bullet. Finally he pulled the bullet free on the end of the extractor and held it to the flames for them to see, the conical shape warped by impact. Then he lifted the lid of the pot, revealing an ellipsis of molten lead. He detached the bullet and dropped it into the pool, then replaced the lid.

After that he started to sit, but one of the others threw him a tin cup long blacked by old campfires. He caught the cup and stepped back to the lion. He knelt and dipped the tin cup into the bucket and came up with a cupful of something. It had to be blood.

That made them old Indian fighters, Callum knew. Like the Colonel. Men who were well versed in killing. Who had come to adopt certain rituals of the culture they fought. Callum had been told of the practice at fireside one night by some of the Colonel's men, liars and truth-sayers by turn. Whether the ritual was a true one among the Indians or just the white man's morbid facsimile thereof, they claimed not to know. The Colonel had forbade any such practice, they said, but they also said he had been one of the thirstiest on the plains, believing that some simulacrum of the strength and spirit of a creature could be transmitted into the killer's blood. The men of the company rumored among themselves within the boy's hearing—for his hearing, perhaps—that among the red men such a practice was confined to the liver of the animal alone, blood-filled and raw, but the liver was a small organ and did not sate the appetites of the white men. So they had taken liberties, as was their wont.

The man stood up with the cup and returned to the fire. He handed the cup back to its owner, the reclining man in the plumed hat. Their leader, by the look of things. Meanwhile, the man nearest Callum picked up a brass picket mold for making bullets.

Callum thought about what to do. He thought of Ava, of her hunger-sharpened face. He thought of the seed of being she carried, a thing whose worthiness to live was not already blacked over by sin. Like these men, like him. And not least, he thought of his own hunger.

He could go up friendlylike and ask them for food. For the horse, the rifle, the matches. The things he and Ava would die without. The men might give him a scrap of something. They might shoot him. He could ask with his pistol instead, but they had too many horses, too many guns. He and Ava, they wouldn't get far. And there was something else he could do. The other thing, that didn't involve asking. But he had done enough of that already, and he didn't want to do it again. Not ever. He decocked the pistol. He would have to take his chances.

He started forward, tucking away the gun, but stopped. The reclining man had sat up and was pointing to a nearby satchel. The man with the bullet mold put it down and reached into the satchel with both hands and brought out a square-shaped glass jar. He handed it slowly to the leader with high and straight-armed carefulness, as if afraid of waking the thing inside.

The leader took the jar and held it toward the firelight and stared a long time into the time-warped glass, at the nearly translucent creature within. He twisted the jar slight degrees this way and that, as if calibrating some kind of instrument, and Callum suddenly wondered if he was trying to see the bone frame and organs of the creature shadow-formed against the fire, the truth of species within.

The man shrugged. He leaned far forward and set the jar on the fire grate next to the molten lead. There was a look of curiosity on his face. The other men watched, the three of them greedy-eyed for what would happen as the temperature rose. They were not watching the trees.

Callum sidestepped until the bulk of the horse blocked his view of the men and theirs of him. Then he came out of the woods, taking long, well-aimed strides toward the horse, leafless patch to leafless patch. The horse watched him and did nothing. He found himself just on the other side of the horse from the camp, his legs lined up behind the horse's. He knew the men had ruined their night vision on the blaze.

"Not sure I understand the need for this, Giff."

"Pay attention, you might learn something."

"Such as what?"

"Such as what hell is like."

Callum was moving toward them before he knew it, propelled. He came up behind the man with the stovepipe hat and pointed the pistol at the back of his head.

Click.

"Take him off the fire," he said.

The man straightened, didn't move.

"I ain't the one that put him there."

"Now," said Callum.

Slowly, the man took the jar from the fire grate. He held it in his lap. Across the fire, the leader—this man Giff—watched the pistol quiver at the base of his comrade's skull. He smiled.

"Big pistol," he said. "You ever use it?"

"You stole our horse, supplies, food. We'll die without them."

Giff pushed his hat back and sniffed.

"And?"

"And I want them back."

Giff smiled again.

"You do, do you?"

"That's all I want."

"Oh," said Giff, "you'll get you more than that."

He went for his gun. Callum shot Giff dead in the heart. The stove-hatted man screamed and clutched his ear; the man to Callum's right lifted his pistol. Callum cocked and fired. The man flew backward, out of the light.

The Walker was empty.

Callum reached down and yanked the deafened man's revolver from its holster and stood over him, aiming left-handed at the man's face. The man lay there powder-burned and blood-eared, moaning. His hat had come off and the top of his head was shiny and bald. He looked up at Callum.

"Mercy," he said.

Callum looked down at him a long moment. He was breathing hard, and he could feel the blood thundering through him. He could feel it beating in his fingertips. Thump, thump, thump. His finger wanted to pull that trigger. To be done with it. He looked away a moment.

The saber caught him on the inside of his left thigh. He screamed. The man let go of the sword and made a grab for the pistol, and Callum stepped back and pulled the trigger right in his face.

It was not like the others. Not something you could unsee. The man's body crumpled before him, the head blasted into the darkness beyond the close halo of firelight.

Callum stumbled backward, dragging the handle of the saber in the dirt. Blood ran down the blade and wetted the pommel; it made indecipherable scribbles on the ground. Callum watched the blade fall from his leg, and it did not hurt, not yet. Still he dropped the pistols he was holding and reeled. The pond circumscribed a clear opening to the sky, treeless, and the stars were bright and high, seeing and cold. They saw what wreckage. They had seen from aeons back, those stars, and he wondered with what all they had seen were they surprised. They did not look surprised.

He looked down at himself, his open palms, his blushing pant leg. The Walker was lying at his feet, empty, and he picked it up and stuck it through his belt. He saw on the leader's hands a pair of fine riding gauntlets. He took these and donned them and took the jar from the fire. He hid the jar back inside a saddlebag, not intending for Ava to know what he'd stolen, not yet. He should have already told her, and now it was too late. He unbuckled the man's gun belt as quickly as he could, his fingers fumbling, and stuffed this into a saddlebag as well. He rifled the men's pockets for currency and found some and tucked it into his coat uncounted. He took up the stove-hatted man's satchel, heavy and clanking with sundry items and a good four pounds of hard bread, and slung it over his shoulder.

He saw two horses standing nervously at the edge of the trees, the rest gone. He knew he should run them down and rope them in, but he wanted to get out of the light. The impulse to run was like a scream inside him.

He swung into the saddle of the black horse and crashed away in the direction of the road, following the creek downward through the wood, the branches whipping blood in streaks across his face. He broke from the trees and struck the road at a gallop, only to stop, disoriented, after some fifty yards. He called Ava's name. Called and called. He needed to quit calling if he was to hear her call back to him, but he called several more times before he could stop himself. He heard her call back from northward on the road, it sounded like. He yanked the horse around and rode in that direction. Slower now, fearful of running her down.

She was on the side of the path a half minute up the road. She climbed into her old spot behind him and he gave her the satchel. He yanked the reins around again and rode hard to the south, descending. He rode the horse hard enough that Ava could not speak to him or him to her, the horse putting long strides between them and the wreckage left in the woods.

They were still riding when the neighboring ridges rose sheer-limned out of darkness, dawning as if for the first time, a cataclysmic upthrust from the ground. Still riding when the sun shot sideways through the forest, and the trees whirled past like black-charred columns in a forest on fire, everything a blur in the violence of flight.

The slave hunter dismounted and led his horse toward the black stain of smoking coals, the ring of bodies outburst as if from an explosion. It was dawn. Cupped in his palm was a small pouch, draw-strung, which the men had watched him worry between his

fingers as he rode. It made a soft rattle in his hand, like stones maybe, or the toyed satisfaction of rosary beads. It gave them chills. A sound like frictive joint bone—a popping ruined knee, or the crackle of a once-broken jaw. It would be in his great white hand, worried, and then gone again, quick as magic. The mystery of its contents garnered no end of rumor. The pouch disappeared from his hand as he approached the scene.

One of the men toed the head of a dead man that lay beside him. There was a neat hole in the forehead, penny-size, the insides blown clear out the rear.

"Hell of a mess," he said.

The mindless wake lay sprawled several feet behind the head.

The slave hunter glanced in that direction. "Yes," he said. "It is."

The men watched him squat before a stray saber. The edge was blooded but dry. Nearby lay a frantic scrawl-work in the dirt. His long-boned index finger unscrolled to a point. It touched the grit that coated the pommel, traced the strange glyphs in the ground. He seemed to cipher them right to left, as one might the strange languages of desert people, until reaching spotted blood coins that punctuated the message like crazed ellipses. He prodded them lightly and touched his finger to his tongue. He stood. He walked to where the prints of a heavy-shoed horse ran parallel to those of a man, the right boot print straight-streaked in ruts, the left toe-struck, until the footprints disappeared and hoofprints lengthened to those of a horse at a gallop. He squatted down and placed his hand into the hoofprints.

Behind him, three of the men were roping in the loose horses. Others were staring at the eviscerated trophy of mountain cat. And the rest were already dismounting, spreading out their bedrolls for a few hours' rest. The slave hunter stood and cleared his throat. The men looked at him, their faces hangdog and coon-eyed. "Back on the horses," he said. "This was him. He's hurt. Bleeding."

Somebody stuck a tired palm in the hollow of his eye socket.

Nobody wanted to keep on, not without a round of shut-eye. "How bad's he bleeding?"

The pouch was again in the slave hunter's hand, popping between his fingers. "Bad enough," he said. He eyed the men and spat. "Best square those bedrolls. I don't mean to share my cut with some bunch of laggards."

Backbones stiffened across the clearing, those of men unaccustomed to such umbrage, audacity. But no one acted on pride. They mounted their horses, their mouths clamped shut, their greed the better of them. After all, this boy—he would make them rich.

Chapter 6

Come midmorning, Callum grew light-headed and cold, colder even as the sun spun white-burning into a pewter sky. His leg throbbed now, a growing hammer beneath the flesh.

The road had forked before them three times in the night, and Callum had always taken the leftmost path, easterly, making no effort to disguise his tracks. They had been descending for some time when the tunnel of trees broke into a meadow of high grass, browned and dry. The long blades rustled in the wind. They left the path for a small knoll, where a leafless tree twisted toward the sky. They rode past the tree, just down the far side of the knoll. They did not want to be seen from the road.

Callum had not looked at the wound in his thigh, as if ignoring it would help. He slipped off the side of the horse, blood-slick, and lay flat in the grass. The ground was uncertain underneath him, undulant. Ava leapt off the horse. He'd hidden the wound from her for most of the night; she'd only just discovered it. She looked at the horse's side and the leg of his trousers, dark from hip to hem.

"Goddammit, Callum."

She knelt down next to him.

"What happened?"

"Saber."

"Take off your trousers."

Callum nodded and fumbled at his buckle. She brushed his hands away and unbuckled him and unbuttoned the fly and peeled the pants down to his ankles. He looked up and saw the upreaching tree silhouetted against the sky, the manifold branches like some insidious fracturing of the heavens. He did not look down at his leg.

Ava lifted his leg and bent the knee. The intake of his breath was sharp, sudden, like the thrust of a knife.

"You're lucky," she said.

"Lucky?"

"Missed the artery. Whoever stuck you knew his business, but he missed."

He heard her tearing scraps of fabric.

"What in the hell happened up there?"

Callum looked off to one side, toward the farther ranges in their wake. He thought he saw the spiraling of dark flecks in the sky. Carrion birds tiny-ranged, still-hung.

"I got the horse back. And our food."

Ava prodded the edges of the wound with her fingers.

"Son of a bitch," he said, gasping.

"I heard shots," she said.

He cut his eyes at her.

"I did what I had to."

She stood and looked down at him. She was tall against the sky.

"You had to shoot somebody."

Callum had begun to breathe hard with the pain.

"Yes," he said.

She sniffed. "That wound infects and you're gonna be a dead boy."

"Just let's bandage it and we'll find something."

"You get anything else from them? Spirits?"

She turned to check the saddlebags. She turned to the one with the jar.

"I didn't get anything off them like that," he said.

She unclasped the flap and lifted it.

"Don't do that," he said. "Please don't."

"What all you got hidden in here?"

The horse was too tall even for Ava to peer inside the bag, so she dug her hand inside and started sifting. Her hand stopped; her face went slack. Slowly, she lifted the jar from the bag by the lid. She held it against the sun, the shape inside newly distorted by the heat-crazed glass.

"My brother," she said.

"Brother?"

"That's what I said."

"But—"

"Miscarried. You took him from my daddy's study."

"I did."

"I couldn't find him before we left. I thought somebody'd stole him."

"Somebody would of. Would of took him off to a carnival show."

"How dare you," she said. She squeezed the jar between her hands.

He felt a long way off from her, and cold. She looked away.

"They were gonna cook him," he said.

She looked at him.

"What?"

"Last night. The men. They were gonna boil him. Over the fire grate."

Ava's eyes became rimmed with whiteness. She knelt slowly at Callum's side, the jar on her knees, and he could feel her fury. He was acutely aware of his thin white legs, his lost blood.

"You killed them," she said.

Callum nodded.

"How many?"

He swallowed. "Three."

She ran her tongue across her teeth, slowly, as if testing their sharpness.

"You did good, then."

He looked away.

"Callum." She took his chin. "You did good."

Callum looked into her eyes, her pupils haloed by blue irises. They glowed with some newly crazed electricity. *Good* was not the word.

"What I had to," he said.

"What you had to," she said. He started to look away, but she held his chin. She looked into his eyes. "What you had to, Callum."

He nodded.

Ava put down the jar and tied a long scrap of her quilt around the wound on his leg and applied pressure. Blood blossomed on the white fabric. Then she got out what was left of the side of meat after the riders' depredations and started to eat. She offered Callum some; he couldn't. The pain had begun to hit him, a long wail from the wound. He thought it would stop but it didn't. It got bigger inside him. Louder.

Wailing through his whole body. He arched his back and drove his shoulders into the ground. He clenched fistfuls of grass and ripped them out and clenched fistfuls of dirt. Ava swallowed her food. She put her hand on his forehead, and it felt cool against his skin.

"Any higher and we'd be putting a tourniquet on your leg at the hip. You'd be lucky to keep the leg. But we got to disinfect. Before it starts to discolor." She bent over the bandage and sniffed. "And to smell."

"Water," said Callum.

She dug in the saddlebags and found their beef bladder: drunk dry.

"We got to get on," she said. "We got to find something somewhere to disinfect with."

He was breathing hard now, the pain like an enemy underneath his skin. To deny its existence the only thing. He gasped for air, not strong enough. It was there, there, there. Pounding. He rolled his head against the ground and searched the heavens, the sun a pale and watery orb in the grayed-over sky. It seemed distant, no help, jealous of its own warmth or shine.

He rolled his head the other way, his eyes white-bulbed, searching.

There: a V of migratory birds, white-flying against the bruised sky. They were geese. He watched them, the gentle working of their wings, long-feathered for wind riding, and the neatly tucked pairs of webbed feet. The bottle-shaped contour of necks and bodies so sleek cutting through the sky, and hollow-boned, like something God-made of the truest reckonings. They flew with military precision, uniformly spaced, formation unbroken. There would be shots to come, lead pellets swarm-blasted from marshes and thickets, some of their number lost, wing-shot, fallen broken from the sky, twist-turning toward the end they all feared. But the wedge would hold, its logic true.

Callum felt tidings white-hatched in his blood, rising, and he wanted so badly to follow them south. Fly past this cold and hard-ridged land and reach some lowland lake or pond. Sun-silvered. Warm. The fall endured.

"Callum. Callum, wake up."

A hand on his face. Gentle, then firmer.

"*Callum.*"

A slap.

He opened his eyes to the gray sky, empty. He looked down. Ava. Her face was dark against the sky. Worried.

"Lost you for a second there. You got to fight it."

He nodded.

Ava helped him to stand. He pulled up his trousers. The fabric was blood-caked and stiff. He walked to the right side of the horse and put his right foot in the stirrup and mounted that way, no pressure on his left leg. But the punctured thigh had swelled and did not like the saddle at all. Ava was working on one of the saddlebags. She was arranging things neatly for the jar. She finished, and he shucked one foot from the stirrup so she could use it to mount. She put her hands in his coat pockets for warmth, like she sometimes did.

They topped the knoll, heading back toward the path, and stopped a moment. The crests of neighboring mountains broke from a sea of cloud, small sharp-pointed hills levitating in the sky. In the foreground lay the path, a narrow strip of black dirt through the meadow. Callum traced the line of it northward, the way they'd come, to the dark-tunneled trees where the woods gave on to the field. It was all quiet save the dry whispering of the grass. It had taken them days to get back the horse. Anyone pursuing them on horseback would have made great strides in overtaking them.

He listened closely for the rumor of hooves on the wind from the north. Listening so hard for danger seemed only to invite the hearing of it. There was the faintest thunder he may or may not have heard. He first thought it was coming downwind from the way they'd come, but the wind was swirling in the meadow and it could have come from the direction they were heading. Or it could be nothing.

He took to the trail, and for the first few minutes he didn't know how he could keep riding for the pain. Each jolt in the saddle stole a breath from his lungs. He tried to go somewhere in his mind. He tried to go to that stratum of quiet sky again, high enough to map a world, all its meanness grown small underneath him. The trying helped, but barely. He could not keep his head above the pain. It was with him every step, insistent. A brother that carried him along, his slouch hat bobbing over the saddle as he rode.

The trail dropped them onto a wider droving road a few hours later. He thought it was the one that went into Asheville. They rode all day with the hope of a farm or cabin where something for the wound could be borrowed or bought or stolen. There was nothing, and Callum had begun to feel a chill crawling up his spine, a flush burning in his face. A slippage between two worlds, like he'd felt the day he was shot. He said nothing to Ava.

Dusk coming, she reached around and put an ungloved hand on his forehead the way his mother had once done. He had the slouch hat pulled low and she had to lift the brim to do it. She drew her hand away after a moment. She didn't say anything.

They kept riding past dark. The moon was out. The wind had moved the fallen leaves to one shoulder, and the white dust of the road glowed with an otherworldly paleness broken only by the fissurelike shadows of the overhanging trees. The leaves had been falling constantly, a slow showering of fire. Many of the trees were nearly naked now. They looked lonely, reaching for the sky.

Now and again he and Ava saw the yellow-lit windows of cabins on the steep hillsides to either side, but they could not find the paths that led up to them. They never saw any. Whether they were hidden by man's disguising or the thick-wooded nature of the country, they didn't know.

They rode a long time into the night. Callum's thigh was thundering and he was cold and his mind was mostly black. They were heading up a long and gradual rise when he felt eyes on him. Eyes like he'd felt with the lion. He thought it could be the fever. The pain. Nevertheless, he scanned the sides of the trail. Nothing.

Then he walked the horse slightly sideways and looked over his shoulder: a pair of lights on the road behind them. Lanterns. He squinted. The flames were slender and tall in their globe-shaped housings of glass. He turned the horse fully sideways and stopped to watch. The twin coronas of light shone bodiless in the black tunneling of trees, dancing in the motion of their progress as though they constituted the gaze of some creature come yellow-eyed and slinking from the darkness below.

"How far, you think? Half mile?" asked Ava.

Callum nodded. "Maybe less."

"Drovers?"

The lanterns were of uncommon brightness. Not candlelit like most.

"I don't think," said Callum. "You got to burn whale oil or kerosene to get them that bright."

"Or be a haint."

He gave her a look.

"Army, then?" she asked.

"I don't know," said Callum. "And I don't want to wait to find out."

He turned to look up the rise of the road. Cresting that rise they would be silhouetted against the night sky, starkly exposed, surely spotted. He looked to the woods alongside the road. The land rose steeply here, like a riverbank. No choice. He urged the horse off the shoulder of the road and into the trees. The horse climbed until Callum reined him on a flat outcropping of rock some twenty yards above and beyond the road.

They climbed off the horse and lay prone on the rock, watching the lights come toward them. Callum swallowed hard. He reached up and drew the rifle from its scabbard. When he lay back on the rock, Ava looked at him.

"What kind of tracks were we leaving on that road?"

"I don't know," he said.

The moonlit dust of the road looked pure as new-fallen snow from where they lay, no prints to betray them. Truth or a conspiracy of moon and dust, he wasn't sure. He thought of what Ava had said, of what spirits might be upon them. Men or ghosts of men—he didn't know which was worse.

The two lights were getting closer now, flickering through the trees below them. Callum aimed the rifle at them and sighted down the barrel. Through a break in the canopy of limbs he glimpsed two riders on horseback. Men. They had their lanterns held low, and Callum realized they were tracking something in the road.

"Shit," he whispered. "Shit."

Ava looked at him, wide-eyed. He looked back down the barrel and endeavored to sight the riders, but the rifle began to tremble in his grasp. Subtly at first but worsening. He tried to steady his aim but failed. He didn't know what was happening. His mind seemed good, unbroken, but the trembling wouldn't stop. It was like the world was coming apart, breaking open.

Ava said, "You feeling that?"

He looked at her, his eyes wide, his head nodding stupidly on his neck.

He looked back at the riders. They had stopped short of where he and Ava and the horse had left the road. They started moving to the far shoulder, not quite opposite the outcropping of rock.

Ava grabbed his shoulder and pointed to the crest of the road. A cloud of dust rose curling against the sky, and through that dust emerged a horned animal, a steer. Then another and another, each with thick dark shoulders and white horns, and then a whole mass of them came, wild-driven and mob-hooved, down the road like a flood. Drovers appeared on horseback alongside them at intervals. They had long staffs from which lanterns swung in flaming arcs above their heads. The cattle descended the road at a growing pace, churning the dust to a mess of hoofprints, thundering underneath the high outcropping of rock that held the boy and girl, erasing any tracks that might have betrayed them.

They watched the herd pass underneath them, a dark muscling of beasts that seethed and roiled like an angry river. Callum raised his eyes from the long shouldering of flesh to the two lantern-bearers watching from the far side of the road, their faces like jack-o'-lanterns above the fires they carried.

The shorter of them was rotund, his grip the weaker, his lantern light shaky at best. He leaned in the saddle and spat on the ground, wiping his mouth with the back of his hand, and Callum saw that it was Swinney.

Callum looked to the taller man, who held his lantern high above the herd, and it did not shake. He was taller than the Colonel in the saddle but narrower, scarecrowlike, with a face so long-jawed and hollow-eyed, he might have seemed to some a punishment for the prenatal sins of his father or mother. At first Callum thought the man was reaching behind himself to scratch his back. Then he turned to speak to Swinney. The left sleeve of his coat was pinned at the shoulder, empty. Swinney nodded at the words of the one-armed man, deferent, his head bowed. Taking orders. Then he looked into the darkness on the road behind them and made a gesture of some kind.

The one-armed man watched the great current of flesh pass by him, as if from some darkened shore. The horse he sat was pale in color, like ash or smoke. The last of the cattle passed, the last drover, too, and as they did, long shoots of flame erupted from the edges of the road into the middle of the herd. Gunfire. The cattle broke into stampede, moaning. The poled lanterns of the drovers fell into the hooved maelstrom like sudden-wrecked ship masts, the drovers churned under alongside their instruments. The herd charged away down the road, mindless, and in the wake of settling dust came the whoops and screams, the silvery arcs of cutting implements, the fallen hulks butchered for feast.

Chapter 7

Ava's chin hovered an inch above the bare surface of the rock. She had her arms tucked underneath her chest for support, her prone body huddled close to Callum's. She had her eyes on the pair of lantern-bearers across the road. She kept them there even as she spoke to Callum, her voice a whisper.

"That round man who I think it is?"

Callum nodded.

"I thought Swinney looked out for you, took you in after the wreck?"

"*Looking* seems about right."

"What about that one-arm son of a bitch?"

Callum wiped his mouth with the back of his hand.

"I don't know," he said.

But even as he said he didn't, the dimmest knowing stirred in him—his gut—like the fragment of an unremembered dream. He kept the rifle leveled on the pair of them, the fat man and the tall, as they urged their horses into the settling dust of the road, their lanterns smoldering in the risen smoke like the very engines of its creation. Their horses trotted back down the road, toward where the rest of the war party was hunched over the dead cattle that littered the ground, busily disassembling them with knives and belt hatchets, joint by joint.

Callum knew they would eat themselves jolly on such a boon. Feast and famine—their way. His, too, for many months. He could even remember fondly some of those times, like the moonless night the Colonel and two others had strode into an enemy encampment in purloined uniforms, replying "Hundred and Sixth New York" whenever challenged. They'd ridden away before dawn with two horses each, a mule loaded with stew meat and hardtack, and various bottles of spirits confiscated from men on picket duty, taking the time to dress them down for their unkempt uniforms and sleep-red eyes.

Callum watched the men begin to light their cookfires in the woods below, splitting their number to each side of the road to allow converging fire should anything of opportunity or threat happen along its course. The game animals were growing fat in the mountains for winter, and slow, but riding in hard pursuit they would not have had much time to hunt. Callum knew the men down there must be hungrier even than their custom. Ornerier, too. So he was surprised when a group of riders detached from the butcher work and came back up the road at a hard gallop, the one-armed man in the lead. They thundered past Callum and Ava's rock and continued onward, cresting the rise of the road as a single dark shape, buoyant-looking and spiny with armament. They disappeared on the other side. Swinney was not among them.

Callum let the hammer down on the rifle and got to his knees. He looked at Ava.

"Let's get out of here while we still got some dark left."

"Out of here where?" she asked him.

Callum looked at the mountains behind them. The slopes dark, unreckonable. No place he really wanted to go.

"You serious?" she said.

Callum nodded.

"I don't see as how we're gonna find anything up there to keep that wound from infecting."

"Don't see as how we got much choice in the matter."

Ava, wordless, got first onto her knees, then her feet. Callum slid the rifle back into the saddle scabbard. He took the horse by the reins and started up the slope, perpendicular to the droving road. Ava stepped forward and took hold of the reins.

"You go first," she said. "Find the quietest way. We'll follow."

He nodded and they started to climb.

It was not steep enough to go on all fours, but close. Callum plumbed the darkness with open hands. Before long his fingertips touched a waist-high maze of leafless underbrush and branches, fallen limbs dead-handed from the ground with the slimmest bonelike branches to snag and break. Other bushes whiplike and thorny enough to draw blood, to leave spoor. And everywhere leaves already fallen, too dry for stealth. They would have to push through it. There was no other way. Even if they could slip through, the horse couldn't.

He looked down on the campfires, the feasting men. They were too far to hear. He looked to the east, the way the one-armed man had ridden. He thought he saw a paleness low in the sky. Not much time. They had to be safely distant come daylight. Distant from the men, the road. The alternative, if they weren't, as unthinkable as it was certain.

Callum pushed his slouch hat off the back of his head so that it hung from his neck by the chin strap, and then he pressed forward into the underbrush, Ava following with the horse, the forest crackling in protest. The sound seemed to carry farther through the unleafed trees, the cold air. It grated him. After a while he cocked his bad ear forward and wished for something to stuff into his good one.

They climbed and climbed, the way steep and dark. He kept his eyes slitted to protect them from naked thorns the size of cockspurs that seemed to haze his every move. Soon he was breathing hard, his face on fire, the stabbing replayed with each step. He looked back at Ava.

"You okay?"

She nodded.

"You?"

He turned around as if he hadn't heard her. A deaf ear was good for that.

The wind was out of the west and brought them the faint scent of burning cattle flesh, something newly vicious to Callum in the smell. He thought of the skinless slabs of muscle over the flames, the red engines of beasts fired black. Fat sizzling along the striations, the pop-pop of gristle. Hard men would be watching, wet-mouthed to feed. Their tongues yellow-coated, slick as worms along their lips.

Fever, he thought.

He tripped on something. His hands hit the ground. Dead leaves, cold and browning. He exhaled and tried to stand and couldn't. He sank to the ground and looked at the sky. The stars were bleeding like so many comets. He snorted and got up. Ava put her hand on his back, but he was already climbing again, all grace gone from his movement, thrash-limbed for progress.

"Callum," he heard behind him. "Callum!"

He kept on. He knew they were cutting a swath through the forest, twigs and limbs pale-broken in their wake—a trail the ineptest could track. But their pursuers would have to strike upon it first. He doubted that, but the thought of the one-armed man wouldn't leave him. The way he took that detachment down the road. The Colonel's men wouldn't follow just anyone—no one they didn't fear—especially with new meat on the fire.

There was wetness down his leg, piss-warm. He found his hands on the ground, clawing upward. He snuck a look behind him. Ava's head was down, her legs pistonlike, her hands on the reins. The horse was calm. The moonlight fell jagged on his big shoulders as he climbed.

Callum tried not to think of his punctured leg. Couldn't help it. His mind was running a course of its own. He had been witness to infection, a man's limb turned green-rotted and foul as that of a fairy-tale monster's, the badness creeping slowly into other parts of him, corrupting him, until he was like the bad place carved out of a piece of fruit.

Callum did not want to end that way, had never thought he would. He tried to disbelieve this newly cauled reality being thrust upon him. To hold instead to an image of hearth fire, Ava beside him, the tidewater of the coast calm outside a fancy set of French doors. Maybe a storm coming inland from the sea. Maybe they would welcome it. Run together to some nearby canning shed, with a tin roof, and await its music.

He stumbled again on something—a dead tree—and pitched forward. His palms struck the ground. His right hand hit the leaves, his left something else: dirt, hard-packed. He turned to Ava.

"There's a trail here."

"Game?"

"Wider."

Callum started up the path, making headway. Before long he could open his eyes wide without fear of catching a thorn or branch. The forest to either side seemed canted toward him, the leaves and branches just grazing the edges of his coat and trousers. Tree roots crisscrossed underfoot, a gnarled stairway of the sort that wood elves might shape out of the mountains for their own secret commerce. Later the path began to zigzag up the slope, lessening the grade. At a treeless overlook, Callum stopped to rest. He sank to his knees, then his backside. His face burned; his leg thundered.

Ava squatted down beside him, near his good ear, the reins held loosely in one hand. They had put good distance between themselves and the road. Callum looked down upon the fires of the Colonel's men, grown smaller but no less threatening. He blinked at them. From this height it looked like the encampment of some heathen tribe, ravenous and fire-crazed. He felt like a hunted animal, treed, the world of his knowing and that of his worst imaginings converged beneath him, an underworld he could not perch above forever. Enemies within him, enemies without.

He thought of how the slightest cut could give portal to disease and rot, as if the world beyond a man's own bodily sanctum was swarming with opportunistic hordes, flesh-hungry, not blighted but blight itself. Like the men down there. Their eyes enlightened by the sight of blood, their bodies affixed with glittering implements of the kill, hands bladed or fire-spitting. He could see them down there, teeming, fire-glazed organisms small as worms from such vantage.

He wished he could be something more than he was,

something wicked and biblical. Something that could come through them in the dead of night. End them. Then they could worry him no longer. Worry him about how they might steal away what was good in his world, what he loved. And thinking of what he would do to them, what secret butchery, he wondered if something mean had slipped into him. Something vicious. For the first time, he touched the pale worm of scar growing along the side of his head, still tender above his dead ear. He ran his finger along the raised luster of flesh.

Ava reached around and stilled his hand.

"Don't do that," she said. "Don't play with it."

He dropped his hand away and nodded, grim-lipped.

"What's wrong?" she asked him.

He looked at her. "I don't know."

She put her hand on his forehead.

"You got a little fever going. That's what. Come on. You don't want to sit here and let it go wild and sick in your head. I can see it happening."

"I don't know if it's just the fever."

She stood up and tugged at his arm.

"It's what the hell I say it is, Callum. Now get on your feet and quit ruminatin'."

He kept his seat on the rock.

"I ain't ruminatin'."

"Like hell you ain't."

"I just don't feel too good about what we got ahead of us."

"Don't say that."

He flung his hand toward the valley. "Look at them down there. Why the hell do they got to come after us? I didn't even kill the son of a bitch."

"They don't know that."

"If I'd of thought of it, I'd of pinned a note on him saying I didn't."

"You really think that of helped?"

Callum shook his head. "You like to think that people, in general, and I mean on the scale of generations, are learning from their mistakes, getting better. But with what all I seen, I don't know if I could believe that."

Ava nodded and stilled herself. She let go of his arm and squatted down next to him, then actually sat on her rear, her arms clasped around her knees.

"My daddy, he used to read the writings of this naturalist in England. You know what a naturalist is?"

Callum gave her a look.

"Well, anyway," she said, "this naturalist, Darwin, he's traveled all over the world, studying creatures of all kinds, some extinct, and you know what he says?"

Callum shook his head again. "No, but I bet you're gonna—"

"He says individuals with traits most profitable for survival are the ones that end up surviving—most the time anyway—so every species of creature is always evolving, passing its traits down the line." She pressed her thumbnail into the leather of the reins once, twice. "Kindly makes you wonder what type of creature we're evolving into, what with so much war. Takes a different sort of person to thrive under such conditions."

Callum felt a meanness well up in him. He didn't know why.

"Sounds awful queer to me. I think I might of preferred your ghost stories."

"You know what else he said?"

"Not real sure I want to."

"He says that shines light on the origin of man, his history."

"Is that so," said Callum.

"It could be there's no real gap between us and the animals, nothing unbridgeable. It could be we all come from a single common ancestor."

"Like from Adam?"

"Like from monkeys."

"He said that?"

"People have."

"And your daddy believed in this Darwin character?"

"He was open to the man's ideas."

"That where he got the idea to put babies in jars?"

The slap exploded inside his head. Afterward he could feel the reddened imprint of her hand on the side of his face, hot as a burn. By the time he regained his bearings, she was disappearing up the trail, taking big steps that matched her overlarge boots.

"You son of a bitch," he told himself.

He got to his feet with his punctured leg as straight as possible, like one of those wooden-legged veterans you always saw in the small towns. He looked down at the fires a last time and was transported back to the tiny lake of fire, the hanging cat, the three men dead. The naturalist's logic maddened him, and he didn't want to think why.

Just then he heard her come half-skidding back down the trail, breathless.

"Callum," she said. "Callum—"

But he was hardly listening. "I'm sorry for what I said," he told her.

She grabbed the sleeve of his coat and tugged. "I know," she said. "But did you hear me? There's a light up there, a cabin." She pointed up the trail, her eyes bright.

"Light?" said Callum, the word flickering through the dark of him.

The trail broke onto a dirt yard speckled with castoffs of a sedentary life—feathers of ill-fated birds and piles of stove ash and rinds of unknown fruits. Scatterings of game bones, molding apples the size of cherries. Amid this offal, a one-room cabin rose errantly against the sky, its walls struck wayward as if by violent wind, its foundation a four-cornered piling of incongruent stones gathered seemingly without regard to size or shape or any architectural soundness. The porch floundered. The tin roof was red-rusted. The whole structure whimsy-walled as something thrown up by some slothful forebear in a single day of work, drunk.

There was a rocking chair to one side of the door, in it a sleeping man with a stovepipe hat and a yellow-white beard that hung to his blanketed knees. He was snoring, and when he inhaled he rocked slightly backward in the chair. He held his breath so long, Ava and Callum looked at each other, thinking he might just have died in his sleep. At last he exhaled a long and corrupt sigh, his airway chittering as though something had been trapped in his throat.

Broken glass twinkled at the mouth of the yard.

Callum looked at Ava and shrugged and stepped forward.

Crunch.

The old man snapped awake, his eyes white-rounded, and like a snake striking from the blankets came a double-mouthed shotgun, sawn short for close-in work.

"Halt!" he yelled over the barrels. "I have here ten gaugies of double-aught can turn ye to Solomon's babe."

There was a candelabra on a table next to him with a single stunted candle burning, its peers melted already into an inch-thick pool of hardened wax on the tabletop. One of the man's eyes squinted into a narrow slit, aiming.

"We're just travelers," said Callum. "We mean no harm."

"I don't like the sound of ye. What's your name?"

"Callum, sir."

"Don't play me sympathies, boy. The Serpent was a sycophant."

"I ain't."

"Maybe I ort to blast you now. Save me the trouble of finding out. I been a misreader of men in times past. I don't like to be anothern."

Ava took a step onto the glass.

"Who's that?" said the old man, swinging the barrels. Callum realized his vision was poor.

"My name is Ava, sir. My friend Callum, he has a wound we're afraid could infect. We'd be much obliged if you could help us, and then we'll be on our way."

The old man leaned back in his rocker and looked back again toward Callum.

"Well now. A bonny one by the sound of her, and mannered to boot." He nodded appreciatively. "Didn't tell me ye were so accompanied." He looked at Ava. "Why you're holding forth with such a ripe young'un as this, I don't know, but I might can hep ye."

"I ain't ripe," said Callum.

The old man ignored him. He leaned forward in the rocker and let down the bunny-eared hammers on the shotgun.

"Name's Lachlan," he said. "Lachlan the Alchemist." He waved them toward him.

As they walked toward the cabin, a neighboring contraption came into view, a bewildering plumbworks of copper tubing and oak barrels. The copper was spit-shined spotless, the joinery seamless, the geometry of tubes and valves strictly adherent to some grand design. A far cry from the cabin that housed its keeper.

"What kind of alchemy you practice?" asked Callum.

A sly look twisted the old man's face. He laid the shotgun crosswise on his lap and leaned forward and reached under the blanket hanging between his feet. He came up with a glass jug the diameter of a tree trunk. It sloshed with a liquid clear as newly sluiced snowmelt, but which rolled heavily around the curved glass, heavier than water. The old man held the jug aloft to the moon. The fluid seemed to quiver, as if possessed by some animate spirit.

"Bottled lightning," said the old man. "That's the hell what."

He unscrewed the cap and touched his broke-angled nose to the rim and snorted. He convulsed with pleasure, his eyes newly awake.

"Take ye a drop," he said, offering them the jug.

Callum stood still, but Ava handed him the reins and stepped forward and took the offering. She cocked her head toward Callum. "Don't mind him," she said. "He's a little young for such."

"Am not," said Callum. He looked at Ava holding the jug under her mouth.

"Best whiskey in these hills," said the old man, nodding toward the jug. "Ask anybody 'bout the white stuff ye get from old Lachlan."

Ava tipped the jug to her mouth for a small pull. Callum watched the milk-white contraction of her neck. She pulled the jug away and gasped, sear-tongued.

"Goddamn," she said.

The old man nodded, happiness in his eyes.

"Y'ain't so mannered with a bellyful of that, hey, missy?"

Ava grinned and swung the jug around until it bumped Callum's chest.

His fingers crept slowly over the jug.

"I've had plenty of whiskey," he told them.

They ignored him. He lifted the rim to his nose like the old man had done and took a big sniff. The burn slammed him like an axletree. His eyes teared up.

"Son of a bitch," he said.

"Get ye a taste. A littlun, a course, young'un-size."

Thusly tempted, Callum choked down a mouth-size swallow of the stuff, pure folly, and spent the next half minute coughing the fire out of his throat.

"Son of a bitch," he said. "Son of a bitch."

"Ain't it, though," said the old man, laughing. "Ain't it." He wiped his mouth with the back of his hand and looked at Ava. "Now you say he's got him the green rot?"

"Not yet. Afraid it won't be long, though."

The old man nodded. "Pour ye a dram of that lightning in it, and clean it good. It'll kill the rot good as any doctor medicine, guarantee you that." He sniffed. "Best clean the boy, too." He shook his head. "Ripe."

"You got a tub?" asked Ava.

"Out back. Fetch it round."

By the time Callum quit coughing, Ava had a tub set before him in the yard.

"Take off your clothes," she said.

"What—"

"Off."

"You heard the lady," said Lachlan. "Be gettin' to it if I was you."

Callum nodded and started to strip down. He went to lay his offings over the saddle, but the horse backed away. Soon he was clutching himself near naked in the yard. The night was cold and moon-shadowed, his bone and sinew adamant beneath the skin.

Ava was inside heating pot water over the woodstove. The old man sipped at the jug, watching him. Callum looked back at him.

"You sleep out here on the porch or something? It must be getting toward dawn."

The old man studied the sky. "We got near on two hours before then," he said. "Anyhow, I don't sleep hardly a wink. Never have. Got the sleeping troubles. I lost a wife once for the awfulest snoring ye ever heard. Told me I was like to kill her. She never could get no rest." He shrugged. "Nothing for it 'cept the whiskey. Puts me straight out. It's real good for that."

Callum stepped toward him. "Could I try another? For the cold?"

"Course," said the old man, handing him the jug.

Callum took a second slug, smaller this time, nonetheless like swallowing a comet. He could already feel the stuff starting to work in his blood.

Ava came out of the cabin with a pot and poured it steaming into the sheet metal tub.

"Get in," she said.

Callum handed back the jug and walked to the tub. He peered inside and saw an inch-deep mirror of water. He touched the metal with the toe of his foot.

"Yow," he said. "This thing's had ages to get cold."

Ava put one hand on her hip. "I'm heating more water. Now just get on in there and take the dressings off." She neglected to watch his pouting as she went back into the cabin with the pot.

Callum stood looking at the ice-cold tub, knowing what it would feel like on his back and shoulders. He heard the old man throat down another pull on the jug.

"No idea what fortune has befallen ye."

Callum looked at him.

"What?"

"Ye got no idea." He lowered his voice, conspiratorlike. "That girl. Bet ye be a dead boy wasn't for her. And pretty as a song. Even I can see that."

"I don't know," said Callum, looking at the blurry reflection of himself in the moonlit sheet of water, the dark and puddled being.

"Yes, ye do," said the old man. "Now I'd get in the got-damned bath if I was you."

Callum put his feet in first. The steaming water was now lukewarm, cooled by the metal. He sank his underclothed buttocks inside, so he was sitting there with his hands clasping his knees, minimizing how much flesh touched the tub.

Ava came back out with a second pot. She poured it in between his legs, some of it splashing his bare skin.

"Shit, girl, that's hot."

"Get that dressing off, why don't you. That's why we're doing this."

"That and the ripeness," said the old man.

Callum gave him the baddest look he could. The old man just grinned at him. Ava started back inside. The old man touched her arm just before she went in the door, gentle and courteous as could be.

"Would you mind fetching a cup for the young'un, Miss Ava? He's got the thirst on him, and I ain't no miser."

She nodded and went inside and reappeared promptly with a tin cup. The old man poured a good-size portion of the clear liquid into the cup. He rose from his chair, no small effort, and shuffled down the steps, across the dirt yard to the boy in the tub. He handed the cup to him.

"Nobody ever taught ye to drink whiskey, did they?"

Callum shook his head.

"Just sip it," said the old man. "Like something precious. That's the hardest stuff ye like to find, in these hills or out."

Callum took the cup. The man shuffled back to his rocking chair, a little buoyancy in his step, whether from liquor or something else, Callum didn't know. He took another sip of the liquor. Like lightning had struck in his mouth. He put the cup down on the ground beside him and slowly peeled the dressing off his thigh. The wound was a puckered mouth, red-lipped. Around it a faint halo of discoloration.

"What happened to ye leg?" asked the old man.

Callum was really starting to feel the drink course through him.

"I got stuck by a saber."

"What for?"

"Stealing back my horse."

The old man rolled a gnarled knot of his beard between his fingers. He squinted at the horse standing at the edge of his yard.

"That's a might-fine piece of horseflesh."

Callum settled himself back against the tub.

"I might of stolen him," he said. "But for good reason."

The old man cocked his head toward the door of the cabin. "For her?"

Callum nodded.

Lachlan smiled. "I reckon God'll pity ye then, same's Adam."

Callum looked at himself, his torso now taking up the bulk of the tub, his limbs splayed over the edges, so that he looked like some tentacled creature creeping out of a cave.

"I don't know 'bout pity," he said. He paused a long moment. "I done things worse."

Ava came out of the cabin then with two pots trailing long traces of steam and poured them both into the tub, careful not to burn him. She went back inside the cabin, and Callum watched her disappear into the far corner where the woodstove must be. The old man set the jug on his knee and leaned forward.

"And now they're after ye," he said.

"What makes you think that?"

The old man tapped the jug of corn liquor with his index finger. "This here is white gold in these hills. That climb's steep enough to skin ye nose. No man goads himself straight up like that less he's after trouble. That or fleeing it. It's a pretty sight up here, but nobody comes just to look."

Callum wiped his nose with the back of his hand.

"I reckon not," he said.

He looked out at the horizon. Pretty it was. The nearest hills jutted visibly into the sky; the farther ones diminished quickly into the night. Above them the stars. They seemed to pulse slightly. Things were going liquid on him. His jaw loosened.

"You're right," he said. "We got some people chasing us."

He looked at the old man. "You ain't gonna throw us out for it, are you?"

The old man patted the shotgun leaning on the wall next to him.

"Just duck ye hear that glass a-cracklin'," he said.

Callum nodded. "I can do that." He cupped some water and splashed his face. All of him was getting looser, but there was power slinking through him, too. He could say most anything.

"Now we got this one-armed son of a bitch hunting us, too," he said. "I don't even know who."

The old man straightened, the jug frozen halfway to his mouth.

"One arm, said ye?"

Callum nodded. "Just a one."

The old man lowered the jug to his knee.

"How tall is he?"

"Tall," said Callum.

"Scarce meat disguising the deader parts of him, bones and skull?"

Callum nodded. "That's a way to put it."

The old man took the shotgun from the wall and laid it carefully across his lap.

"I don't know what ye done to have the man sicced on ye. Not sure I want to know."

Callum sat upright in the tub.

"You're talking like you know him."

The old man nodded. "Of him. I know of him. No mistaking the description. Name's Clayburn. That be his Christian or surname, I don't know. Seems he ain't got but the one."

"Who is he?"

"Bounty hunter. Been hunting fugitives since the forties, slaves mainly. Be a rich man he didn't have a bad habit of killing off them darkies fore he collected the bounty on 'em."

"What happened to his arm?"

"Manassas. Good for the Yankees he got discharged so early, I reckon."

Callum grew conscious of his own jaw, agape. "Son of a bitch," he said. Then he narrowed his eyes, suspicious. "How'd you come to know all this?"

"Them drovers," said the man, gesturing toward the valley. "They bring news from all over. I go to the road twice a month. Sell my stock. Ye didn't think I brewed all this whiskey just for my own thirst?"

"Son of a bitch," said Callum.

"He is that."

The old man held the jug hovering in limbo between his mouth and lap, his bad eyes glazed distantly in the candlelight.

Callum ground the heels of his hands against his forehead. "I had a awful feeling about that hollow-eyed son of a bitch," he said. "If you just want us to get on—"

Just then Ava came out with a pot and a foamy rag, headed for the tub. Callum straightened.

"What're the menfolk talking about out here?" she asked, her spirits high. "Nothing scrofulous, I'm sure."

Callum looked at old Lachlan, Lachlan at him.

"Course not, Miss Ava. Nary a cuss fouled these tongues, not gentlefolks like us."

"Uh-huh," she said.

The old man nodded toward Callum. "Ye got ye a real good boy here, I learnt me that. Look after him good, he'll do ye likewise." He swallowed on a dry mouth. Gathered into himself. "It's a evil moment in the world, this war. Evilest I seen, or will. Sticking together is about all there is left, I reckon." He lifted the jug right to his lips. "That and good whiskey, a-course." He took a long pull on the liquor, longest of the night.

Ava allowed a one-cornered smile on her mouth. She dumped the last pot of hot water into the tub, and then she took the rag into her right hand and went to work cleaning Callum's wound.

Callum reached quickly for the tin cup and drew the liquid through clenched teeth. Her scrubbing was unmerciful—had to be. When she was finished with the soap, she rinsed the rag in the water. The only place to do so was a dangerous spot between Callum's legs. He held his breath. Ava washed the soap out of the wound with the clean rag, and then she took the tin cup from his hand. She took a long gulp from its contents, followed by a fierce shake of the head. Then without warning she poured a long stream into the wound. Callum clenched his windpipe against the scream, but it came anyway, a high-pitched screech as the white liquor sizzled—so it felt—in the raw flesh, killing whatever had taken up residence under the skin.

When it was over, she took another deep slug from the cup. Callum did the same. Then another. He looked over at Lachlan, and the old man had gone double on him, man and ghost of man. Callum looked heavenward, the stars grown tremulous. They swirled like glow bugs. He looked at Ava. She was wrapping a new dressing around his thigh, the material torn from her quilt. Her fingertips were light against his skin, and she took great pains to position the dressing just so, sliding her fingers underneath it here or there to test the snugness.

"Ava," he whispered.

She turned to look at him, her face smooth and white, her eyes dark and strong. Her pupils, steel-specked as always, went wide a moment. Dark-welled, as if to take in more of what she saw. Her hand hovered on the inside of his leg, where it had stopped. Callum opened his mouth to say the thing in his chest. His heart beat, beat, beat. Ava suddenly pulled her hand away and stood.

"Don't just sit there," she said. "You're like to catch your death." She started back into the cabin. "I was warming a blanket for you by the stove."

Callum stood from the tub, alone, his innards warm despite the gooseflesh that bound him, his belly hot. He slicked the water off him with the flats of his hands—this arm and that, front of leg, back of leg—trying not to wet the dressing. He looked again to the sky, his feet pressed against each other for warmth, his head tottering a little atop its perch. The liquor roared in his temples. The stars were quivering, the once-mapped arcature of night undone, made liquid, star fates scattered so wildly he could make of them what he would. His heart swelled toward them, uncaged.

A moment later he turned to old Lachlan, both of him.

"Thank you," he said.

The old man leaned forward in his rocker, speaking in a forced hush.

"Don't thank me, damn ye. Get!" He jabbed his thumb toward the cabin door. "Fore ye catch ye death." His eyes were smiling.

Callum hopped out of the tub and skittered naked across the yard, sliding wet-heeled into the dark depth of the cabin. He could see little at first save the open door of the stove, the split hickory red-warm as his warmest vision of hearth fire. He stood shivering before the flames, clutching himself. Then a heavy blanket enveloped his shoulders, Ava beside him, and he realized she was within his swaddling blanket, not without, her body thin-shifted and warm. She pressed against him, and he felt his cold hide begin to warm, go supple, melding to her contours, her heat, even as another part of him grew hard.

Lachlan yelled in at them from outside.

"Spare blankets in the trunk next to the cupboard," he said. "Don't mind me. I ain't slept horizontal since '49."

Callum looked at Ava.

"Want me to get another blanket?"

"No," she said. "Don't."

Chapter 8

He woke into perfect darkness. Then, slowly, the shapes of the world began to limn themselves out of the void: a stove, a cupboard, a slanted table. He thought the dark of slumber would adjust his vision to the absence of light, to better it, but the case seemed different, as if his eyes had been looking someplace else. The world of his dreams, perhaps, unremembered save for the omnipresence of fire.

The rhombic shape of the front door rose into his vision, rising dawn-pale as from murky water, and a strange song whittled into his hearing. A sound like the death rattle of a stricken animal. It was the old man sleeping, he realized, sounding like he could die at any breath. It was a good man who could remain so cheery, so big-hearted, despite such handings-out.

The boy looked down at himself: naked save his underclothes and bandaged leg. Ava's arm was slung across his waist. It seemed dangerous, haphazard—a thing she'd never do awake. Outside the door, the world was taking shape out of the high-country mist. Blued timbers sprung of the fugitive reality of dawn, ghostlike, perfect hidings for ambushing men. He looked down at her arm again, the thinly fleshed sinew, the crescents of her nails moonlike and clean. How they remained that way despite their journeying was a mystery far more unfathomable than trinities or conceptions or sundry other such holies of old.

He didn't want to move but had to—the night's whiskey wanted out. He slid himself from under her arm—carefully, carefully—and stood beside the bed. She looked softer somehow, unhardened, the girl she was. The reality of the world for a moment at bay. She lay on her side, her dark hair scattered across her pillow, her shoulders, her mouth. Only her nose and eyes and forehead were bared to him. He bent toward the latter, his lips an inch above her temple. He made to transgress that final margin, in daylight a mile's breadth, his lips softened stealthlike, his young joints quiet in their bending, when a sudden sound of crackling glass ripped him away and out the door. He landed both-footed in the dirt yard, crouched, looking for a gun to go with his underpants.

No one.

He looked to the horse. The horse looked at him, his loose lips chewing sideways on what grazings he'd found on the edge of the old man's yard, his front hooves planted on the perimeter of broken glass—the sound of false alarm.

Callum rolled his eyes. His leg throbbed from the action, and he felt a fool.

He turned back toward the house, pivoting quickly on the heel of his good leg. Too quickly—when he tried to stop, the world just kept whirling sideways on him, dizzied and unchecked. Something rattled sickeningly through the interior of his skull, like a dislodged marble. He reached out his arms for anchor, staggering to the tub just in time to eject his stomach's meager oddments into the filmy water. After that, just dry heavings, thick spit filming his lower lip and chin.

The old man opened one eye at him.

"My likker don't give no hangovers."

Callum convulsed drily toward the shallow well of vomit. He could feel blood vessels sparkling red under his eyes. He straightened, finally, and wiped his mouth with the back of his hand.

"Like hell it don't."

"Well, I don't give no money-back guarantees, ha. Drinks good while ye keep it down, though, don't it?"

"I don't remember," said Callum. The taste was so terrible in his mouth, he thought he might be sick a second time.

"Ha, ye remember," said the old man. "It ain't no popskull. Keeps ye memory intact. That's the truth, be it detriment to some."

Ava came onto the porch barefooted, half-dressed, the shift she wore light enough against her body to swell Callum's throat like one of those red-chested birds, his voice trapped.

"Morning," she said.

Callum nodded and turned to attend to the horse, unspeakable reactions wrenching his body. He tried to focus. Before his bath the night previous, he had hobbled the horse narrow-hooved at the front legs to keep him in check. This out of habit, the horse so trustworthy that he might've left him untethered to graze. But the horse didn't seem to mind either way. Callum had been stealing horses a long time and he'd never encountered one quite like this. Not even the cremello. It was so strong and good. Not submissive. Rather, the will he imposed on the animal seemed so within its capabilities, it had no grounds for complaint, such was the scale of its power.

He approached the horse to unhobble him, his spine sharp-boned toward Ava and the old man, and the horse eyed the front of him, his slight engorgement, with a dark and knowing eye. Callum realized that the horse had been so good to them, and he so much the opposite, the horse thief who seldom even called the animal by its name.

"Reiver," he said, patting him between the eyes.

The horse lifted his head away, as though he had no use for such.

Callum bent down and untied the rope that spanned the muscled black legs. Loosed, the horse made a trotting circle of the yard, high-stepping as if to loosen his unbounded legs. Afterward he bent again to graze for the ride to come, however long. Callum looked toward the cabin. Ava and the old man were watching.

"Some horse," said the old man.

Callum said nothing, just watched the horse like it was his own. Maybe it was. Maybe deserved to be. He leveled the hard flat of his hand against his face, swiping free flecks of vomit and saliva, baring his own teeth with the hard pull of his hand. Then he looked around the yard, the trees silent and still in the mist.

"I reckon we better be getting on," he said.

Ava nodded and began moving around, getting things ready.

Callum tucked one of the horse's front legs between his knees. He was checking the tender-creased frog for embedded flecks or shards when he heard the crunch of glass behind him. He swung around, unarmed, and caught the explosion of pink mist even before the resounding thunder of the ten-gauge. He snaked the repeater from the scabbard and leveled the barrel at the trailhead, expecting the full assault of the Colonel's men.

Nothing came. He listened a long minute: silence.

Then the old man: "Nother goddamn likker poacher," he said. "I seen him on the road three days ago, posing as a drover."

The body had been blown fully backward into the trees, out of sight, sliding down the steep and rocky trail like a sack of feed. A large-bore shotgun lay on the broken glass, everything spattered brightly.

"You sure?"

"Course I'm sure. Think I can't tell a stranger?"

Callum stood wide-eyed and naked save his underclothes, the rifle hanging limply from his hand. Ava had retreated inside the cabin. Her head poked out from the edge of the door.

Callum looked at Lachlan.

"You want me to go see he's dead?"

The old man shook his head, sad.

"No. That double-aught ort to done it." He let down the unfired hammer with a trembling thumb. "Just leave him be. Powerful disencouraging to like-minders."

Callum wiped his mouth with the back of his hand, his eyes wide.

"I reckon," he said.

He slid the rifle back into its scabbard and gathered up his clothes, sticking his legs straight into his trousers and hopping to yank them to the waist. He buttoned the fly quickly but left the belt unbuckled. He opened the saddlebag nearest him and took out the brace of purloined pistols. They were navy sixes, .36-caliber, both loaded and capped. The men had dripped hot candlewax over each of the caps to seal them from rain or moisture. He threaded the holsters butt-forward on his belt, one a side. Then he ran the belt through the buckle and pulled it tight as the tightest punch hole.

He thought of the Walker. He felt surer with it at his side, but the chambers were all empty now and it would take too long to reload. He was not even sure he had the right-size shot, had not rifled that far through what he'd stolen from the men at the pond. He put on his long-sleeve undershirt, his regular shirt, his coat, his riding gauntlets. Ava came out of the cabin in her high boots and quilt.

"Well, I reckon we got to get on," she said. "Don't want to overstay our welcome."

The old man had been watching the boy dress so quickly. Now he looked at her, hurt-eyed but knowing.

"Was a pleasure, Miss Ava." He reached underneath his blanket. "A jar of the white stuff," he said, handing it to her. "Ye just keep that young'un over there from overserving hisself," he said, winking at her.

Ava took the jar from him and gave him a hug, then hurried across the yard to the horse. Callum boosted her onto Reiver's back. He whipped himself into the saddle and walked the horse closer to the old man's porch.

"I want to thank you for everything," he said.

Old Lachlan held out a flat and sullied hand.

"No need," he said. "Even a old son of a bitch like me ort to have him a moment now and again to give Old Peter a second thought."

Callum tipped the brim of the slouch hat in parting, as he'd seen men do who wore such hats, and then he rode the horse around the side of the cabin and back onto the trail. He felt he'd marred the farewell somehow, not given himself over sufficiently to the task, but there was nothing to be done for it.

Not now. They were surely never to see the old man again. Much as that should bear no weight on courtesy, it somehow did. The whiskey robber had shown them that they were not safe here—that they were foolish to feel anything but.

The day was early, the mist as yet unbothered, and only the nearest trees seemed fully real. The world beyond lay shrouded, ethereal. The path was rock-studded, slippery with green moss, and the horse's iron-shod footing rang out in the stillness. They soon found themselves on a narrow spine of trail, the land dropping away steeply to one side. Callum realized they had eaten neither dinner nor breakfast, nor had they offered the old man any of the stolen hardtack or salted meat in their saddlebags.

"That old man," he said, "we ought to given him something for what he done."

"I know it," said Ava. "But he wouldn't of took it anyway."

Callum nodded, knowing she was right. He felt bad about it, but there was nothing to be done. And he had bigger things to worry over. For he had underestimated the loyalty of the Colonel's men, he realized. He had not thought they would pursue him this far. He knew of no bounty upon his head but that which they might have pooled together of their own meager resources. Apparently to hire a bounty hunter of some renown, notorious even, and notorious men did not come cheap. And Swinney in on it, too. The man who had been almost a father to him. Who had dragged him from the beach after the wreck and nursed him in his little thin-walled progger's shack, set on a marshy plot crowded with spoils from his shoreline prowls, collecting the wash-up from the Cape Fear wrecks.

They had eaten shrimp from the big man's nets, fried in

flour and lard, and mullet he smoked and served for breakfast instead of bacon. They had gone to port once a month to sell Swinney's latest trophies—compasses and officers' trunks, barrel kegs and medicines in watertight ampoules. Anything that washed up upon the river's banks or spits of beach. During the nights they could hear the booming of shore batteries, keeping them in business.

Come spring, though, old Swinney had other engagements. It was time for war again, and he had to head west to rejoin the Colonel's troop. He told Callum he could stay there on his own, living in the little shack, but Callum did not want to spend a single minute in the little boat that took the old man on his errands of fish and spoil—the only way to survive. He did not want to be out on the water again. Not ever. But he was good in the saddle, he said, and he could handle a gun. He could ride with Swinney's band. The old man didn't like it, but when he left on his horse, equipped for war, the boy was behind him, jogging along. And soon enough, after they passed the first farm, the boy had a mount of his own.

Callum thought maybe if he could isolate Swinney, he could talk some reason into him, but how he could do that was beyond him. His immediate task was to get them the hell away, south, and worry about pleas of guilt or lack thereof when opportunity struck.

Down the long slope beside them ran a small stream. Glittering. A magic little ravine in the earth. He watched for silhouettes against the glitter, bushwhackers lying in wait. A white sun clocked along its arc into a bright blue sky; it gave little comfort. He worried that Lachlan could have been mistaken. The intruder a scout whose failure to return to camp might give them away.

Deadfalls of broken timber littered the forest to either side, but the trail was mainly clear of obstruction. They ducked under the low branches and squinted into the undergrowth, afraid.

That night they slept in a huge bowl of earth left in the wake of an uprooted blackjack oak. The tree lay some several feet away, dead, the gray-whorled mass of roots clutching the air. Some past winter's ice storm the culprit, the weak soil overtaxed.

Feed gone, Callum loosened the saddle and hobbled the horse and set him to graze. He and Ava huddled beneath the wind that soughed through the cold forest like some lonesome song. They made no fire, the body of the dead whiskey poacher—or whoever he was—yet warm in their minds.

Callum's leg no longer throbbed. The liquor was doing its work. Only the faintest red tracery haloed the wound now, no longer angry, and it was beginning to scab. He tried to pick at the nascent crust, but Ava stopped him. She cleaned and dressed the wound again. She felt his forehead. She said his fever had broke.

The next day they found themselves walled in by steep land on either side. This was the notch in the mountains they'd seen from the droving road. The pass. Trees grew sun-straight from the slanted ground to either side, and they rode with their eyes cocked up the slopes for men lying in ambuscade. Highwaymen or irregulars or bounty hunters. Boulders and stones and scree fallen from either side littered the trail. The horse wended between these with high and careful steps. By noon they were descending the far side of the pass. They broke upon a green-grassed bald on which a handful of meatless and bone-ridden cattle stared dumbly at them. They galloped across the soft turf as fast as they dared, acutely aware of their exposure to the sparse stands of trees on every side.

No shots.

Callum's fever had gone, but the image of the bounty hunter yet haunted his mind. Details he'd not previously remembered came forward to render the man in more complete a shape. He wore his right pistol with the butt facing backward instead of the cross draw preferred by cavalrymen. Like the Colonel, he wore a saber on his left hip, low-slung, and above that a second pistol in a shoulder rig, butt-forward. These tools, just visible, jutted from beneath an unbuttoned wrist-length cape that failed to broaden the look of his shoulders. His horse was smoke-colored, with a black mane. A big horse, tall as Reiver but not as stout. The man wore no hat; Callum remembered that. And he knew to fear a man who went hatless of his own volition, for it meant he was accustomed to tracking through dense woods and brush—tracking men like they were animals.

"That one-armer," said Ava, as if she'd read his mind.

"What about him?"

"I dreamt of him last night."

"Yeah?" said Callum. He didn't like where this was headed.

"Uh-huh," said Ava. "He told me he was a ghost."

"Shit," said Callum.

She shrugged.

"I told him where he ought to take himself then. Told him they had a nice warm place for him down there."

"What'd he say?"

"He didn't. Just kept huntin' round for his arm, like he'd misplaced it."

They continued to bed down fireless, using small sips of the old man's liquor as a heat-promoting tonic. The liquid fire warmed their bellies, numbed their saddle sores, eased the awkward conjoining of limbs and blankets that kept them warm in the absence of fire. One time, after she'd fallen asleep, Callum ventured to place his ungloved hand on Ava's belly. It was still flat. Would be for some time. Still he tried to detect, by touch, the life of the thing inside her. He'd heard of soothsayers reading an object this way, its portents and history. He pictured a creature like the one in the jar but smaller, small as a lima bean, and he allowed himself to envision a future in which it had grown into his life. A vision in which he stood drinking coffee in a set of Y-backed suspenders on the sunlit boards of a front porch, his own, husbanding a plot of land and fathering loves however sired.

"What you ruminating at now?"

His eyes snapped open. She was watching him in the dark, a wry smile on her face.

"Nothing."

"Like hell, boy. I can see the wheels turning."

"The future, I reckon."

"What you see in it?"

"I don't know." He swallowed. "You, maybe."

One corner of her mouth climbed higher.

"Ain't you a little young for me?"

He started to pull his hand away. "I wasn't the other night—"

She grabbed his wrist, staying his hand—a strength he hadn't expected in her grip.

"Callum," she said. "I was only kidding." She rolled over in her blanket, pulling him close against her, his hand held in the hollow between her breasts, their bodies fitting together like two spoons stacked in a drawer. "I was only kidding."

The trees were mostly bare as they rode, the hills a leafless brown save small copses of sharp-pointed firs like the ones in fancy drawing rooms at Christmastime. The fallen leaves allowed the riders to see much farther and deeper into the woods, though anything in the woods could see out equally as well.

Ava was not sick so often in the mornings now, but sometimes she rode with her chin tucked into her shoulder, her eyes closed, her face waxen with a sweaty sheen. Unwell. Callum wished he could do something, but the best he knew was to keep mum. Mainly he did. One morning, though, when she wasn't sick, he saw her feeling her stomach, below the navel, with her hands. He was still swaddled down in his buffalo blanket; she didn't know he was looking.

"Which'd you rather?" he asked. "Boy or girl?"

She turned to him, startled, and swallowed.

"I don't know," she said. "Reckon I should, though."

Callum shrugged. "Girls are good."

She nodded slowly and looked down at herself.

"Yeah," she said. "A girl can't be so much like him."

More rolling green balds in the days that followed. These they crossed with bated breath, heeling the horse for speed. Rarely did they see livestock in these hills, though they saw rotting mounds of old hay and telltale herd prints around watering holes and streams. The meat was mostly gone, eaten or stolen or sold. Several times they heard the far-off howling of hounds, but there was no telling what type they were. They could be cattle dogs, guards, strays, man-hunters. Callum told Ava they were cattle dogs.

The horse kept on, seemingly tireless. Reiver. They watered him whenever they could, and he seemed stronger on grasses than feed. Callum was glad that of all the horses he could have stolen, this was the one he had. He believed there were great animals like there were great men. He told the horse this once, but it only shook its head, like it always did. Callum rubbed him down as best he could in the evenings, massaging the dark shoulders and flanks, but the big horse paid him no mind, munching on whatever grasses or plants or ferns presented themselves.

The horse made him think of the cremello that he had given away. The one no one would buy. It turned out everyone knew the Frenchman who owned him, an accomplished duelist who had killed ten men with swords. He reportedly made his slaves fight one another for sport, bare-chested in little arenas of cut cane, where the loser was whipped if he could still stand. They were mighty wrestlers, his Senegalese imports—capable of killing by hand—and people said more than one of his enemies had met them. No, no one would buy the great cremello, and the Frenchman and his men were hard upon him—had been for days—and Callum simply let the animal go in the middle of a mud street in New Orleans, in some dirty little quarter along the river where the saloons floated like barges on the muck. He let the reins slide from his hand. It was raining, and dusk, and the bone-colored horse was black-legged from the mire. It had looked at him once, its blue eyes electric in the gray, and then turned and walked jauntily up the street, the commerce freezing around it, everyone turning to look. Callum had turned and run the other way, toward the docks.

They stopped to rest the noon hour in a stand of pale-barked trees. Sweet birch, Ava said. The trunks had long horizontal fissures, the bark patterned silver and light green. The ground was littered with fallen catkins that looked like little caterpillars.

Ava broke the end off a low-hanging branch.

"If the sap was running, we could stick a bottle on the end here, catch us a whole mess of it. It's good to drink."

"It's not running now?"

She shook her head. "All the sap goes to the roots in fall. That's why the leaves turn color and die."

She broke the branch in two and rubbed the pieces together.

"Smell that," she said. She held up the waxy place where she'd rubbed.

"Like medicine," he said.

She nodded. "Wintergreen."

"Maybe you ought to chew you some."

She stuck him in the gut with the branch. Fast. She was smiling.

Later they lay down to eat their meager ration of hardtack, softened slightly with water from the beef bladder. They crawled to the edge of the trees and looked down upon a tidy cottage, whitewashed and smoke-spired. In the yard, a rawboned woman was splitting log after log with a heavy maul, red-faced with effort, her forearms rippling in the sun. Behind the cottage stood an elevated outhouse, and behind that a grove of yellow-hearted stumps. A baby cried inside the cottage, no one to soothe it. The woman kept on, machinelike, yelping as she split each log. Baby could cry and cry—no matter, not if the coming cold slipped through the doors and windows unbattled.

Callum looked at Ava. "Could of been you, I reckon."

She nodded. "I done it before. Two years running I did." She pulled his hand to her arm, under her quilt. "Feel that," she said, making a muscle. It was small but hard as river stone.

"Where's yours?" she asked, smiling. She reached for his arm.

Callum shook loose and stood. "We better get on."

She cocked her head at him.

"What's wrong? Afraid mine's bigger?"

"Shit," said Callum, dismissive.

But he was.

Toward dusk they left the road along a scarce tangent of trail. They needed a place to bed down for the night. The trail ran crookedly amid a thick and shadowy growth of firs. They flushed a brace of grouse, fat-bodied birds that had taken up shelter in the evergreens. As they skittered through the air, Callum wished for the shotgun lying beside the would-be whiskey poacher. They would need meat soon.

This path broke onto a sparsely wooded ridge. Long-fallen hunks of rock covered the slope, each of them bearing furry green moss. Delicate ferns peeked out of their cracks and fissures, as if those little plants had been what split the mighty granite. Beyond this the ridge verged unto a small valley. A small highland village sat upon the valley floor, hunkered in shadow.

Callum, silent, dismounted. His eyes were wide, captive. He crawled to the cliff's edge.

He couldn't believe it.

There, in the failing light, a long string of varicolored horseflesh alongside a low-roofed building. A tavern. The windows of the place were all lit up, flickering. It was full.

"Son of a bitch," he said.

Ava appeared next to him. She was prone, squinting. "What is it?"

"Them."

"No."

"I guarantee you it is."

"How can you tell?"

"I just can. What other force of so many riders would be all the way up here?"

"We better get out of here," she said.

Callum slowly shook his head, his eyes on the valley.

"I got to go down there."

"You got to what?"

"I got to talk to Swinney. Tell him I didn't do it. It wasn't me that killed the Colonel."

Ava reached over and took the lapel of his coat.

"What you got to do is get back on the horse with me so we can ride the hell out of here."

Callum kept his eyes on the tavern, the windows' inner glow. "You're the one asked me to ride you out of harm's way, and that's what I been doing."

"That's right," said Ava, "and I'd like to see you follow through."

"If I tell Swinney I didn't do it, maybe they'll leave us alone."

Ava yanked on his coat lapel so he would look at her.

"Listen, Callum, that ain't gonna do it. Just telling him that."

"How do you know?"

"Please just get on the horse with me and let's get out of here."

"I aim to," he said. "Soon as I come back."

"And what if you don't?"

He gently removed her hand from his coat and got to his knees, then his feet, and started back toward the horse. He could hear Ava coming behind him, could almost feel the angry words pent in her throat.

He wanted the Walker for this. In the stolen satchel he found a powder horn, felt, and shot. He set the pistol to half cock, freeing the cylinder to spin, then began measuring powder into each of the six chambers, rotating through them one by one. He cut wads out of the felt, then set one over the mouth of the first chamber. He seated a lead ball over that, then rammed it home with the loading lever, gritting with effort. The men of the troop had always said that round balls were better man-killers than the army-issue conicals, but you had to cast your own and they were hell to load. He found a snuffbox full of caps. He forced one onto each of the nipples with his thumb.

He unbuckled the brace of pistols and hung them over his shoulder, then straightened his coat and buckled them over the outside of it. He stuck the Walker through one side, his sheathed bowie knife through the other. He uncoiled a long length of rope and tied it to a nearby chestnut, then started back—rope in tow—to scour the ridgeline for a path into the valley.

Ava followed behind him. He found a steep slope of dead leaves, populated by a few bare-limbed trees. He crouched at the edge of the slope and spread handfuls of dirt across his cheeks and forehead. He was studying the geography of the descent, the various trees and thickets where pickets could be posted between him and the tavern.

Ava stood behind him, arms crossed.

"You go off like this and I might not be here when you get back. Reiver, neither."

Callum looked at her. "I have to do this."

"You die down there, you better hope I live a real long time. Because that's all the goddamn peace you're gonna get. Soon's I die, I'll be hunting your sorry ass through heaven or hell or wherever they see fit to send fools like you. You won't ever hear the end of it."

Callum sat at the edge of the decline, his boots hanging over. He looked up at her, making his eyes as big and round as possible.

"Please don't go."

Before she could say anything, he reached over and squeezed her calf through her boot, then stuck the rope in his teeth and slid over the edge on his backside. His boot soles struck the base of the first tree dead-on. In this fashion he picked his way down the slope, leaving the rope at the bottom for when he came back. If she left him and took the rope, the climb back up would be treacherous and long. Probably not a climb he could make before daylight.

He squatted a long time at the base of the slope, studying the terrain, letting his eyes adjust. The clouds were with him. No moon, no stars.

Up here the picket line would be loose and infrequent—probably it would. There wasn't too much for them to worry over in terms of security. After a time he spotted the mark of many a lazy picket: the red cherry of a pipe or cigarillo flaring in the darkness. From the height of the ash, the man looked to be sitting or squatting against one of the few trees that dotted the valley. This one stood to his right. Callum looked for a second picket to his left. He couldn't spot one, but the only cover—several trees and thickets—was a good ways away. He reckoned he could slip through the line unnoticed, striking a direct course for the tavern.

The ground to cover was less than a quarter mile. He accomplished that distance at a quick pace, keeping his head low so as not to silhouette himself against the granite slopes thrust upward from the valley behind him. The rock-strewn grass made little sound or prints under his boots. There were some bare-looking fields, and he skirted these as best he could, a small dark figure scurrying along the ground, propelled by that audacity of youth the gummed old men of the land were so pleased to denounce from their rockers, flanked by their spittoons and surrendered hounds.

He thought if he could just tell Swinney he was innocent, it would do them some good, at whatever risk. He did not know if Swinney would believe him. Was not sure it mattered. But he felt compelled to voice the words into the old man's ear, to show them to the old man as he would some doomed artifact in a disappearing world, just so someone else would know of its existence. He had to.

Ahead of him the tavern pulsed with light and sound. The rest of the town was dark-windowed and silent. A seeming ghost town. The doors surely bolted or barred against the ruckus, no candles to tempt or invite the band of riders. Next to the tavern stood a long and narrow storehouse of some kind. Feed store, maybe. He faced the rear of it. Beyond the building lay the dirt main street of the town. A porch lipped the rear of the storehouse under a tin awning. On the porch, cartons and sacks sat in nearly complete shadow. Nearer him, an old wagon sat rotting in the yard, vines grown around a busted wheel.

There were no windows in the rear of the tavern, only on the sides. Light bled outward from these, making strange shadows against the side of the storehouse. A cryptic drama, the dark shapes of men warped and reeling against the wood-planked wall.

Callum hid behind the old wagon, watching. He was about to cross to the porch of the storehouse when a man burst from the side door of the tavern. He lurched across the alleyway and caught himself against the side of the storehouse. He leaned his forehead against the wall, and it seemed he might stay that way. Then he turned and used his butt to jolt himself back to standing. He belched. He staggered a ways toward the rear of the tavern and faced the wall, unbuttoning his fly. He steadied himself with one hand and let fly a fine stream against the side of the tavern, heedless of the backsplash flecking his boots and trousers. After a moment he put his other palm against the wall and stared down at himself, brow furrowed, as though his organ were an object of no small curiosity to him.

Crouched behind the wagon wheel, Callum watched the gold arc steam against the unpainted clapboard, a dark hill-shaped stain. Many another such mark soiled the side of the tavern, some overlapping. Callum was pleased to see them. They were fundamental to his plan.

The capacity of Swinney's bladder had long been a subject of conversation among the men, so frequently did he dismount to relieve himself. It was common knowledge that a child of four years could have outlasted the fat man were they to imbibe equal measures, and shame him handsomely if the drink were whiskey—which for Swinney it often as not was, and would certainly be so on this night.

The man finished, buttoned himself, made his way back into the tavern. Callum crept across the open space to the rear porch of the storehouse. He leaned his back against the wall and slipped as far into the shadows as he could. He slid the crate at the top of a stack beside him a few inches sideways to make a slit. Now he could watch the side door of the tavern, and who came out of it. He took the Walker in hand and lowered the hammer down from half cock so that it would make the strongest statement possible when he thumbed it back.

He watched, hardly breathing, as men staggered outside to sully the wall. Men he recognized. They were dust-ridden from hard riding and red-eyed, and he saw new details upon them: light blue trousers with yellow striping, steel-frame Colt's revolvers holstered or belt-stuck at least four to a man, spit-shined U.S. belt buckles worn upside down. He thought of the empty cavalry horses they'd seen pass some days before, wondering if their fallen riders had provided such souvenirs.

He settled in to wait, remembering the night big Swinney had taken him in. The night of the wreck. Callum had been on deck, under a moonless sky, as they made the run into Wilmington. He was what the crew called a monkey, doing whatever odd jobs were needed: by turns messenger and servant and nurse. The ship was a side-wheel steamer, narrow-built and long with a shallow draft. It had been constructed in the English shipyards, just for running blockades, and it was painted dark gray to match the sea at night. They were coming in from a stopover in Nassau, where shirtless blacks had loaded them with supplies from a merchant vessel out of England. Three hundred barrels of gunpowder, Callum was told, and five thousand Enfield rifles. Cartridges, too, and caps and swords. The supplies would be shipped by rail to Augusta or Richmond, to the depots there.

They were running without lights, as they always did.

Coming across from the Bahamas they'd been burning coal, leaving a bent tower of smoke in their wake, but they'd switched to smokeless anthracite as the coast neared, so as not to give themselves away to the Union men-of-war blockading the coast. This was not their first run up the Cape Fear River into Wilmington, and Callum knew the river itself was as treacherous as the warships that guarded it. He knew that was why pirates before them, like Blackbeard with the candles in his gnarls, had called it home.

They were going to shoot the narrow passage into the river, New Inlet, under the protection of the big gun batteries at Fort Fisher. They were in the shoal waters along the coast, still out of range of protective fire, when they were spotted by a three-masted corvette off the starboard bow. Immediately it sent up a signal rocket to mark the blockade-runner's position, a glowing hook against the sky. Callum was sent aft to tell their signalman to fire their own decoy signals at right angles to their course.

It was too late. Another enemy sloop hove into view, emerging from a hidden cove, and opened up with its thirty-two-pounders. Callum felt the night tremble as the shells streaked overhead, ripping the air apart. Then the ship quaked beneath him, struck, and he lost his legs, falling flat on the planks like a landsman. There were shouts of a fire belowdecks, and he scrambled to help. The captain ordered hard a-starboard and full steam, and they were soon within range of the eight-inch guns of Fort Fisher.

The sea erupted all around, driving back their pursuers, but black smoke was churning out of the ship. Crewmen with handkerchiefs tied over their mouths brought two badly burned men to the deck. Callum fed them water between their moans. Then the crew started bringing the powder kegs topside, rolling them over the gunwales into the river. They worked quickly, like men who wanted to live. But the fire was spreading, and soon seamen were jumping ship, even officers. Callum was not sure what to do. The port was too far. He would jump.

One of the burned men grabbed his ankle.

"Don't leave me," he croaked.

Just then the first powder keg ignited, a blast that bulged the deck, illuminating the spaces between planks. Then darkness. The next thing he remembered—clearly—was the beach, and the old man scouring it for loot that washed ashore, not expecting to find a boy spit up as if by the incoming tide.

Callum watched the tavern for another quarter hour. Finally, Swinney's rotund body swelled through the door and trod down the side of the building. He was walking heavily, uncertain, one hand sliding along the boards to impart confidence, the other resting on the vast protrusion of his belly. He was facing the wall, fumbling to open his fly, when Callum came up behind him. He thumbed the pistol's hammer to full cock.

Click.

"You old ash-shitter."

Swinney turned slowly around, white-eyed with fear, his fly half-open.

"Boy," he said.

Callum reached out and gripped the lapel of the older man's coat with his free hand. He pulled him out of the light and around to the far side of the storehouse. The pistol was sufficient prompting. There they stood across from each other, old man and young, the pistol quivering long-barreled between them.

"You shoot that thing off, you'll be dead in a heartbeat," said Swinney.

Callum decocked the revolver with one hand, unsheathing his knife with the other.

Swinney pincered the paste-ridden corners of his mouth between thumb and forefinger.

"Best watch them comeuppins, boy. They could be out for you."

"That's what I'm here about."

Swinney said nothing.

"It wasn't me that killed the Colonel. It was some soldiers came out of nowhere. Regulars, in uniform. It wasn't me that did it."

Swinney nodded slowly. "I didn't figure it was," he said.

"You didn't?"

Swinney shook his head. "No."

"Then why the hell y'all chasing us?"

Swinney blew a long sigh out of his mouth, bulging his cheeks. "Bounty."

"What?"

"Bounty, boy. Money."

"I don't understand."

Swinney laced his fingers together and rested them on the top of his belly. He looked down at them a moment, then back up.

"Back in '62 the Yanks put a bounty on the Colonel's head. Five thousand dollars. Same's they done Mosby and some them other Partisan Rangers. Colonel was furious. Called it unsoldierly and unsporting and ungentlemanlike and everthing else." Swinney tugged at his beard between steepled thumbs. "So you know that train he robbed, got him unstrapped of his commission?"

Callum nodded.

"He took them banknotes and railroad gold and made up a bounty his own. *Posthumous.* Five thousand dollars to whichever man could kill the man that killed him. Made Old Lawyer Sawyer with the spectacles keep a copy of the will in his saddle. Made him the *egg-secutor.*"

Callum felt a tremor slip across his bottom lip. He took a step closer with the knife.

"Well, that's all fine and dandy, Swinney, but I didn't kill the son of a bitch. Might would of, but didn't. So you can just call off the dogs, and I'll be on my goddamn way."

Swinney's bulk deflated.

"Wish it was that easy," he said.

"What about it ain't?" said Callum. "I didn't do it. That's the truth. Plain as day."

"You got any evidence?"

"I didn't know I'd be needing any, seeing as how I didn't do it. Thought the truth'd be enough."

"The truth?" said Swinney. He turned his head and spat a dark clot into the shadows, as if doing away with the word. "Problem is, it looks awfully like you was the one done the killing, and that's the most profitable truth for everbody. They're all planning to split that bounty money, with twenty-five percent going to the bounty hunter and twenty-five to the trigger-puller, and the rest divided evenly. Good dividins for everbody. I believe you weren't the one that done it. But you got to realize my voice is just a single one among so many others, too many, my truth trumped by all else's. None of these sons of bitches gives a good goddamn whether you done it or not. Old Lawyer Sawyer decides whether the head brung in is the right one, and don't think he don't got his own head to worry about with so many notes on the plate."

Callum's eyes seared, wet, his lips quivering beyond his will. A mad impulse gripped him. He wanted to wound Swinney however he could.

"You yellow fat-bellied son of a bitch," he said, looking for the hurt in Swinney's eyes. When he saw the pain, it didn't help him. He wiped his mouth with the back of his free hand.

"Well, you sons of bitches are gonna have to chase me from here to Northern Virginia, maybe farther north than that. See how you like it up there."

Swinney didn't take the bait.

"You be careful, boy. We heard Atlanta's occupied now. Sherman."

"What's that matter to me?"

Swinney shook his head. "Nothing, I reckon." He wiped a single finger hard across his bottom lip. "I'll do for you what I can. But listen, this bounty hunter we hired up, he's getting somebody to meet him with his dogs soon. Can track a horse good as a nigger. You ain't gonna have long after that."

"Clayburn," said Callum.

Swinney's jaw dropped, surprise in his face.

Callum smirked. "Don't think I ain't been watching you, Swinney. You and the rest of these sons of bitches."

Swinney straightened from the wall. "Then you know you got to stay clear of him," he said. "Get you some distance. I reckon we didn't even quite know what we was getting into when we hired him up on the border. Thought he was just a good tracker. The best. And had some skin in the game. Some blood."

"Blood?"

"Don't you know? You know every damn thing besides. Clayburn, he's the Colonel's brother."

Callum's voice stuck in his throat.

"Not that that seems to matter," said Swinney. "Not to him. He wants that bounty, same's everybody else. But this son of a bitch—" Swinney shook his head. "The man's got ways and means—"

Callum didn't want to know.

"You just worry about your own damn self, Swinney. Like maybe I ought to gut you right here, make sure you don't go telling everybody in there I'm out here. Telling *him*."

"I won't," said Swinney.

"Maybe I ought to make sure."

"Goddamn you, boy. I said I wouldn't. Like I wasn't the one pulled you flat-bellied from the beach that time, took you in."

"Yeah, well maybe you ought to left me. Hell of a lot easier way to go than being hunted down like a dog."

"Boy, you got your own self into this mess chasing after that damn girl."

"She ain't just a damn girl, Swinney."

The older man's eyes grew suddenly softer, sadder. He might have been looking upon some damned specimen, a firefly in an airtight jar. His bottom jaw moved back and forth inside the gray of his beard.

"I'm awful sorry, boy."

Callum stepped forward, the point of his knife prodding Swinney just below the navel, prodding him hard.

"Awful ain't half as sorry as you are," he said.

Then he pulled the knife away, unblooded, and shot off into the darkness, gone, Swinney left gasping all the air he might have lost. Slowly the big man sank against the wall, holding his face in his hands.

Callum was fifty yards from town, wet-eyed and running toward the far-off slopes, toward Ava, when he tripped over a sleeping figure he'd missed on the way into town. A picket. He was thrown face-forward into the dirt, then up and lunging back with the knife in hand, without thought. He drove the blade across the waking man's throat before he could cry alarm. Then stood. The wound bubbled and gurgled like a mouth, trying to speak. Callum stood over the sight a long moment, watching, unable not to, then bolted. He ran and ran, running until his lungs seared like burning wings, as if fleeing what the wound was trying to tell him.

Chapter 9

Callum did not know if the rope would be there for him. He did not know if he deserved it to be, if he deserved to escape this place. Perhaps he was a creature marked and fated to remain here, his sins worth whatever bounties had been set upon his head. He ran in headlong flight, panic-struck and reckless, as though the valley he crossed were the floor of some nightmarish underworld, every rock and bush and tree an enemy leering from the darkness before him. He felt wholly alone, forsaken, the only man he'd trusted lost to him, maybe the only girl as well.

He saw nothing for a long time. The far-off ridge was mottled and dark, scarce moon to illumine anything. When the line of rope appeared finally upon the slope, he spurred himself harder, collapsing finally at the foot of the ridge. Stars swarmed his vision, crooked and quick. The ache in his thigh had become a thunder. His face burned; he could not quit from heaving. His limbs had gone willowy on him, weak. He rolled onto his side and vomited.

He could not stay here. He pushed himself onto his hands and knees, studied the valley for pursuers or pickets. Nothing, just the hovering red ash of the other posted man, unalarmed. Callum's breathing began to slow. He turned and grabbed hold of the rope and began the ascent, using roots as footholds in the loose ground. It felt like his arms might quit him.

They didn't.

Ava was waiting for him, squatting on her haunches near the edge where she could peer down to watch him. When he crested the slope, she stood and turned wordlessly from him and walked to the horse.

They rode unspeaking until dawn, and then kept on riding. Ava had let the horse graze while he'd gone into the valley, and they didn't need to stop. When finally they did, the mist yet unburned from the ground, he told her all that had happened, end to end. She did not say *I told you so* like he'd thought she would. She only nodded, as if what story he relayed was no mystery to her, as if she'd seen it all coming.

When he told her what last thing he'd said to Swinney, his eyes welled up and his throat took to convulsing on him. This seemed to surprise her least of all. They were sitting underneath a large oak. He lowered his head between his knees and buried his face in his palms. He tried to stop the sadness from welling out of him. She rubbed a slow circle between his shoulder blades with her palm. He pressed his wet face against hers. He remembered the soft cheek of his sister and mother, both lost so long ago, and the rough cheek of his father, too, whose face he could hardly remember. Everything before this shore like a myth to him, unreal, all his memories sunken in the earth so dark underneath the peat. But this, that cheek—it went to the core of him, to all he'd lost.

Ava had begun talking to him. "It's going to be okay," she was saying, her lips just inches from his good ear. "We're going to make it to the coast. To family. Peace. Away from all this."

If they kept moving south, they would break out of the mountains soon, into hills and lowlands. He knew this from the droving road. And the prospect of crossing open country with so many riders upon them—many of them sprung of these lands—did not sit well in his mind. A group of their size would move faster across such ground, enjoying the advantage of a citizenry to tell them what they'd seen passing through, and whom. It was a long way to the coast, and the odds seemed to be multiplying against them.

Even so, Callum found himself nodding to Ava's words. They were rhythmic, recurrent. He was nodding as much to soothe her as to soothe himself, he realized. And all the time wishing for a second good ear, so he could listen for the distant howling of hounds.

The riders stood around the slit-throated man in a ragged and unrealized halo. They were shift-footed and long-shadowed here at dawn, the night's whiskey scum fermenting on their tongues. The slave hunter was taller than the rest of them, his cape clean and eyes clear, no drink to cloud or sunder him from the sight at hand. He squatted down to the corpse, the mouth and throat red-gaped as if in song, a dry-dark puddle of unstaunched spirit encircling the head like some blasphemy of sainthood.

The bounty hunter placed two fingers along the gash, tracing the edges as if they could tell him all he needed to know of time and origin. There was grit in the wound, the flesh carved with the slight raggedness of a well-used blade. The laceration a single action, no slowing or second thought.

He spoke without looking at the men. "Build a fire," he said. He took the knife from the dead man's belt and held it out behind him, handle-first. "And put the blade in the coals." Someone stepped forward and took the knife from him, gingerly, so as not to cut or threaten to cut the hand that held it.

Clayburn stood and drew a silver case from his coat pocket with his one hand. His hand crept over the stained pewter like a great white spider, his fingers long-boned and bloodless. He removed a thin cigar, then shut the case with his pinkie. He put the case away and at the same time drew from his coat pocket a cigar cutter, ivory-handled with a cutting hole on one end, a tab button alongside to work the razor. He stuck the cigar in his mouth backward and cut the nub end and turned it right side around and lowered his hand to his side. He dangled the cigar cutter on the crook of his finger, by the cutting hole.

"Who was posted to either side of this man?"

Two men stepped forward a half step.

"You didn't see anything."

One of them shook his head, hat in hand. "No, sir," he said. He looked at the ground.

The other shook his head, too, and spat on a nearby rock, then squinted into the far sky. Clayburn cocked his head and watched the black-juiced clot seep partly into a crack in the granite. He stepped across to the man and caught him by his wrist. He yanked the man's fingertips to his nose and flared his nostrils and sniffed. Before him the man stood frozen, both he and his comrades wide-eyed.

"Smoking last night on picket duty, were you, friend?"

The man's head quivered horizontally. "I ain't stupid," he said.

"We missed him because of you."

The man started to speak again, but Clayburn moved a long finger to his lips to shush him. The man's eyes were wide a long moment, then darkened. He tried to pull away. Clayburn wrenched the man's arm under his own, locking them arm in arm. He raised the cutter.

"The hell?"

Clayburn clipped off the tip of the man's finger at the outermost joint. It made a sickening pop. Then he turned and thrust himself away from the embrace, standing suddenly empty-handed as by some magician's legerdemain, cutterless.

The man lifted his disfigurement to eye level. It began to spurt, spurt, spurt—a startle of red in the morning grim.

Clayburn watched him silently, intently, as if in study.

"Hurts, don't it?"

The man screamed.

"Fetch him that blade from the fire when it's hot enough," he said. He turned away. "He can burn it closed." The ring of men parted for him as he walked back to his horse.

Later the men scoured the ground for the cut-off end of the man's finger. They found nothing, no sign, and when somebody said something must've run off with it, nobody laughed.

"Atlanta," she said.

Callum looked at her. They were nooning beside a brook that ran through a cold blue meadow. The wind sheared through the grass. Cold coming.

"What?"

Ava gestured at him with the dry cracker she held.

"Swinney said Atlanta was occupied, right?"

Callum nodded.

"Maybe he was trying to tell you something. They can't go anywhere near the Union army, but I bet we could slip in there easy, just the two of us. It'd be a lot closer than the coast, at least for the time being."

They were already nearing the eastern edge of the Blue Ridge. Callum looked out to the east and south. Sharp ridges softened into lower hills, lower and lower, rolling toward the central pine barrens. Beyond those lay the swamps and plains, far out of sight. It was a lot of open ground to cross, with fewer places to hide.

"You don't think we could make it?"

Ava had a big bite of the stolen hardtack in her mouth. She swallowed and shook her head. "I been seeing the look on your face," she said.

"What about a couple days back, all that talk about the coast?"

"Just trying to make you feel better."

Callum pursed his lips and squinted into the distance, then back at her, wishing the idea had been his.

"Atlanta, then," he said. "We'll start heading southwest. I reckon that'll keep us in the mountains until we're pretty close to the city."

"I got a good idea or two, don't I?"

Callum nodded. "Pretty good." He grinned. "For a girl."

The block of hardtack was like a rock when it struck him on the nose.

The afternoon sky darkened like a threat. Before long, rain was falling slantwise and cold. The day seemed many hours ahead of itself, dusking already, a surreal and unchanging grayness of light. They pulled their coats around themselves as tightly as they could. Callum tried to give Ava the slouch hat to keep the rain from seeping cold into the crevasse of her spine, sliding down the ridges of her slim-muscled back. She wouldn't take it.

They'd been on an old wagon road since noon, descending, parallel ruts through rock and dirt. Within the first hour, runnels of fallen rain flowed through the wheel grooves. These grew to torrents by late afternoon, dark-running, and the horse walked the elevated ground between them like a causeway. Finally the water overran its channels, flooding, and the road itself began to slough forward, downward, a single mass of sludge that swamped the animal's hooves to the fetlocks. Reiver high-stepped and shook his head and snorted.

Callum rode slumped in the saddle. Wet, cold. The sky crashed above them, thunder and the echo of thunder sounding through the valleys. The naked mangling of branches above them whirled and clattered, raftering the storm like the antlers of crazed beasts.

He looked back at Ava.

"You cold?"

She smiled, her face stretching with effort.

"In my head I got a fire roaring red in the stove. I got a bearskin blanket over my chest, my feet in a pot of hot water."

"Just you, huh? Hogging all the heat?"

"I might could let you in, if you want."

"Shit," said Callum, "and leave my steaming tub?"

"I got you out of one before, didn't I?"

Callum couldn't argue with that.

They came upon a stream crossing before dark. The

streambed was shallow-cut from soft ground. No high banks, no aeon-smoothed river stone. But the water ran high now and swift. Leaves and debris cascaded in the current, twirling in the eddies and crashing against crag rock and deadfall that littered the banks. There had been a primitive lashing of saplings to corduroy the crossing for wagons, and these were wrecked and scattered against a wind-felled tree that lay several yards downstream.

Callum sat the horse before the edge. He leaned forward over the stream and saw the reflection of himself whipped and harried in the current, his edges torn away like lickings of flame. He became aware of his heart accelerating, some undercurrent reacting to the slender rips of flood.

"What is it?" asked Ava.

Callum shook his head.

"Nothing," he told her, telling himself the stream was shallow, the horse strong. He urged them forward into the current. The horse went under to the belly. The stream foamed at their boots. A vision struck him of the horse's footing being ripped from beneath him, the three of them carried away. That fallen tree trapping them under, crammed and drowned. But the horse shouldered the current unfazed, propelling his head forward and back, forward and back. They reached the far side, Callum's hands white-knuckling the reins. Ava pulled her hands from his coat pockets and touched his fists until they relaxed. They rode on.

They broke onto a vast rolling meadow just after sundown, the rain unabated. They decided to push for the trees on the far side. A jag of lightning fissured the sky. Their surroundings were exposed, stark white. Huge hunks of white-lit stone rose half-buried from the earth, then darkness. Callum wondered how they'd gotten there, those stones. They were too big for man. Only giants could have strewn them. Some monstrous antecedents, perhaps, warring over a long-forgotten insult or dispute.

They dismounted in a stand of trees. Callum loosened the saddle's girth straps and set the horse to graze. They huddled together, shaking. They wet what meager hardtack they saw fit to apportion themselves and choked down the white mush. They refilled the beef bladder from a streak of rainwater coming down from a leaf.

Ava went off a little ways for nature's sake. She was gone longer than normal, it seemed. Her wet-blown hair clung clawlike to her face when she returned from the trees.

"What is it?" asked Callum.

"Nothing," she said, sitting beside him. "I got some spotting is all."

"Blood?"

She nodded.

"Is that normal, with a baby and all?"

"Some is, I think."

"Was it more than some?"

"No," she said. "It's just I couldn't tell at first in the dark."

"But you'd tell me if it was."

"I would."

"Promise?"

"Promise," she said.

They clawed out a bare spot on the ground and put down a bedding of leaves and buried themselves as tightly entwined as they could, the coming hours promising to be storm-ridden and cold beyond any previous imaginings of misery. They lay a long time, listening to the rain patter down through the trees, their breath smoking in the dark.

"I was afraid," said Callum.

"What?"

"Earlier today, crossing that stream. I was afraid."

"I noticed before. It's okay. Everybody's afraid of something."

He shook his head. "It ain't. It's the reason we're in all this. The reason I fell in with the Colonel's troop."

"I don't understand."

"After Swinney took me in, I could of stayed on at his shack without him, hunting for what washed ashore from the wrecks. But I was afraid of being out on the water again. After what happened. He didn't want me to come, but I did."

"Callum, you hadn't been with the Colonel's troop, who knows what that first son of a bitch would of done to me."

"But look what happened anyhow."

"That ain't your fault, Callum. None of it is."

"I don't know."

"It ain't. You didn't know what would lead to what. There's people in the world claiming to have the second sight, and maybe they do, but you aren't one of them." She touched his arm. "Besides, it brought you to me."

Callum felt a pang in his belly, warm.

"You think stuff happens for a reason like that?"

"I don't know. I think you can find a reason sometimes if you're willing to."

"You look like a pretty good reason."

She wiggled closer to him, smiling. "Tell me a story," she said.

"About what?"

"I don't know. About the future. Let's see if maybe you do have the second sight."

"Hell."

"Come on, I seen you ruminating. I want a story."

"Well," he said. "Just for you."

He thought he had no story to tell, but he was wrong. He began to tell her of a boy and girl and horse—orphans all—racing through a bad land, and of the city that would save them, so warm and safe, and of the coast after that. The words came in a low lullaby voice he hardly knew he had, strung together almost without thought, and he knew for the first time how fathers at bedside told stories of their own invention, devised even as the story unfolded, and how easy for folk- or fairy tales to pattern the words, to lend them power and weight. He spoke of sunlight and hearth fire, swept streets and new-risen bread, of Irish-born soldiers of the North who might recognize his family name or exploits, welcoming them with whiskey and hurrahs. All these images bright-lit and fictive, a world apart from the cold ground that clutched them.

Dawn broke over the sawtoothed ridges to the east, the sky a featureless gray. Bursts of wind tore across the open meadow, rendered in waves of white mist-rain that cut through their coats and gloves. Mud caked them from head to foot. Their fingers were stiff, their hands palsied as they readied the saddle for the day's ride. Callum was tightening the girth straps when Ava yanked his coat sleeve and pointed back the way they'd come. A rider on a dun horse had emerged from the trailhead behind them, the one that gave on to the meadow. The horse's breath steamed in the cold air, and he was dark-painted with mud. The rider raised a set of brass binoculars with one hand. His other held a long gun propped on his knee. A scout. He lowered the binoculars and started to shoulder the rifle.

Callum pulled Ava behind Reiver's barrel-like chest and drew the rifle from the saddle scabbard. He dropped prone, half-hidden by a nearby tree, and leveled the rifle on the rider.

"You can hit him from here?"

"Nuh-uh," said Callum, sighting. "But I can show him I'll damn well try."

A fire-filled puff from the other man's weapon, and Callum fired, too. The shots clapped across the open field, crisscrossing. Callum heard the incoming ball crack into the bark high above him. His own shot gave no effect he could see, but the scout thought better of his tactic and disappeared into the trees. He'd be riding hard to alert the main force.

Ava was already up. Callum boosted her onto the horse and slung himself into the saddle. He whipped them into a gallop toward the parallel tracks of the wagon road, his heart manic, his hat brim folded back on itself with speed. Soon the road dropped out of the meadow, into the dark channel of trees. Here Reiver sank into a black mire, slogging and snorting in what muck the storm had made of the road. Some minutes later, Ava turned herself around on the huge haunches, riding backward.

Callum looked over his shoulder. "The hell you doing?"

"I don't intend to get shot in the back," she said, locking her hands behind her around his waist.

Callum did not know how far ahead that scout had been of the main party, how long it might take him to rejoin them—days or hours or minutes. Regardless, the bounty hunter had pushed the men closer than he'd expected.

At the next forking of the road, he bore right, then rode until they reached the first creek crossing, wide but no more than knee-high. He led them into the current and turned them downstream for several paces, breaking low-hanging branches that crossed above them as if they'd been snagged while making for the other fork. Then he turned them upstream, west, no tracks on the stone-laden creekbed underneath the horse's hooves. Reiver was careful on the smooth stones that quivered beneath the shallow current, fugitive shapes, but soon they struck a new trail heading south, hardly more than a footpath. Maybe an old Indian trail, maybe just one used by deer or wild hog. No matter. The path was single-file—slow going for a larger force.

They rode this trail hard, crashing through dead limbs until an hour later it dropped them upon a wider trail. It was rockier than the old wagon road. They were descending from here on, the horse's iron-shod hooves ringing out on the rock-covered road. Hours later they broke out of the woods onto a bluff that overlooked a black river. The water was high-running and foamy at the banks, the surface light-speckled with afternoon sun.

There was no bridge or ferry, not here, and Callum cursed the fear in his belly. He reckoned their best chance of a crossing was back where the old wagon road hit the river. He didn't know how far he'd diverted them from that road, only that time had been lost.

Driven stock had trampled a grassy thoroughfare along the banks and bluffs, and at least they made good time riding downriver. An hour later, a flat-bottomed ferry appeared on the far bank. Callum dismounted and pressed his good ear to the wagon road: no sound, not yet. He climbed back in the saddle and watched the water, black-running like the midnight sea in which all those men had been sunk, drowned, their dying bubbles breaking on the surface all around him. He looked downriver. Maybe there was a bridge that way. But no. He had other fears to contend with now—he felt Ava's body against his own—and more of a future to fight the past. He urged the horse to the river's edge and hailed the ferryman, who waved and began crossing toward them, hauling on his guide ropes.

Ava looked up the wagon road, then back at the ferry.

"It ain't the fastest thing I ever seen."

"No, ma'am. It's surely not."

The ferryman was little more than a boy, twelve perhaps, his small frame swallowed in a handed-down gum blanket that made streaks of the fallen rain. Several feet from the bank he halted.

"Ten bits to cross," he said.

Callum dismounted and dug into his pocket, his hand coming up with a crumpled fistful of notes—those he'd taken from the men at fireside.

The boy's eyes widened a moment, then squinted again, suspicious.

"Them's U.S. dollars, right?"

Callum shrugged. "Mostly. I got both. You can have your pick."

The boy, satisfied, pulled the ferry into the bank.

"My mama says them Confederate notes ain't worth a shit in the woods," he said. "Not these days."

Callum wasn't listening. He stepped lightly onto the flat-bottomed vessel with one foot, as if he could measure its seaworthiness through the sole of his boot. The horse snorted behind him. Callum placed both feet onto the deck. The horse fairly nudged him aboard.

The ferry boy was watching him with a troubled look. He spoke to Ava out the side of his mouth.

"He ain't some kinda dumb, is he?"

Callum was standing at the centermost point of the deck, straight-backed, his feet close together. He was the maximum distance from the current foaming and eddying around each of the edges.

The boy looked at him. "This here boat was built by my daddy's daddy, so you don't got nothing to worry about."

Callum didn't seem to hear. The boy shrugged and turned to his ropes. Ava watched the riverbank behind them as the ferry pulled away, watching the place where riders on the wagon road would emerge. The boy was laboring hard, his breath loud and steady. He looked from Ava to Callum and back again as he worked the ropes.

"You kids on the run or something?"

Callum wiped his mouth with the back of his hand.

"Say," he said, "there any bridges over this river hereabouts?"

The boy snorted. "Ain't nobody needing a bridge over this river, not when they got ferries like this one." The boy grunted through another pull. "Any bridges I ever heard of round these parts been burned or blowed to hell anyhow."

The ferry was moving toward midstream now. Slowly, slowly, with each pull of the rope. Callum, like Ava, took to watching the shore they'd left.

"And what about the next nearest ferry? Where's that at?"

"This here is the onliest one for near on thirty mile upriver or down," said the boy. He took one hand off the rope to pat the deck.

Callum looked at Ava, she at him, a sad bridge between their eyes.

The boy was still talking. "But anybody with any sense in 'em comes to this one anyhow. Specially the womenfolk.

They'd much rather a cute littlun like me than them toothless sons of bitches you're like to get anyplace else."

When they struck the far shore, Ava led Reiver off the deck. Callum lingered behind a moment. When the boy turned around, Callum was pointing his pistol at him. He gestured with the barrel for the boy to disembark ahead of him.

The boy leaned and spat.

"You got to be shittin' me," he said. He stared a long moment into the barrel of the gun, disbelieving. Then he looked up at Callum's face. He dropped the rope and shuffled off of the boat. Callum followed. On dry ground, he told the boy to cut the guide ropes, setting the ferry adrift.

"I ain't got a knife," said the boy.

Callum, still holding the pistol on him, reached under his coat and handed the boy his bowie knife in the sheath. The boy took the implement. Unsheathed it. Hefted it in his hand a moment as if noting the craftsmanship. Then he turned and hurled the knife far out into the river.

Callum watched the knife arc glittering through the air, end over end, its reflection tumbling across the surface until the two blades disappeared point-first into each other, a white burst of spray.

The boy held out the empty sheath as if to hand it back. "You think I'm cuttin' loose the ferry my daddy's daddy built, you got another think comin'."

Callum looked at the boy.

"I was figuring you'd want to be the one to do it."

"Not goddamn likely."

"I'm sorry, son, but this is just the way it is."

"Son? You ain't my goddamn daddy. He's two year dead, and you're hardly a day older'n me, you son of a bitch." He lunged at Callum. Callum stepped forward and drove his forearm under the boy's chin and thrust him over his outstretched leg, onto his back. The boy lay pinned and fighting, red-faced, tears streaking his face. Behind them, Ava had gotten out her folding knife. She sawed through the guide ropes. The ferry, sundered, began to swing toward midstream on its single radius of rope, pivoted by the far shore. Lost. The boy lay there, watching, the fight draining out of him.

Callum unpinned him and stood. The boy sat up and watched from his knees, his fingers in his hair, fisting and yanking. His face was red and wet. He was silent.

Callum dug into his pocket for the wad of bills. He started counting off notes, U.S. ones. He counted off a goodly sum and looked at Ava. She nodded. Callum folded the bills once over and placed them in front of the boy. The boy looked at them. Picked them up.

"They got blood all over 'em."

Callum nodded. "Reckon they'll spend anyhow."

The boy crushed the bills in his palm.

Callum boosted Ava onto Reiver's back, then mounted. They looked back at the boy. He was still facing the river, his fists balled small and powerless at his sides. Beyond him the northern shore, empty and far.

Chapter 10

Four days on wagon roads and horse trails. A cold wind, unrelenting, took the place of rain. Snow dusted their shoulders past dusk on two occasions, and they pushed harder and deeper into the nights, dropping down out of the mountains in darkness. They hardly stopped, hardly slept. Come morning the world would dawn white-haunted with mist, the trees emerging before them like shadows of what they were. Sound carried farther through the sparse wood at morning, eerily clear, and first light no longer afforded them solace or relief or anything save fear of exposure.

Come nightfall they feared what they couldn't see. The crack of broken wood, the rustle of dead leaves gained weight and force, striking through Callum like a blade to the bone. It was like the fleshy hide that bound him was worn too thin, and the whole world had gone sharp-edged on him, sight and sound. On his bad side, he could hear only faint mufflings, too easily shaped or misshaped by his imagination into something sinister. He knew Swinney would know which ear had been blown bloody and unhearing, and so might the other men know and attack from that angle.

What kept them going was the nearing of the city, the army of bluecoats into which they might slip unmolested, their pursuers daunted. They crossed the state line and redoubled their pace. They rode day and night, stopping no more than an hour or two at a time. Just long enough for the horse to feed, for them to shovel crumbs into their mouths. The meat was gone, the hardtack nearly. Ava started taking turns at the reins while Callum slumped behind her, asleep.

Gradually they found themselves pushing ahead of the coming winter, the turning of season. It was different here. There were leaves yet unfallen on the trees, blood-colored and gold over green-brown fields that held grazing livestock like some kind of heaven. They thought of poaching a hog or cow but why stop—so near was refuge, the city of Atlanta. It had to be close. Better to push past hunger, hard-riding beyond regard for anything save the ribbed engine of flesh that carried them. This they maintained at all costs, feeding Reiver the best they could, whispering words of encouragement into his tall ears. There was good grass and shrubs for him, and even as they rode he would extend his neck and snatch hanging leaves and standing brush to eat. Callum loosened the cinch whenever he could to avoid sores, and he checked the horse's hooves each day for thrush or cankers, for sand cracks or bruises or puncture wounds of any kind. Reiver would lift his feet for inspection, obedient as any soldier, before they rode on.

One night, they sat on the bank of a stream that crossed a meadow, staking Reiver to graze. Ava lay back against the earth, her hands folded across her belly.

"That story you told before—have you ever been?"

"To Atlanta?" He lay beside her, shoulder to shoulder, his hat against his chest, and looked up at the stars. "No, I just heard stories. We were mostly in the mountains. The Carolinas, Tennessee."

"Did you ever think of running away, making for the coast yourself?"

Callum rubbed his thumb along the brim of the hat, looking up.

"I can't say I really did, much as I should of. Not then. I don't know—bad as the Colonel's men were, I reckon it'd been a long time since I felt I belonged someplace."

She nodded. "I used to think I belonged in that valley. Couldn't really imagine myself anyplace else. But when the letters quit coming from Daddy and Jessup, it was like the light went out. I got to feeling closed in, the walls of the house and the hills past that. Feeling this darkness scratching at the door, skittering cross the roof." She paused. "I was starting to think of hurting myself."

Callum rolled onto his side, propping his head on his hand.

"Then we turned up, done it for you."

She nodded, squinting at the stars. "Sometimes I worry I didn't fight him hard enough. Like maybe I deserved what I got."

Callum turned fully onto his stomach.

"Look at me," he said. "Nobody deserves that. Nobody. Only one got what he deserved was the Colonel, and a long time coming at that."

She rolled up onto one elbow, brushing the hair from his brow. Her face was close to his.

"Roll back over," she whispered. She nestled her head into his shoulder, her leg on his thigh, her hand over his heart like a pledge. "You think they got coffee in Atlanta, not just the chicory stuff?"

Her knee was touching his groin now; he could feel himself engorging. He licked his lips.

"Girl, they just might, and sugar, too. Butter to fatten you up—"

There was a crack from the woods, as of a stepped-upon limb, and they bolted upright. Before they knew it they were on the horse, in flight, the creek left far behind.

Soon they began chancing the clay roads under cover of darkness. These crisscrossed the hills, red-beaten by day, empty by night save the odd mule cart or ranging head of cattle. There were no low-hanging branches to snag or slow them, no potholes to break a horse's leg like the crack of ax-felled timber. Few creatures but the raccoons and nighthawks to bear witness to their passage, and scarce evidence even of these, as if some curfew had been imposed on man and beast alike.

They were hard upon a road that wound among homesteads all hill-settled and black-windowed with sleep when Callum first glimpsed a strange glow in the night sky. Sunrise, he thought. But no, it couldn't be. It was the wrong hour, from the wrong direction. He looked to the stars. They were obscured in a scud of low-hanging cloud. He looked back at Ava. Asleep.

The tiniest fear began to simmer in his gut, like some reflection of the fired sky. He couldn't say why. Before long his eyes were burning. He didn't know what was wrong with him. He wiped his nose with the back of his hand. It was stopped up, runny, the mucus dark.

Ava stirred. She sniffed.

"You smell that?"

"Smell what?"

"Something burning."

The road swung upward before them to crest the highest hill of the night, and crest it they did, boy and girl and horse, the three of them struck suddenly rigid in the road as before them a firestorm raged upon the city of their hope. A hundred fires, a thousand. Every last thing ablaze save a single mountain of bald stone upon which great mirrored flames reeled and surged, the city below it thrust heavenward in snarling fury, in leaping spires and spits of flame, a fortress raised up in terrible light. Glowing cinders raced into the sky, the remnants of homes and markets, depots and factories, and the fires jumped easily from place to place, hungry to feed, the flames building upon one another in ever greater ramparts.

This once-great railway terminus, its iron rails radiating outward to the great cities of the South—it was like a heart destroyed, ground black beneath the flames. Smoke poured from the wreckage, so much darker than the surrounding night, churning in great towers against the sky, monuments raised as if to the wrong kind of god. Now and again the smoke pulsed, as a thundercloud would, swallowing up explosions of powder stores and munitions, and rockets tore across the night like panicked messages. Flames scrawled wildly through the outer streets, climbing whole buildings in an instant, shooting out of windows and doors, and the avenues were full of burning wagons, caught fire before they could escape.

They were miles distant, the riders, and they could almost hear the roar.

Callum slipped off the horse and walked to the edge of the

road and sat. He stared, disbelieving, for a long time. He could hardly breathe, like the fire had sucked the air from the night. This was beyond hell, beyond any biblical image of torment. This was real, and it was happening as if it happened just for them.

Something broke loose inside him, came screaming through his clenched teeth. He grasped fistfuls of hair and twisted and yanked, screaming bulb-eyed, blood-faced, until all of the air had been retched out of him. His lungs empty, his vision starry. His head between his knees.

When he looked up, Ava was sitting beside him, watching the city burn. She was calm, her face like porcelain, hard and smooth. The far-off flames licked the risen contours of cheek and bone, vanished in those gaunt hollows long-carved by the world she'd known. After a while she reached over, not looking, and took his hand.

"The coast," she said. "We got to keep moving."

Callum nodded. He took a deep breath and stood. Ava, too. He turned and looked to the descent of the road behind them. He was afraid to look too long, like he might invite things he did not want to see. They got back on the horse, and Callum settled himself as far toward the rear of the saddle as he could, as near to Ava. He clucked and Reiver started them down the road. Now and again through the night they caught sight of the distant inferno, and that bright city, however flame-ridden and damned, seemed only to darken the lonesome outlands before them.

The two boys appeared barefoot from the woods with a pair of hounds on rope leashes. The dogs were harnessed by an intricate series

of knots and slipknots, and the slack of the ropes was spooled around the boys' chests and shoulders. They stood straight-backed and rigid before the slave hunter's smoke horse. They were his sons.

"Where's the rest of them?" he asked, frowning at the two dogs.

"Yonder," said one of the boys, throwing his arm behind him. There was a log house with V-notched corner timbers, and before this a dog kennel with expensive wire fencing. "Inside."

The riders nudged their horses forward, the slave hunter leading. He rode up to the very edge of the kennel and looked a long time at the dead hounds it housed, the streaks and scrapes and pools of blood gone dark. He looked at the exploded skulls, the black blood of punctured guts, the spilled intestines and shot-scattered brains. He looked a long time to where one of them, Star, had dragged herself gut-shot to a corner to die.

His favorite.

"We took Polly and Sergeant into the woods when they come through. We couldn't get 'em all. They say Sherman put out a order for all nigger dogs to be shot."

Clayburn lifted one leg over the saddle, dropping off it without turning his back on the kennels. He took the leash ropes of the two surviving hounds, both in hand, and tied them around his saddle horn. Then he stood over the two boys. They did not flinch, waiting. He cuffed one on the cheek, then the other.

"You boys should've cleaned this up already," he said. "You do it soon's we're gone."

They nodded.

Clayburn nodded and held out his hand behind him, toward the riders, not looking at them. His fingers were open, his palm white.

"Mr. Swinney," he said, "let's see that scrap of coat."

The fat man took a deep breath and looked around him at the other riders. Nothing but hard eyes, the kind that told him they'd rip those rags from his saddlebags themselves if he didn't surrender them.

He wiped the back of his hand across his beard and then rode forward, digging through his saddle for a scrap of the oversized coat the boy had been wearing on his sickbed, before the girl had made him another. The dogs quivered with desire, wet-mouthed, waiting to be loosed.

❧

A cold sun broke through the trees, watery and pale. In the west, columns of smoke hovered wind-bent over the razed city, the ruin itself hidden somewhere beneath the close-pressed horizon of hills and fields. The odor of burning pine stung the air, acrid, and when the wind was right a pall of ash descended upon horse and riders and road. When this happened they rode with bolts of torn fabric covering their faces like highwaymen or bandits. They saw no one about. The slanted shacks and porch-wrapped houses were shut-doored, silent.

"You think it was a accident?" asked Callum.

"I don't know," said Ava. "I don't know if I want to know."

The trail had branched sometime in the night onto a narrow-tracked farm road, skirting east of the city. Black and russet cattle ranged in the fields to either side, sharp-boned and lean, their backs ash-dusted like a faint powdering of fresh fall. Callum found himself watching them huddle and graze. Found himself lusting for the slim red muscles, the white-marbled fat beneath their hides.

"We got to eat," said Ava. She touched her belly as she said it, not knowing she did, and Callum didn't know if it was the hunger or the baby that pained her, or both.

"I know it."

Callum looked around for house or barn or man. Saw nothing. He rode them off the road into the rolling pastureland. The herd lowed as they passed, unalarmed. Callum rode to a far edge where a large cow and her calf stood near the trees. Both were the color of rust. He dismounted the horse and drew his pistol, then thought better of it.

"Borrow your knife?"

Ava nodded. She handed it to him from somewhere under her quilt.

He walked toward the cows, unfolding the small blade from the handle. He looked at the big one. He did not want to kill more than they could take. He looked at the smaller one, grazing close behind its mother. Its bright eyes welled with his reflection, and it became nervous. He started talking to it. Comforting it. Speaking in a low and soothing murmur. He got close enough to lay his free hand on the notch between the eyes. He rubbed it there. It looked up at him. He flicked the blade across the neck from underneath, laying open the artery. The calf screamed, and its mother, seeing, leapt backward with a long moan. But she could do nothing. The small heart continued to beat. It pumped in mindless cadence, machinelike, all that life spurting red-bright and rhythmic into the morning sun. The calf staggered and sank to the ground, then laid its head down as the spurts grew weaker and weaker, a fountain dwindling. Callum watched the white wisping of the calf's breath diminish in the cold air. The once-bright eyes became glazed, unseeing.

He pulled the dead calf into the trees, and Ava rode the horse in behind him. He turned the animal onto its back, russet with a soft white belly. He drove the knife into the rear of the animal, between the legs.

"Not that hard!"

He turned, and she was already jumping off the horse.

"You can't go that deep. You're gonna pierce the rectum, spoil the meat."

She crouched beside him and put her hand on his shoulder.

"Let me see the knife."

He handed it to her, watching as she cut delicately into the rear of the animal, opening a vent, and pulled out the tube-like organ.

"You got a string or something? We got to tie it off so it won't leak."

He got her a length of pigging string.

"Perfect," she said.

Then she made a small incision at the base of the abdomen, sticking two fingers into the cavity to guide the blade up through the downy belly, toward the breastbone.

"You got to use your fingers," she said. "Make sure you don't puncture something you shouldn't."

She cut the membrane that lined the ribcage, the thin whitish one that held everything in place, and reached in among the organs, pulling out the heart, lungs, windpipe. Together they rolled the animal on its side. Out spilled viscera in coiled piles, and so much blood—a flood of it over the fallen leaves. It was bright as anything. Steaming.

She went for the backstraps first, those tender lengths on either side of the backbone. Callum unstrapped the bedroll and laid it open on the ground, piling in a bed of dry grass and leaves, and she laid the bloody cuts of meat in neat rows as they came free from the animal. She'd taken off her quilt and she was red to the elbows from the work. Finished, she rinsed herself from the beef bladder while Callum rolled up everything in the bedroll. He could feel the warmth of the meat, even through all that tight-rolled wool and grass, like there was something still alive in there.

"We best get a couple miles from here," he said. "Make sure nobody runs up on us enjoying their stock."

Ava nodded and took the roll, handing him the knife.

"You hold on to it."

"Your knife?"

"Our knife."

They mounted and rode back across the field and onto the road to find a place to avail themselves of their poached meal. They were on the road an hour longer, the sun's ascent not yet noon-high, when spires of new-risen smoke appeared along the horizon before them, east of the city. As the day progressed, they watched these columns of smoke track eastward along the sky, as if locomotives were racing from the city on course for the sea, heralded by buzzards and crows.

"Ain't looking like an accident now," said Ava.

"Not by a long shot," said Callum. "Only the army could do that."

"What's there to burn thataway?"

"Between here and Savannah, I don't know. Looks like they aren't being real particular about it."

"Least it's not us they're after."

Callum leaned and spat. "We get in their way, I don't reckon it'll matter."

The rough track they were riding grew sandy for several miles through a thick wood, pines grown dark and arrow-straight from a floor of cones and straw. They crossed creeks that ducked and twisted through the terrain, and the trees latticed the sky so close-clutched and crooked they could hardly see the smoke or sun. The earth they rode was red, rust red, and when the trees would clear and the land open, they could see the dry creeks and washes that scored the hills like wounds.

Toward noon the sky darkened, as if by storm, and they could hold out on the meal in the bedroll no longer. The track opened onto a channel cut treeless through the wood. A railway, or what was left of one. Massive stacks of torn-up rail ties were piled, smoldering, as far as they could see in both directions. Blue towers of smoke hung over them, and where the tracks curved out of sight, yet more smoke spiraled out of the trees.

They looked from the sky back to the ground. In the grass, once-straight iron rails lay scattered, newly demented into violent angles, acute and obtuse, as if by the hand of some race of men with such cruel strength to torque them. But the power, Callum saw, was one of mind: The angle-pivots were blacked with heat, like smithy's work in the grass.

Ava tapped his shoulder and pointed across. Callum looked. There, on the far side of the tracks, a rail had been twisted around the trunk of a pine tree like an iron necktie, the wooden neck choked and scorched. Up and down the tree line he saw other rails tree-bent in like fashion, a whole piney wood manacled in iron. An entire railroad ripped up, ruined. The force it took, the sheer scale, dried up his mouth.

"Jesus," he said.

They sat the horse a long time, listening at the edge of the trees: nothing. They rode out toward the nearest pile of cross-stacked wood. It was red-hearted with heat, the outer ties ash white. They dismounted the horse and unrolled the blanket. They pierced the rough-cut steaks with whittled sticks and squatted side by side. The red flesh hissed over the coals.

"Wonder what future people will think," said Ava. "Finding all this. The trees gone, all these irons dug up from the ground. Hundreds of them. Thousands, maybe."

"Nobody's like to forget this," said Callum. "Not soon, I reckon."

"I don't know," said Ava. "You'd be surprised what people'll forget."

Callum looked at the loop-bent irons, imagining what people who didn't know better might think. How they might think them the shackles of forgotten giants, or the letters of a lost language. The ruinations perhaps of an angry god, bending a once-straight world to his will.

Ava turned her meat over the fire.

"They squeezed their fun out of it, you can tell."

Callum nodded. You could see they'd tried all sorts of shapes, testing their creativity. Mainly a single bend or loop, but there were a few triangles. Trees coiled as if by iron snakes. A couple of *M*'s or *W*'s—someone's initials, no doubt. And there, down the line, a crude pentagram leaning against a tree.

"Reminds me of the Colonel, almost."

A kind of growl in Ava's throat. "What fun he had?"

Callum nodded. "You know, he was a tenor before the war. Like in a choir or something. And he could mimic a baby wailing like nobody else. We'd come up on a encampment, and he'd let out a cry, just out beyond the line where a single sentry could hear. It was perfect, just like a baby left all alone in the woods. He'd perfected it. Of course the sentry'd hear and come investigate. The Colonel'd cut his throat, then leave him there to be found come morning. He'd come back to camp just beaming after. So proud of himself. He was having the best time. He might do it two or three nights in a row, and each night the other sentries would stay closer to camp. Scared. Before long they were too close to warn of a force come riding through in the night."

Ava shook her head, as if to get the thought out.

"Bastard," she said.

They stared at the meat awhile, letting the smell waft up and around them. Callum's mouth was wet now, a hot spring bubbling up. After a minute, Ava pulled her steak from the fire and eyed it good.

"Not quite there, but I don't think I can wait."

"I ain't," said Callum, biting into his.

Ava watched him, a grin trembling across her mouth.

"How is it?"

Callum didn't bother to swallow first.

"Heaven," he said.

The steaks were unbelievably tender, like something for dessert. They ate them with their hands, tearing them with their teeth, and put more on the spits. They had two cuts apiece, then three, the red meal smeared across their lips. They smiled at each other, over this greatest of feasts, like wild things from the woods. Callum felt the fat and muscle warming his gut, like it might really replenish his thin-worn flesh, his beat-up spirit.

He got up and walked to the horse and retrieved the jar Lachlan had given them, unopened since the mountain storm, and brought it to the fire. Ava raised an eyebrow at him. He unscrewed the cap and took a big slug. He handed the jar to Ava and she did the same, her sip almost dainty in comparison. Callum felt one corner of his mouth turn up.

"Don't want to start him too early, huh?"

"Or her. Rather not birth me a little tosspot."

"I don't guess you got to worry too much. One thing I'll say for the Colonel: I never seen him drunk."

Ava exhaled through her teeth, handing him the jar.

"Little blessings," she said.

"He was a Irishman, now then you might have to worry."

She grinned, watching him have another slug. "It seems so. Was your daddy a big drinker?"

Callum handed her the jar, beginning to feel himself swoon on the meat and mash.

"I heard he had a taste for the poteen, that pot liquor they made, but he was never mean or nothing that I recall."

She handed back the jar. "I thought you didn't remember him."

"There's a couple things I do."

"Like what?"

Callum squinted one eye, holding the jar against his chest.

"His jaw. Scratchy and square and red, like a brick. I remember rubbing my face against it."

Ava nodded. "My daddy wore a beard, and when I was a little girl I used to sit in his lap evenings while he read and try and braid his chin whiskers. Thinking back, I can't believe he'd let me."

Callum leaned back, rubbing his nearly vacant chin.

"Tell you what. When this here beard comes in full, you can braid it anytime you like."

A wicked light came into her eyes.

"Can I sit in your lap while I do it?"

"Girl, there's another thing you can do anytime."

Afterward they rose, sated, into the smoky twilight of the noon hour, a man-made dusk yet haunted by the soundless echo of screaming iron, roaring flame, the step and fall of marching boots. Callum knew the power that had wrought such damage upon the land was enemy to the power that pursued them, and so he tried to take some small comfort in the ruin all around them. However much he could. He walked back toward the horse, his blood thick and roaring. He boosted Ava onto the horse and helped himself into the saddle.

The horse moved out along the ruined railroad. Callum knew they should keep to the trees, but the smoking sun was upon their shoulders and necks, the fired rail ties radiant in the cold like a pathway made warm especially for them. The horse stepped carefully between the heat-bent rails, the cold grass crackling underneath his hooves. His angular shoulders flexed and relaxed, flexed and relaxed. The movement was uniform, soothing. Callum's eyes grew heavy, so heavy. He could not go to sleep. Should not. His head dipped. He caught himself and lifted his chin. Again. Again.

He let himself float upon his perch above the ground, lulled toward the dark and womblike beckon of sleep, distant, a seeming reprieve from the meanness of the outer world. He felt Ava slowly reach her arms around him, as if in embrace. She took up the reins, riding them toward a path into the sheltering pines, out of the open.

❧

Callum dreamed. He dreamed of riding horseback through hills snow-laden and naked, no cover save a handful of leafless trees upthrust from the ground like the crippled hands of supplicants. Arrested, perhaps, in the final throes of some clawed-after resurrection. The sun was dark as a hole stoved in the white and featureless sky, and cold, an inverse of the self it lent to the world of men. A freezing wind skirled across the land, whipping powder in wind-torn tracings off the sharp slopes, stinging Callum's face with nettles of ice. He went to raise a scarf over his mouth and nose but found nothing on him, no clothes, his body naked to the pale flesh, the sharpened bone.

There was something on the horizon behind him. A blot, black as india ink, but alive, moving. He watched it bleed down the crest of a distant slope in the dark-flowering blush of something spilled. He watched it gather quivering and lakelike in the bottomland a single moment, only to burst suddenly forth in a shape wild and amorphous upon the hills, black-surging, emerging as it approached into a running of wolves. Beasts begotten of a single point and singular still, their eyes like carved marbles of ice with black stavings of sight by which to track him. The furred rush of them dropped into and out of sight as they tore across the hills toward him, leaving no prints he could see in their wake.

He turned and whipped the horse for speed, surmounting the nearest slope, dropping suddenly into a valley littered with the burned-out wreckage of machines. Strange machines wrought of iron and brass, none recognizable, all trailing long streaks of soot as though someone had tried to slog them to a place upon the barren expanse he didn't know where. He shot past them upon the dense-packed snow and glanced over his shoulder. He saw the hoofprints of the horse pooling ink-dark behind them. He realized the beast was melting away underneath him, giving out its black liquid of being with every step, the hounding wolves seeming to rise and multiply upon the dead-pooled remnants.

When the legs of the horse had given fully away, the belly

struck the ground. The legless chassis of horseflesh rolled screaming underneath him, and he was flung forward across the snow. Then up and running, the wolves right upon him, and on the far side of the next-nearest snowdrift lay a huge and sunken hole like the mouth of a mine shaft drilled vertical to the core of the world. He stood upon the edge of the abyss and looked back toward the wolves, which were not wolves now but men on horseback wearing the flayed and gutless hides of wolves. As they came down upon him so hungry, so vicious, he knew if he stood his ground at the edge they would be taken with him into the well of darkness from which the twisted black hands had clawed so long to rise. The wolves crested the nearest snowdrift high and dark and mighty and the dream ended.

Callum woke. Ava's arms were encircling his small waist. She was holding the reins. Straight shafts of pine stood close upon every side of them, the forest hazed by ragged traces of smoke. Slants of late sun struck here or there through the overhang of branches.

They had been a long time in the smoky wood when they forded a slow-moving creek and broke upon a rolling field littered with leavings of a battle months old: crumbling earthworks and blasted trees and long trenches like mass graves. There were ammunition pouches, emptied, and dented canteens and haversacks forsaken by men fleeing or dead. A single weathered slouch hat, upturned and punctured, rolled in lazy circles when the wind nudged it.

Callum looked to the west and saw why a battle had once taken place here. The land rolled nearly unobstructed toward the city. The once-great cotton warehouses smoldered now amid the neat outlay of streets like so many great boxes of coal, and the hulking depots that lined the railroad yards had been scorched black, their windows gaping upon the wreckage before them. Skeletal remnants of storefronts flickered, fire-hollowed, and much of the city had simply collapsed, imploded, nothing save for piles of blackened timber and here or there a lone chimney, scorched. The air was strange and dusky, a red sun hanging over the scene like some savage ornament.

They stared upon it all for a long time. From the hilltop the previous night, the flames had been lurid, unearthly, the surface of a sun against cold space. Here, now, they saw there was truly nothing left for them in this city. No shelter, no army. A city charred and ash-ridden, to be reconstructed along some dim blueprints of memory or not at all.

From an outer quadrant of the city came a white flash and resounding boom. An ignited arsenal. There followed the staccato crack of other munitions, cartridges or packaged gunpowder, the city warring upon itself. They turned the horse and rode quickly along the edge of the battlefield, close to the trees, and gained a new trail, east, in the wake of new smoke. Callum watched it drift through the pines. If there were anything to daunt the men pursuing them, it was an army of their enemy willing to torch so mighty a city and blaze like-minded for the sea. This hope sung in his chest a moment, but then he looked back a last time at the city. He could almost hear the echo of heavy boots, the crunch of broken glass, the screams of a night ago. He turned away, the feeling of lightness lost.

They decided to bed down that night near a shallow river, more like a stream. Several white cravats of churned current were visible in the starless dark. The water and rocks were murmuring to one another as they always would, their talk ever-changing with rains fallen or unfallen, rocks lodged or dislodged in the drunken eddies and rips.

Ava began to gather up kindling for a fire. Callum looked around, the world hidden in such inky shadow, a fire beckoning to anyone in the night. Not least the riders hard upon them somewhere in the angular ridges and ravines of pine through which they'd come.

"You think we ought to risk it?" he said when she returned with an armload of tinder.

"I think we have to," she said. "I think the cold's coming again."

Callum watched her words cloud as she spoke.

The morning cold lay frost-spoken upon the shadowed pine and river rock. They unwound their limbs from the weathering embrace in which they found themselves. The fire was nothing but embers, and Reiver was ready to move. As Callum went to relieve himself in the woods, the horse positioned himself in front of him.

"Just give me a minute," said Callum.

They forded the shallow wash of the river and followed the same trail they'd struck from the battlefield. Within a half hour it curved and ended into a much wider road of reddish clay. The thoroughfare had been churned mightily by boots, hooves, wagon wheels—the passing of an army column. The clay of the road had frozen this way, a treacherous and unending range of miniature peaks, jagged and uncertain enough to thwart the horse. Instead they rode upon the shoulder, hugging themselves against the cold.

When the sun loomed higher, it illuminated a glittering sky, the cold smoke light-spangled by an infinite sum of flurried ice. They followed the road into a town, no other way to go, and found themselves surrounded by unpainted buildings, some just burned-out husks, and everywhere a whelm of stone-faced women and girls who looked at this curious pair of riders without seeing them. Some of the women stared out from broken windows, some from slanted stoops, one or two upon their bare and blackened knees in the cold, hands clasped. There were sundry items yanked willy-nilly into the streets. Thickly padded chairs and sofas ripped open by excavating saber. Bolts of calico and silk. A mahogany hutch overturned in the middle of the road, the sterling silverware thrown across the ground like the glittering spillage of a wounded machine.

Toward the city square there was a grand piano set rakishly in the road, as if they had entered a world where people with fine English pianos chose to play them in the streets for all to hear. Callum reined in the horse alongside the instrument and looked into the brassy innards straight-strung beneath the propped hood.

"He played good, I'll give him that."

They looked toward the voice. A woman sat in a rocking chair on a nearby porch, knitting. She looked up at them.

"Who did?" Callum asked.

"That Pennsylvania boy that drug it out there with his friends. Played like some kind of a prodigy, you ask me."

"What did he play?" asked Ava.

The woman shrugged. "Bach, Beethoven, Mozart. All the

Germans he could play. Dutchman himself, by the sound of him."

"So the army came through here?" asked Callum.

The woman had a length of sharp-pointed bone through the bun of her steely gray hair, same as the needles she knit with. She nodded. "You ever think," she said, not looking at them, "you ever think how many songs will go unwritten because of this war, unsung? Paintings unpainted, discoveries unmade? You ever think of that?"

Callum and Ava looked at each other.

"Probably you haven't," she said. "You the ones would write them anyway. You or ones like you."

She looked up at them from her knitting for the first time. Callum looked at her and was suddenly aware of the people around them in the gray light and cold, people at the corners of his vision. They were gape-mouthed, broken. Not this woman, though. She looked right into him.

"You seen any more of that army behind you?" she asked.

"No, ma'am."

The woman nodded, satisfied, and put down her needles. She began unwinding the thick-wound ball of yarn. Callum and Ava watched her, somehow enthralled. Its diameter grew smaller and smaller. After a time a glint of gold peeked through the yarn, then another. When she was done, she held a gold timepiece in her hand, the subterfuge of yarn unspooled in her lap. Her mouth moved toward a smile but didn't get quite that far, her bottom lip trumping her top, her eyes hooded toward what the watch hands were telling her. She watched them a long moment, as if deciding whether to forgive them for some lie they told her.

"You ain't no thieves, are you?" she asked, her eyes so

set on the pocket watch that Callum and Ava weren't sure if it was them she was talking to or the watch hands. In a moment she looked up at them, as if to resolve the question.

Callum and Ava looked at each other. Ava looked at her.

"No, ma'am," she said. "Not if we can help it."

The woman sucked at a tooth and looked squint-eyed in both directions, and then slipped the watch furtively into a pocket sewn in her dress.

"Everybody's gonna have to be something they don't want to after this," she said, sweeping the square with her eyes. "You two best be getting on. Sit a animal like that round here long enough, people liable to get suspicious."

They looked around and saw eyes upon the horse, sizing up the high legs and thick musculature for banknotes or food or maybe just some quick-triggered hope of escape.

Callum clucked and Reiver started to move forward, but Ava pulled at his shoulder and the horse stopped. Ava looked at the woman.

"We got some people after us, ma'am. A one-armed man and some others. Probably best you keep your distance they come riding through."

The woman did not quit her knitting. "I'll be right here," she said.

"We don't want you to have more trouble than you got here already."

"I hate the Yankee much as the next one, love, but I lost me a husband and two boys already. This is what it takes to bring my last boy home, so be it."

"I don't think you under—"

"Don't you go telling me what I know and don't, girl. I'll

be right here, knitting this here scarf. Winter's coming, and my boy's like to be cold without one."

Ava bit her lip, nodded, and tapped Callum's leg. He clucked and the horse moved on along the road. At the intersection ahead they kept east, following in the tracks of the marching army. They looked back once, both together, and saw the old woman bent yet at her knitting. Her scarf.

Her hope.

That day they passed beneath the shadow of the great stone mountain that stood just east of the city. It rose bald from the land, like a giant lump of sugar, ungreened save the scantest patches of vegetation. The early snow had turned for a time to rain, and torrents bounded down channels long-cut in the granite dome, crashing and glittering under the thawing sun.

"Hell," said Callum. "All them falls, you'd think it sprung a leak at the top."

"You know what this mountain is?"

"A hell of a rock?"

"It ain't," said Ava. "I mean it is, but what it really is, is a pluton."

Callum looked over his shoulder at her, furrowing his brow. "A *what*?"

"Melted rock from beneath the earth's surface, bubbled up and solidified. My daddy always held with the Plutonists, not the Neptunists, about such things."

"Oh he did, did he?"

"That's right. Pluto was god of the underworld, you know."

Callum grunted. "How'd your daddy come to know so damn much?"

"Books, mainly," said Ava. "But not just that. He went to the University of Virginia, the school of medicine there. Doctored people and animals both. Anything that was hurt, in any of the hollers close. I think it bothered him sometimes, what all he saw. He came home all the time in blood. I think he wanted to understand what made it all work. Lot of people think science is at odds with such, but I think it was in all those workings he was looking for some kind of a god."

"You think he found one?"

"I don't know," said Ava. "I'd of liked to ask him."

The road beyond the mountain was slop, a red slop that coated the horse's legs like paint. Reiver snorted as his hooves sunk nearly to his knees, and Callum could hardly imagine how the army's wagon trains had made it through such a mess. Smoke still poured from the eastern horizon. They crossed a bridge over a muddy red river and forded soupy streams that cut across the road. In late afternoon they crested a high hill and saw before them, for the first time, the full scope of the Union march, a ragged blue line strung crookedly across the countryside, mile upon endless mile, a column composed of men and horses and cattle and wagons, jostling as they made their way, looking from this distance like the roiling current of a new river breaking across the land, pushing east toward the sea. On either side of it was fire, a wide swath of advancing flame and smoke, as if the land were being sucked so dry it simply combusted under the sun.

"Jesus wept," said Callum. "Hand me that spyglass, would you?"

Ava rummaged in one of the saddlebags, finding him the

telescoping spyglass that had been the Colonel's. Callum extended it and looked through the eyepiece, the far-off world brought big and close. He saw whole regiments marching ten abreast, their muskets bristling like forests in the sun, and men driving cattle before them in bustling herds. He saw men on horseback, their saddles festooned with live chickens and turkeys, the birds flapping and squawking at their upturned world, and infantrymen knee-deep in road, pushing wagons and ambulances and caissons through the mud. He saw artillery pieces on their tracked conveyances, the barrels coal-black and mean-looking, the cannoneers trudging alongside, and open wagons piled with rugs and shiny loot. And behind it all a wake of blacks in mottled dress, carrying sacks across their backs or on their heads, with children led by hand at their knees.

"How many you think it is?" asked Ava.

"I don't know. I never seen so many people in one place."

"Let me see."

He handed her the glass.

"Jesus," she said. "There must be ten thousand of them."

Callum spat. "I wouldn't say there wasn't."

They rode on. Everywhere were burned barns and granaries, even farmhouses, some of them with people picking through the ruins, prodding the ashes with sticks or pokers as if they might turn up something that hadn't turned black and brittle as dust. They were stone-faced with glassy eyes, and they didn't even look up as the horse passed along the road.

Come dusk the riders began to hear a far-off thumping in the air. Drums, but not of war. The last trace of sun flared along the western horizon, cold-gone, and a new fire rose in the east, the clouds red-bellied over the trees. Darkness swelled, stars abounding through smoke and cloud, but the eastern horizon remained red-lit, flickering. And still the drums.

They took a wooded track off the main road that forced them to ride low against the horse, the cross-hanging branches broken only high enough for animals of lesser stature. Stalks of firelight began to rise through the trees that stood before them. Callum stopped the horse and got off. Ava, too. He led them off the trail, through the trees, as the drumming grew louder, deeper. Rhythmic. The sound the world might make if it had a heart, and they moved toward it, silently, as if entranced. The elbow of a creek edged out of the dark. They stepped across. The trees began to thin, open, and before long they were crawling on all fours toward the edge of the tree line.

A clearing opened before them. In it were black men, a ring of them dancing, their bodies cut jagged against a towering blaze. Their drums haunted the edges of firelight, palm-struck. Their fire rocketed into the sky. The house that had presided over them was but a smoking hulk, nothing save the brick-mortared chimney still standing through the flames.

He and Ava watched them a long time, their throats constricted. They watched the unbonded slip and flow of their limbs, the writhing concordance of their bodies. The backs of the men had grown wide and cruel under generations of burden, like wings or the muscle for wings yet unspread. Several of them bore slender blisters of scar, pale and lustrous as worms in patterns of crisscross or cat-o'-nine. The breasts of the women hung heavy and oblate under their shifts. Callum and Ava watched and watched. They had planned to ride the night nearly through, but they did not want to leave the edging of trees that hid them so close to the fire, the drums, the men and women full of song.

The sun was red, dying, when the riders tore into town upon the heels of two bloodhounds. The hounds had black faces, slack-jowled and long, like whiskied men of another life condemned now to this sorrowful occupation of scenting blood and shit, of heeding the barks and cur slaps of angry men.

The woman was in her rocking chair, nothing for supper to eat, her needles scraping against each other like the arms of a fly on a loaf of bread. The sharp points of them went still when the two hounds stopped in the road before her house, sniffing just where the horse had stood.

A man on a smoke-colored gelding sat his horse before her porch, not looking at her, looking instead at the gouges on the steps, the ruts in the road where the piano had been dragged. Behind him hovered a group of riders in what some called the multiform, no sign of rank or allegiance among them beyond the quality of their horses, the way they sat them. Some of them spat and grumbled; others scoured the square for something to look at, women maybe. A few stared unblinking at the man on the smoke horse. None got off his horse to hunt the broken buildings for something of worth. It was obvious this town had been emptied, undone.

The two dogs circled the spot where the black horse had stood. They stopped, unsure which way to go. The woman watched them. The boy and girl upon the horse had been so mud-caked and hungry-looking they'd given her a glimmer of hope for her boy. That youth could survive so much. Desperation, hunger, murder. She could see it. What it made of them, she didn't know, nor what her boy would be. She didn't care as long as he was breathing.

The man dismounted the horse and looped the reins around the porch balustrade. He mounted the porch steps with a mechanical clop-clop-clop that disturbed her somehow. She saw that he had only one arm under the cape he wore. He stood blocking out the sun, so that she and her rocker were eclipsed in the long lance of his shadow. Dark come early, and cold.

"Which way did they go?" he asked her.

She made to keep up her knitting. "Who?" she asked, looking with a spurious air of concentration at the most recent work of her needles, as if she'd made a mistake that might or might not require rectification.

He stepped closer. "I don't have the time, woman."

There was Georgia in his voice. She worked her tongue along her tall bottom teeth, her receded gums. "Manners, neither, I reckon."

He stepped so close that it was unnatural not to look at him. Still she refused. She looked at her own hands, the splotches where the sun had left its mark, the once slender-boned fingers grown fat-knuckled and gnarled like those of an old crone. Out of the corner of her eye she could see his single hand, fleshed the color of bone, creeping slowly up the side of his trouser leg. Each finger moving with a mind its own, and slow, a grotesque mimicry of the webbed predators that resided in the corners and nooks of her home.

Suddenly her hand was seized in a vise of five tiny arms, hard enough to bruise, and a band of cold metal slid over her ring finger. Then she saw what it was, the razor fine-honed to a wink.

"Tell me which way they went at them crossroads," he said, nodding ahead, his thumb on the trigger.

"And you Georgia-born," she said.

"Tell me or lose the finger."

She inhaled big into her sunken chest. "I lost worst," she said.

She looked away, waiting for what she expected to come. It didn't. He removed the cigar cutter. He was silent for a long moment. She could feel his eyes on her and her handiwork.

"Who you making that scarf for?" he asked her.

"Myself. Winter's coming, you know."

"No," he said, "you knitting that for a man." He bent in close and examined the design, the neat stripes. "For a boy," he said. "Woman your age only gives that much love to a boy."

Her limbs went hot and willowy. She thought of sticking him in the eye with one of the knitting needles, but they felt too heavy to lift.

He knelt beside her.

"Think of your boy, woman. Think of him making it home, only to find his mama dead. Maybe the one good thing left to him, hung broke-necked from the rafters like a nigger." He leaned in closer, his breath whiskey-hot, unrighteous. "What do you think that would do to him?"

Slowly she lifted a finger in the direction the boy and girl had gone. Her hand palsied, her eyes downcast, her aim yet true.

Dawn. Ragged shapes of light began to puncture the far tree line. Closer, the fire smoldered, dull red coals pulsing in heaps of ash. Cold smoke hung lazy upon the air, the naked chimney black-bricked by so many hours of fire and soot. Everywhere long traces of ground fog whited out the grass and clay of the clearing.

Callum blinked the sleep from his eyes. He was not sure what had woken him. He looked around, saw a small black boy crouching behind a fallen tree several feet away. Callum waved at him. The boy raised one hand over his barked bulwark and waved back. Callum raised himself off the ground on his elbow, and he thought first of food. He gestured for the boy to come toward him.

"Have you got anything to eat, by chance?"

The boy nodded yes.

"It ain't all burned?"

The boy shook his head. "We got some hid."

"Could you bring us something?"

The boy froze, his head cocked, his eyes going wide.

"Dogs," he said. "*Dogs!*"

"What?" said Callum, looking around. "What?"

"I got to go," said the boy. "Got to tell everbody."

He turned to run but looked back over his shoulder at Callum. He shot his hand into the pocket of his overlarge pants and tugged hard, tugging free an apple. He underhanded it to Callum, then shot away across the clearing toward the far-off huddling of negro cabins, the soles of his feet so much lighter than the rest of him.

Callum strained to hear whatever the boy had heard, frantic, turning his good ear this way and that. Finally he caught the distant bark of a dog, then another. He shook Ava.

"Get up," he said. "Get up."

He turned, unhobbled Reiver and untied his line from a nearby tree, his fingers slipping madly on the hard knot.

Ava was coming unsteadily to standing. "What?" she was asking, her eyes half-closed. "What is it?"

He took her roughly by the arm and hauled her toward the horse, unspeaking, and boosted her into her place. Then he cinched the saddle and stuck his foot through the stirrup and hauled himself upward. His hand slipped off the dawn-slick pommel. He fell flat onto his back in the leaves, hard.

"Callum, get up! Callum!"

He opened his eyes to Ava looking down from the saddle, her hands on the reins. She held out her arm and shucked one foot out of the nearest stirrup. They grasped each other at the forearm, and he struck one foot through the stirrup and climbed onto the back of the horse. She whipped the reins even before his foot was out of the stirrup for hers. They tore across the clearing, past the charred ruin of house, toward the road they'd left the evening before. Callum looked behind him and saw the negroes fleeing their cabins for the woods, quick with fear.

Ava struck them upon the road, the clay red and hard-churned by the army that had passed down it. They crested a rise and dropped so fast their guts sang quivering into their throats. They landed charging steeply downhill and found themselves in a white sea of fog, the road but a rumor before them, the trees like the faintest shadows out of the corner of an eye. Even so Reiver shot them forward, forward, forward, into the blindness, and Callum, unsaddled, could feel the power of the horse's haunches exploding underneath him, a violent mechanism seemingly unbound by the weakness of flesh. He knew the sun must be crowning the horizon, if not the trees, but he could see nothing, no light beyond the blankness of fog. Callum pulled one of his pistols and twisted to look behind him. The fog swirled between the narrow channel of trees.

He knew the dogs could not pace the speed of the horse, and he had not heard any barks over the clamor of Reiver's hooves for some time. He twisted to look again, and this time something was there: a slender blade of shadow in the fog, a vision of horse and rider flickering like a candle flame. He raised his pistol to aim. The barrel jolted at the end of his arm, above their pursuer, below. Momentarily the rider disappeared into the fog, then loomed visible in another spot, and he could not tell if it was the same rider or another.

He thumbed the hammer back and the gun kicked unexpectedly, triggered by a jolt in the road. A cloudburst of smoke was left hovering in the fog until the rider tore it through, dark tendrils torn ragged and swirling. Now more riders could be seen in pursuit, horsemen seemingly born legion of smoke. He fired twice more into the shadow shapes of them; they came on undaunted. He started to worry them something spawned of an addled mind, dubious imaginings. Then the first blast of shot erupted bulblike in the fog, and another and another.

Plenty real.

He turned back to Ava and swelled his lungs to make himself as big and wide behind her as he could. He imagined his back like that of those slaves he'd seen. A terrain cruelly built, inviolate, shield-shaped like a symmetric battering of flesh. He closed his eyes and tried to believe something of such stead bodied the stitching of his coat. He encircled Ava's waist as tightly as he could, determined to hold on even if he were hit.

He felt Ava's body hesitate a moment, then tense, urging the horse for speed. He looked over her shoulder and saw a throng of blacks on foot parting before them. They were clothed in tatters and shreds and nearly all of them shoeless, with bindle sticks over their shoulders or bedrolls. Pilgrims. They watched wide-eyed as the horse passed before them, and then they were gone, and all around the horse on every side was a bristling of bayonets. Men blue-coated with haversacks looked up gape-mouthed with surprise, fear, bringing to bear their rifles amid the clicking of cocked hammers.

"Johnnies!"

A riot of shots erupted on the road behind them, a clash of steel, their pursuers having ridden head-on into the rear guard of the army column. Ava turned Reiver around and around amid the sudden chaos of fire and smoke, the blood and screams. The heads of men and horses reared disembodied from the miasma in frozen visages of gritted teeth, fear, the glint-eyed lust for blood.

Callum looked down and saw an infantryman's face swing toward them, spinning, sweeping his rifle out of the fog. The soldier saw who sat at the reins—a girl—and swept past them. His barrel emitted a long tongue of flame into the belly of a man upon a horse opposite them, an old battler of the Colonel's troop. The man screamed and fell, twisting from the saddle. His horse dragged him away by the stirrup.

A gap yawned open in the melee. Callum slapped Reiver's rump even as Ava saw it. Reiver bolted off the road and through a wet ditch. He leapt a rough-cut pasture fence and they raced away across the open ground.

The sun hung over a land burned dry of fog, only the smoke left to threaten its dominion. Girl and boy and horse traveled down a line of trees grown guardlike on either side of a stream between cotton fields. Ava reined Reiver in at a cut in the bank. The stream's current rippled in the sun like shard glass on stone. Prints of hooves and paws and feet, shoed and unshoed, indented the bank, a catalogue of many days and nights past. Together it looked as though the beasts of the field had warred here for power of the drinking hole, a stoving mob of all species.

They dismounted and descended the bank to drink. None of them left more than the tracest prints in their wake, not even the horse. It disturbed Callum, somehow. Just the cold, he told himself. The ground too hard. But still it seemed strange to him, like they were not of such weight and substance as the things that had come before them. He wondered if ghosts knew they were ghosts. He was not so sure they did.

He knelt before the stream and touched his hands to the bank. No, they were here. The ground was just that cold, just that hard. It glowed in his palms.

Ava knelt beside him. The three of them bent to drink together. He looked at Ava, her reflection. Her face was moon-pale, sharp-cut as a man's with hunger and plight, her handling of both. She cupped a handful of water to her mouth, drank, then looked serious-eyed into the stream, as if watching for the right moment to drink again.

"I believe those Yanks might of shot us if it hadn't been me at the reins."

"I know it," said Callum.

"If you hadn't of fallen off getting on."

"I know."

She bent again to the water, her two faces converging, and Callum thought of what she'd said, the slip of fate that had put her in the saddle instead of him. A sudden upwelling stole his breath, a spark of something wild-born, fearless, and he surged forward as her lips came glistening upward from the stream and pressed his mouth against hers. She placed her hands on his chest to push him away, as he thought she might, but she did not push. She had let him do the other things, and now she let him do this.

After he pulled away, she licked the remnant stream water from her lips. She seized him by the lapels of the coat she'd sewn him and kissed him again, hard, then held him at arm's length. From there she cocked her head at him, a strange faraway expression coming into her eyes.

"You know, you're just about the age my baby brother would of been had he lived."

Callum rubbed his chin. "Oh?"

Ava hovered there a moment, eyes lost to some interminable distance, and then they were back again, blazing into his.

"I might," she said.

"Might what?"

"Have plans for you."

"Yeah?"

"Yeah," she said, patting his cheek.

Before Callum could reply, she stood. She set her hands on her hips, elbows cocked, and looked at Reiver.

"I reckon I ought to be the one taking the reins from now on," she said, arching her back. She set her front teeth into her bottom lip, restraining a grin. "Seeing as I was the one got us out of that mess."

"Shit," said Callum. He was on his butt, his palms splayed behind him on the ground. He squinted one eye up at her. "Only if we got Yanks around us don't want to shoot a girl."

"A girl?"

Callum pursed his lips. "A pretty girl?"

She offered a hand to help him up. When he reached out, she briskly retracted her arm.

"Oh, excuse me," she said, a rip of smile splitting the hollows of her face. She turned to mount. She climbed into the saddle, then slipped behind the cantle onto the horse's bare haunches, bowing a little in mock courtesy. Callum smirked and mounted, taking the reins. He reached into his coat pocket and held out the apple behind him, for her.

"I shouldn't," he said.

She took the apple. She pressed herself against him, resting her chin on his shoulder. "But you did." Her breath tickled his ear. She wiggled slightly, and her breasts felt heavier than they used to. Swelling, perhaps, with motherhood. He could almost feel the twin pricks of her nipples through his coat, awake and alert, asking him questions to which all of his answers were yes. *Yes, yes, yes.* She took a bite of the apple and handed it back.

They rode on amid the slow roll of cotton fields, riders newly buoyant and sweet-mouthed. Above them hung the ashen sky, hourless and strange.

They stood in a dense copse of trees, ash-floored, their horses saddled behind them. Men going about their palpations of torso and limbs in a surreal quality of light. The sun above them an elliptic orb, fog-diffused, a paleness over the claustrophobic membrane that domed them. The black stakings of the trees cast lancelike darknesses across the ground.

A quarter of their number could not be accounted for. Scattered, shot, taken prisoner. The remaining troopers toed black streaks in the ashen ground. The crackle of dead leaves and clang of weaponry, old soundings of dominion, as muted now as the light that bathed them. One of their number groaned from the base of a tree, and the others saw blood leaking through the broken pilings of his teeth, rich and bright. To a man they wished they could clamp shut his mouth for the sake of quietude, for however long it took to silence him.

None did. The big man, Swinney, had walked into the diagonals of light that cut through the close huddling of trees. They looked at him. He grasped the cuff of one overlong coat sleeve in his palm to keep it taut. He wiped his forearm under his nose like a schoolboy. A long worm of snot glistened on the fabric when he dropped his hand.

"I don't know about you, but I think I had about enough of this.

It's one thing to goose-chase a son of a bitch across a whole state. It's a whole other to do it straight on into the heart of a goddamned army."

Men, their heads down already, nodded.

"I say we haul it back up into the mountains before the mob of us is digging holes in a prison up north somewheres, for to sleep in. Tree-high walls and nigra guards to keep us in."

They nodded again. Conceding.

"You yellow son of a bitch."

The men looked. It was Clayburn. He had his back to them a few feet off. A bright sluice of piss came spraying from between the triangular propping of his legs, slicing right into a gopher hole in the ground. At the same time they could hear the open and shut of his cigar tin, the snip of his cutter. When he turned his head over his shoulder again, he had a new cigar between his teeth. He'd kept his aim true on the gopher hole, no-handed.

"That army is marching in two columns. Only safe in numbers, and they know it. Like a herd of something. Them foraging parties is light infantry, too cocked for plunder to be a problem. We haunt the edges of everything, and they know it."

"Didn't seem that way today," said somebody. "Seemed a whole lot different, in fact."

Clayburn let off several final spurts, short rockets that disappeared into the ground. He finished and turned around. No time to button himself, but buttoned he was.

"You've seen what the Yank is doing to this state, this far south. You think anybody's going to stop them? And what do you think we'll have to come home to then." It wasn't a question. "Catching this little son of a bitch is all we got. It's either that or go hiding in the mountains with winter coming."

He ground the tobacco sideways in his jaws.

"Now Mr. Swinney here, I think we all know he's got some kindy

soft spot for the boy. Who knows, maybe designs beyond that. I heard a queerer things myself."

A few of the men chuckled.

Swinney's face reddened. "Now hold on," he said. "The truth is, I just don't think he done it, the killing."

Clayburn let his eyes slide over the big man, his pudgy fingers.

"The truth?" he said. He spat. "I don't think that's for us to decide. We got us a trustee for that."

He looked over at Old Lawyer Sawyer, a slight man in round-rimmed spectacles with an unshaved shadow of beard. A pale man, meant for offices and libraries. Not for any of this.

"Now Mr. Sawyer, Esquire, whose head is it gonna bring them bounty of U.S. notes from that bank in New York?"

The men seemed to lean toward him almost imperceptibly, the trees, too. The sun itself so close, the thin man could feel the speckling of sweat underneath his skin.

"The boy," he said. "The boy will."

Along the horizon before them hung yet more towers of smoke, still as brushwork in the colorless wash of sky. Callum knew they must be crossing the gap between parallel army columns advancing across the state, crossing the no-man's-land that divided them. They were a night and two days trekking south along farm tracks and byroads that ran through sparse forests of pine where the understory lay browned and fallen, through vast cotton fields with farmhouses ransacked by foraging parties. Yards littered with upturned furniture and smashed china and bolts of calico and other fabric that fluttered like spent ghosts. Grounds perforated by ramrods in the hunt for buried treasure, the outbuildings fired to coal-colored hulks, the ruins slowly disintegrating. Long whirls of ash were carried off by cuts of wind, like the whip of powder from snow-laden roofs.

"I just realized," said Ava.

"What?"

"The genius of it."

Callum looked over his shoulder at her. Her eyes were wide, staring.

"Of what?"

"All this. *Sherman*. Think: Nobody's going to want to fight any longer, they don't have nothing to come home to."

Callum looked at a dead dog by the side of the road, shot, its tongue blue and stiff.

"It's hell is what it is."

Ava nodded. "Exactly."

Everywhere they saw only women and blacks and the youngest of boys, as if some plague had taken just the men. Before an unravaged homestead they saw a mule-drawn cart piled with jumbles of household sundries to a height nearly comic, an errant tower of bed frames and grandfather clocks and ladder-back kitchen chairs cobbled together by irregular lengths of rope and improvised knots. Standing before this ill-fated chariot, the refugees: a long-faced woman with her brow all shadowed under her bonnet, her two small boys beside her with sullen faces puffy and round. Little men who already bore a visible spite for the world in which they found themselves. The three of them watched the two riders pass through their land. They stood frozen, grim, as though posing for a daguerreotype. Around them moved the blacks, their onetime slaves, helping to load the wagon still higher.

The single apple was long gone, and hunger hard upon them now, a darkest coring in their bellies. Even so, they made no move toward the farmhouse, the cart. Something hard in the faces of the woman, the boys, deterred them. Something perhaps the two riders carried in their own faces, hammered visages of bone and flesh that floated through the land like the war masks of primeval clans, each of them rival to all others. Callum watched the cart being loaded and his mind was full of stratagems, predatory, of how he might hold them at gunpoint while Ava rifled their pockets for food, yanked open their cupboards and sacked their root cellar.

He closed his eyes, shook his head. He looked away, toward the trees. As soon as he did, the hunger was back in his belly, hollowing his insides, making him want, want, want. He worried what it could make him. Something he didn't want it to. He remembered the flesh of that apple, their only food in three days. Snow-white and red-skinned, sweet as any gift. It seemed only to make him hungrier. He reached one hand inside his coat pocket. Felt Ava's fist balled there against the cold. Felt the hard ridging of her knuckles, the small hand bones strung like some delicate instrument. He gave his heels lightly to Reiver, accelerating past the scene at the farmhouse.

That night, they bedded down without dinner. They risked a fire, knowing the Colonel's men would still be off somewhere regrouping, licking their wounds. Ava laid down her quilt, then stood staring into the flames. Callum watched her touch her stomach, almost absently, like she sometimes did. He knew it was still flat, hard as a board beneath her dress.

"I'm sorry we don't got anything to eat," he said.

She looked at him. "You got nothing to be sorry for," she said. She looked back at the fire, keeping both hands on her belly. "I'm hungry, but it ain't that."

"What is it?"

The tendons in her hands stood out. "I don't rightly know. It's just it feels so heavy sometimes, inside me, knowing it's partly him. I don't want it to, but it does."

Callum sat up quickly and swallowed hard. "I'm sorry," he said.

"Ain't your fault. I've said that before."

"I was thinking," he said. He paused. His heart felt weak and strong at the same time, beating fast.

"Yeah?" she said.

"Yeah," said Callum. He rubbed his mouth with the back of his hand, looking into the fire. "I was thinking you could maybe just pretend it wasn't him that put it there." He paused and looked up at her, crinkling his brow. "Like maybe, one day, you could just pretend it was me."

Ava looked back at him, her eyes going wet. She knelt down on her blanket and put a hand on his knee and looked into the fire.

"Maybe," she said.

Callum stared into the fire, too, this miniature of hell growling before them, the red embers somehow pretty despite, and when he looked up again Ava was waiting for him, her eyes the fiercest blue. She kissed him slowly, her tongue searching his. She ran her hand up the back of his neck, threading her fingers through his hair, and then she pulled him onto the ground, clutching him in the cradle of her thighs, her heels hooked into the backs of his legs. She rocked herself against him, her eyes widening, locked into his, her breath ragged in her throat.

"Yes," she said, and he didn't know if she meant yes to him or to the question of the child. She must have known, for she lifted her mouth to his ear: "To all of it."

Two days south, they sat Reiver on a knoll over a small plot of land. There was a house, a barn, a smattering of crooked trees. The gate of the hog pen had been trampled by its inhabitants. Everywhere they lay arrested in the outspill of flight, a pathetic diaspora of swine flesh shot or bayoneted in the field between the pen and the creek. Only the hindquarters of the stock had been taken. The unbutchered remainders, hulks pink and gray, lay slumped in perverse auras of blood and viscera, their front hooves spraddled before them as if to drag their unlegged bodies to safety. The riders had been four days without food. Here was their boon.

Chapter 11

For two days they followed a black jag of creek that cut eastward between cotton fields and emptied pastures. Most of the picking was done, but here or there late-planted cotton had exploded into seas of stormy bolls, ash-dusted, hovering low over the fields like so many thunderclouds. Always Callum was glancing over his shoulder, every ridge and shady grove pregnant with menace. Any moment their pursuers could bloom darkly upon a distant hillside, emerge out of a bottom or ravine like something loosed out of the ground.

Often a watering path would intersect with the creek. They would ride its soft ground away, leaving tracks, and then return by another direction. Whenever they met a larger road, they would mingle their prints with those of its regular commerce, hoping to leave a record of disappearance in this direction or that. They never remained long on the road, though. Not during daylight. They didn't want witnesses. Before them, the smoke hung in a dark stratum recalling the much-rumored factory skies of the North.

They avoided the burned towns, mills, gin houses, planters' factories when they could. They wanted to avoid the souls left wrecked in their wake. People desperate. Violent. But everywhere was destruction. Cotton, king of the land, smoldered wherever they looked, in scorched fields and tumbled black barns and warehouses. It shrank as it burned, curling into itself like a spider might, the stacked bales collapsing into smoking heaps and mounds. Seeing all that, Callum knew it wasn't just the will of the people that Sherman sought to break, like Ava said. It was the South's very ability to fund itself, to turn the cotton into guns and cannons and shells, hardtack and haversacks and men-at-arms.

They saw gristmills toppled into the streams that served them, damming the current in a bubbling mess, their waterwheels canted out of the water like something from a destroyed steamship. It rained, and the coals were still so hot they hissed. There were sawmills fired black, and storehouses and granaries and single-crib barns that would hardly have fed a family for a single long winter.

The second day, the creek cut straight across a plantation, and they stopped at a little distance to survey the place.

"Think we ought to chance it?" Ava asked.

Callum was squinting at the place. Everything was burned, even the big house.

"I think it's all right," he said. "I don't see anybody around."

They rode on, in between the fallen structures, tie beams and king posts jutting out of the wreckage like blackened bones. There were smoky bottles gathered in the ashes of the dairy, a big horned anvil sitting upright on the floor of the blacksmith shop, its oak base burned from beneath it.

Not even the slave quarters had been spared. They sulked in their rows, hardly recognizable, whispering smoke. There was no sign of the inhabitants.

Someone had tried to save the gin, they saw. It had been dragged from the structure that housed it, and it sat now in a little dirt yard by itself. The boxlike frame was scorched, as was the spiked cylinder inside it, spun by a hand crank to separate the seeds from the lint. So charred, it looked like something more evil than what it was. A torture device, perhaps, for tearing flesh from bone. Something you could stick a man's hand in if you needed him to sing.

Farther on was a mule-driven press for baling cotton. The mule was still in its harness, chained at the end of the turning arm. It had been unable to escape the fire's heat, trapped as it was in the circular orbit of its labor, the rut its hooves had cut. The animal's inner side was burned terribly, a gruesome new country that attracted flies.

Ava climbed down off the horse. She looked up at Callum.

"You got the knife?"

He handed it down. She walked up to the mule, unfolding the blade.

"Somebody should of done this already," she told it. She touched it on the head. "I'm sorry they didn't."

She reached under and cut its throat.

The following day they struck upon another railroad, torn up and bent like the others they'd seen. There were long straight stretches of railbed, and Callum knew the army must have heaved up whole miles of track at once, blue-coated men lining the rails as far as the eye could see, each upending his own crosstie. The ties had been stacked and burned as before, the rails twisted and corkscrewed around the oaks and pines. They rode some ways along the track, wending through the debris, now and again passing old boxcars thrown from the rails, heeled over and rusting in the trees like ships run aground and others left abandoned on forgotten sidings. The cars swarmed now with runaway slaves of every color—coal and chocolate and caramel and sand—living in the square-mouthed caves, the dark squalors jumbled with debris.

"Freedom," said Callum.

"If that's what this is, they need a new word for it."

"You think any of them would trade it back?"

"I reckon not."

Two men, twins, sat perched upon one of the boxcars like giant birds. They were squatting on their heels, their bony knees nearly as high as their shoulders, and they had long jaws and shaved heads. Callum waved at them as he passed, and they waved back, both raising their inner hands, chained together at the wrist.

Callum stopped the horse.

"Y'all want me to bust them irons?"

The men smiled, identically, and scrambled down from the roof.

"All right," said Callum. "Pull the chain tight."

He pulled the pistol from the saddle holster.

The two men leapt back toward the boxcar, but the door was jammed shut. They cowered against it, shaking, their bleached palms held before their faces.

"Jesus," said Callum. "Somebody done a number on y'all, didn't they?" He decocked the pistol and pointed it away. "I ain't gonna shoot you, but it's the only thing I got."

They nodded and came forward. They stretched the chain between the two of them, quivering, and Callum tried to touch the barrel to the middlemost link. They were shaking too much. He couldn't.

"I could do it, suh."

Callum turned to look. It was a sorghum-colored negro come out from the woods, wearing a chewed straw hat over a thin cotton shirt.

"They ain't 'fraid of me," said the man. "Not like they is you."

Callum's hand tightened on the pistol. He looked at Ava. She said with her eyes what he was thinking: no. He saw other faces peeking from the woods, from behind trees and out of brambles.

"You," he said, pointing to an old woman with a ball of silver hair. "You can do it."

The woman crept slowly from the trees.

"I ain't never banged no gun," she said.

"It ain't hard," said Callum. "You two, stretch that chain across that tie there."

The brothers did. The woman came up to the horse.

"Don't point it at nothing but that chain," said Callum. "You got to cock the hammer first. I'm gonna give you this smaller one. It don't have the same kick."

He handed her one of the smaller Colts, keeping the big Walker in his right hand. She took the pistol across her open palms, the way a priest would something at Mass. She squatted on her heels in front of the stretched chain, taking the pistol in both hands now, the barrel wiggling like a tuning fork. The two brothers were no longer afraid though they probably should have been. She used both thumbs to pull the hammer back. She put the barrel up to the chain and closed her eyes and pulled the trigger.

The chain blew asunder and she dropped the pistol, leaping back.

"Lort God!"

Callum laughed—he couldn't help it—and the runaways watching from the trees began slowly to smile at the event, realizing they could. Soon they were chuckling, their hands over their mouths. The woman took up the pistol, careful, as if it might go off again, and handed it back to Callum. He took it, his right hand still on the Walker, and they rode on. The two brothers waved with the same hands as before, as if the chain had never been broken.

Later that day, a town of some size began assembling before them, the largest they'd seen in some days. They thought of going around, but heavy curtains of smoke lingered on the outskirts, the places where arsenals and depots and factories would be. So they rode on into town, going slow, cutting their eyes left and right. There were big brick homes set back from the streets, largely intact, with broad green lawns and deep-shaded porches, here or there a broken window or smashed-in door, a dug-up garden or scorched portico where a flag had been burned. There were few men about—just women young and old, and children rolling around in the dirt and leaves. They did see a trio of white men come from behind a house, dressed in what looked inmates' garb, with candlesticks and crystal gathered up in their arms like firewood. The men saw them and ducked out of sight around the corner.

"Jesus," said Callum. "Who let them sons of bitches loose?"

"Who you think?"

"Sherman don't seem the pardoning type, not from what I've seen."

Ava patted his shoulder. "Why not, when those boys'll do such good for society?"

The town opened into a giant square at its middle, a grassy area in the center of which stood a great building of brown stone constructed of various-size blocks, the walls topped with toothlike battlements such as a castle might have. It had not been burned, but the grounds were covered in debris of all kinds, spewed down the steps and onto the trampled lawn. There were big leather-bound books with yellow pages flapping in the breeze, and loose papers of all sorts, and paintings of wigged men in fancy dress staring up at the sky. There were state bonds and notes strewn about, none signed, it seemed, and a scattering of heavy wing-back chairs not meant for the out-of-doors. A great many were smashed or upset, as if they'd given offense to the sitter.

Callum walked the horse into the square, closer.

"What the hell is this place?"

There was a round-backed woman bent behind an overturned pew of some kind, muttering at something on the ground. She had on a coarse gray sweater with holes at the elbows, her legs hidden behind the nicked-up wood.

"Ma'am?" said Callum. "Ma'am?"

The woman looked up, her hair frizzled and silver around a rugged red face.

"Yes?" she said. "Yes?"

"What is this place, ma'am?"

When the woman came from behind the pew, a large goose followed along beside her, waddling at her feet, attached to her wrist by a small leash. It had beady black eyes and a pointed beak, an imperial air that said it shouldn't be crossed.

"Boy, this is the State House, don't you know? Everybody knows that."

"Oh," said Callum.

"I was in there the other day," said the woman, nodding. "I was, too."

"Here?"

"For the assembly, boy. In the Senate Chamber. Them

blue-bellies parliamenting, drunk as lords, too. I never seen such legislating."

"They pass them some new laws?"

"They did too, boy. What was they? Ducky, you remember?" The goose looked at her. "That's right," she said. "That's right. They was resolutions. One, that secession was a indiscreet ordinance, and injudicious as well, and ought well be discouraged furthermore. They said that. And two: that the aforementioned ordinance was naught but a damned farce, in fact, and hereby repealed. And three, that Sherman would play him the devil with the ordinance of secession, and with the state, too. *Vi et armis.*"

"What's that?"

"With force and arms, boy. Don't you know Latin?"

"It's been a while," said Callum.

"Anyhow," said the woman, "I got to be getting on. I can smell 'em on my heels."

"Who?"

"Them damn loon hunters, boy, from the asylum. They hunting us that got loose."

"Oh," said Callum.

"Tell you what, you see 'em, you tell 'em I left with Sherman's army. You tell 'em I was on the arm of a real pretty boy from Indiana. A officer. You could do that for me?"

Callum looked at Ava, who was smiling.

"Yes, ma'am," he said. "I believe we could."

They slept that night in an abandoned house on the edge of town. There was no wood for a fire, and they didn't want to burn the furniture. They slept fitfully, without fire, in a room with two ways out. Several windows had been broken by looters, and Callum spread the broken glass at the entrances, like Lachlan had done at the edge of his yard.

"Feels strange, don't it?" said Ava as they bedded down.

"What?"

"A night indoors, after so many out."

"It does," said Callum. "I can't help but feeling trapped."

"Get over here and keep me warm."

"Yes, ma'am."

They lay enmeshed beneath Ava's quilt, Callum's buffalo blanket used as a pallet. She had her head against his shoulder, her finger tracing the patchwork that covered them.

"I've never seen the ocean," she said. "Just know it from books and such."

Callum squinted, as if seeing it again.

"It's got all these different colors, like moods almost, and same for the motion. It can be glass-smooth or corduroyed in ridges, risen up in hills and mountains even. Whatever its whim. You get the feeling how small you are, that's for sure. How little you count."

"Did you like it before the wreck?"

"Like it, I don't know. I didn't see much on the way across. They had us packed in like cattle belowdecks, worse even than the workhouse. I can still remember the stench, so thick you could hardly breathe. Now the blockade-runner, well, anything was better than Louisiana at that point."

"What about the coast?"

"The coast ain't so bad. There's all these islands, each of them surrounded in marsh grass, and a whole maze of creeks and inlets and backwaters. They got that Sea Island cotton down there the Brits pay big money for, and I know they dike and flood the marshes for rice."

"Sounds like easy living compared to the mountains."

"I don't know if I'd call it easy, exactly. The heat's fearsome—Swinney used to say that—and the mosquitoes, too. In summer you might think you died and went to hell, same's Louisiana. Big planters got most of the land."

She nestled closer to him, nuzzling her cheek against his shoulder.

"These Goslings, you think they'll let us sharecrop a little plot, raise this baby up right?"

Callum slid his hand over her belly, warm beneath the muslin. As he did, Ava hiked up the dress to reveal the bare flesh of her navel, warmer still, a softness coming into her eyes he'd not seen.

"I hope," he said, palming her there. "Blood is blood, right?"

By dawn they were on a minor road out of town, coming soon upon a high bluff, below it a slate river vented with dark rips of current. Trees reached sideways from its banks, wet and black. They could not see the bottom. To the south, just before a bend, they glimpsed the empty pilings of a destroyed bridge.

"Confederates burning the bridges to stop the advance," said Callum.

"Don't look like it's working," said Ava.

For they could see, nearby, the littered waste that marked the army's crossing. Toeless boots and busted wagons and the bodies of lame animals left at the river's banks.

"Nuh-uh," said Callum. "They got those pontoon bridges now. Something like this don't slow them but for maybe a day. It's putting bridge blowing out of fashion. Colonel used to get all steamed up over it. It was one of his favorite pastimes."

They headed downriver, looking for a bridge, a ferry, a fording. A hundred yards downstream, they found hoofprints leading down into the water. They could not see any reciprocal tracks on the far bank. They kept riding. Later they found a flat-bottomed ferry partially wedged beneath a dead tree in the middle of the river. Only the warped triangle of a single corner was not submerged. Around its edges the current grumbled and foamed. A spotted dog stood on the only section that was dry. He was balanced on front and rear paws that nearly touched, so narrow was his stance, his space. He watched them pass along the shore, dipping his head now and then to look at the water roiling underneath him. They could see his ribs. He barked twice at them. They kept moving.

At the next bend they crested a bluff and heard voices. Song. Through the trees they saw people in the river, women mostly. Their pink flesh was quivering through wet pinafores, their shoulders quaking. The hems of their dresses fluttered sideways in the current. They were singing, their voices plaintive and strange, their words hardly decipherable. No matter, the loss could be heard in the cold strangle of their voices. They were facing a young boy with a girl's face. He stood on a rock far out in the current, barefoot, unshaking in the cold. His hair was curled and gold, his mouth gaped in song. His lips an ellipsis of the brightest red, as if painted.

The horse halted, no prompting from Callum. None conscious. The sound moved through the trees, high and lonesome. The world seemed sharper, clearer. These were poor people. It could be seen in their bony fingers, their notched backbones, the jagged blades of their shoulders. All these articulated against the thin, wet membrane of their clothes. The slate river in which they stood was fired with fallen leaves, gold and crimson. For a strange moment, Callum felt they were singing just for him, him and Ava, like the chorus to a play the singers would never see. The young boy looked up toward the bluff but didn't seem to see them among the trees. Callum coaxed the horse forward. He hoped the boy's vision was lacking, not prescient.

They rode on, looking for a place to cross.

"There!" said Ava.

Callum looked where she was pointing. There was a spot where the near bank had caved under the hooved descent of a cavalry force. On the far shore they could see the treaded swallow where the horses had struggled black-legged up the bank. It didn't look too old.

Here was the place.

Callum watched the river crash around the angular hunks of rock that jeweled the river. This was the longest crossing they'd faced. The most treacherous. Only the river stone closest to the shore could be glimpsed, pale under the dark current. Farther out it was too deep, the bottom lost. He waited for the fear to burn in his belly, that yellow bile. He waited, and nothing.

He looked over his shoulder.

"Ready?"

Ava nodded.

He clenched Reiver's wide ribcage with the insides of his legs. The horse stepped carefully down the bank, his head lowered, and entered the river. The cold gunmetal of the current stunned them when it reached their boots, their knees, their thighs. Callum had known some cold in the mountains, fuel too wet to burn. Fingers white. Noses red. Peckers held with both hands when taking a piss, to keep them warm. That was a long battling with the element. Attrition. But here was cold quick to the bone, sharp enough to kill.

Reiver rocked back and forth, fording, his hooves probing the bottom. The river broke against his body as against a giant black rock, the current eddying in dark whirlpools that slid downstream, unraveling. The shore neared; they began to rise out of the water. The sheen streamed off his body like shed armor. He climbed the bank, dipping his head with effort, and finally stood to blow on the high safety of the bluff. His black coat smoked in the air.

"Good boy," said Callum, patting the enormous neck.

The horse turned his head to him, one dark planet of an eye lashed like a slattern's, and blinked. Cool, unpanicked. Then he dipped his head to graze. Callum just leaned back in the saddle, against Ava, and let the big horse eat.

The terrain on this side of the river was immediately flatter, wetter. Gray beards of moss haunted the low overhang of the trees. Before long even the smoke seemed changed, a dusky pine haze that coated outbuildings and cotton fields. Harder to see, harder to be seen. By sundown, Callum could make a fist and see pale fissures revealed at his knuckles, the rest of his hand dusted like that of a smithy or coal miner.

He knew a number of rivers cut across the state, some parallel. They had strange Indian names that he couldn't remember, not exactly. Some started with an *O*—he remembered that much. He reckoned they'd crossed one. More lay before them.

The sun had fallen low against their backs, a fiery peach, when they crested a small rise and looked down upon a vast expanse of cotton fields and pasture, angular green planes partitioned by red roads. The plowed reaping land contrasted with worthless islands of scrub pine, some oak, many of these cradling the smoking hulks of torched homesteads and barns. The army's advance was clear, the land jetted with smoke. It was as though they were merely hacking into the earth until the hot core of the world bubbled up in fire.

"I remember my daddy talking about this," said Ava.

Callum looked at the devastation, raised an eyebrow.

"He some kind of soothsayer now? Future-reader?"

Ava shook her head. "More the opposite. He said these prehistoric shorelines cut across the land at places, specially down here. Said the land, it goes suddenly flat like this because it used to be underwater. All this"—her hand swept a panorama of the vista before them—"all this used to have fish swimming in it. Sea monsters with giant teeth that aren't even around anymore."

Callum looked out over the smoking red land and imagined the low reefs of cloud as oceanic leviathans, creatures flicking their tails through a lightless depth.

"Bullshit," he said.

"Serious," said Ava. "They can still find remnants, images compressed in rock that look like something from a whole other planet."

Callum rubbed his chin. "So not only do we got a team of sons of bitches on horseback to contend with, now we got to worry about giant sea-ghosts swimming in the heavens over us?"

Ava leaned against him, patting his leg.

"There, there," she said. "I'll protect you."

Her hand stayed on his leg.

The next day they hit mires of lowland swamp. The trees grew straight out of obsidian water, the surface coated here and there with specious green islands of lilies and algae. They cut southward until finding trails corduroyed with new-cut saplings. The going was slow, wet, dirty. The army had left a stench of shit in their wake. The soldiers could not venture very far from the road here. Their shit and the shit of their horses and mules littered the road and roadside in ropy piles, each of them crowned with emerald flies that swirled into the air when passed, tiny whining cyclones, before alighting again on their mounded bonanzas.

At least there was little way for their pursuers to flank them here. Still they were relieved each time the trail broke out upon dry ground, cutting between fields shot through on the margins by yellow geysers of goldenrod. They were growing hungry again, the bellyfuls of pork long gone, and Callum watched the beetles and other black-legged husks tick across the serrated leaves and egg-shaped blossoms.

"You ever ate a bug before?"

"Once I did," said Ava. "On a dare."

"What kind?"

"Just a worm."

"I don't think I could stand the wriggling."

"Well, it wasn't still *alive*. Daddy'd fried it. He bet me I wouldn't do it."

"What he bet you?"

"I don't know. He just bet me."

"What was it like?"

"A little baconish."

"Bull," said Callum.

"Honor bright."

"Huh," said Callum.

That didn't sound half as bad as it should have.

That night they camped in a dense grove of sycamores that clouded a hill high above a creek. The trunks branched hydralike low to the ground, so that every tree was like many, an open head of branches whose dead yellow leaves whispered drily in the breeze, walling them in. Perfect cover from searchers. They led the horse into the maze of limbs and tied him off, then crackled down into a makeshift bedding of dead leaves and blankets as a cold breath came skulking across the ground. Ava was shaking some, more than Callum thought was good, and he held her close from behind, his body a shelter for hers.

The cold, he thought. It kept coming. They were heading south, away from the worst, but the season was sweeping rapidly toward winter. He knew the trees they'd left in the mountains were naked now, wintry and dead-seeming, and the seasonal flaming of the land through which they rode as ephemeral as fire itself. Their days-long ride within its ken an unnatural protraction, the land darkening behind them. Dying. Toward the coast the world changed, he knew. There were trees that held their leaves the year long, evergreen, and could provide better cover and shelter to those in flight from the wintering lands, from the furred riders who roamed them on smoking horses. And before falling asleep, he wondered if given something fast enough, a machine or beast heretofore unfathomed, a man might outride the night itself, racing apace with the sun under a sky of eternal light. Never lost, never cold.

He was drifting to sleep. Down in the creek bottom below them, the windows of a small cabin flickered from the burning heart of its woodstove. The porch pillars were made of tree trunks, the branches amputated to six-inch nubs.

Midstream of the crossing one of the horses spooked, a lightning-strung mare stolen from some stable of former privilege. She was chest-deep in the river, her chestnut shoulders bolding and articulate, when she went suddenly walleyed at some shadow of fish or snake darting under the surface. She reared for the near bank,

screaming, charging the horses behind her. Three of them were knocked from their feet. They rolled into the slate current with their riders atop them, a mess of legs and teeth and hooves and screams that careened downstream, rock to rock, until all of the screaming stopped. The record of anything out of the ordinary lost altogether in the river's voice, jagged-toothed and sweet.

The slave hunter sat his horse, safe already on the far bank with a tracking dog slung sleepily over his knees. He watched the majesty of channeled stormwater swallow the panic so quickly. So absolutely. Then he turned and rode on into the trees.

Twice that day they lost the trail, the scent. Both times the slave hunter would not be thwarted. He wrangled the path right out of the wild, cutting for sign with bent spine, labored breath, prodding the earth with the same hand that held his horse's reins. He could tell the Colonel's stolen horse by the stamp its iron shoes left in soft ground. One of the front shoes did not match the other. It was slightly out of shape, hammered in place of a thrown original, and did not carry the mark of a former cavalry unit as the other did. He could tell the tall horse by the head height of its riders as they broke trail branches and stripped foliage through the woods. He could identify the horse's stool by sight, his dogs the same by scent. He knew the distinct patterns of fire-making the riders used. The way they built their architecture of kindling and kicked their fire to ashes. The way the boy pissed a zigzag over the smoking coals. All these things they did not know they did—the hunter knew.

But in the swampy glades the trail was easily lost, hoofprints hidden beneath a sheen of opaque water. They pushed on along the corduroy roads, pushing far past nightfall. Nowhere to stop, this slop no place for bedding down. The men rode slumped on their horses, single file, bitching over their shoulders in hushed voices. They were saddle-sore, hungry, cold. Sleep had been scarce, pickings scarcer. The ones who did not bitch slept. Some did both, grumbling into their bearded chins, the words profane or inarticulate. But the charred land through which they rode these long days, charred or yet still smoldering, seemed only to fuel them. The razed homesteads and mutilated stock. The dead-faced whites and white-smiling blacks. All these signs like the revelating Horsemen of the Book might leave, judgment come early upon this kingdom. And in the wake of this loss, the bounty of the boy's head was only of greater import, for men such as them would have little place in the world that stood scorched and remnant before them.

A scream woke them, curdling through the morning dark. They did not jolt or straighten, by instinct. The dead crackle of their bedding could betray them. Instead, their eyes flicked wide at one another, pale halos at the whites. The sun was not yet up. Slowly they flattened themselves beneath their mounding of quilts, blankets, and coats—slowly, slowly—and crept to the edge of the grove, the protest of fallen leaves drawn out to the thinnest sound, broken and unpatterned. Callum eyed Reiver over his shoulder. The horse had gone still, one eye hunting the bottomland for the next stab of sound. They looked through a dense clutch of branches to the dark string of the creek scrawled below them, the rusted cabin roof. The door of the place stood open, as did the door of the woodstove inside, a stovepiped iron with a belly of fire. The cabin pulsed with inner flame. The light spilled down the front steps and into the yard, a red pool in the mist.

There was a large laurel oak in the front yard, dead, its naked branches twisted outward into a broad crown. Shadowy figures swarmed beneath the penumbral gloom, their shapes mottled by the play of firelight. Callum squinted, his eyes adjusting. They were in ragged uniform, their shell jackets blue, their heads covered in plug hats and kepis. Foragers. Maybe ten of them, some with burning pine knots. One of them threw a dark coil of rope over a low-hanging branch and noosed the end. There was a scream again, then a strangled gurgle. A girl's voice, clamped shut at the throat.

She was on her knees by the mules and wagon, held in place by a skinny soldier with no beard. Callum looked back underneath the tree. There was an old man trembling there in pajamas, his feet bare. One button was undone at the trapdoor seat of his pants, one half globe of bare ass revealed. One side of his face hung slack; a thin strand glistened from his mouth. They looped the noose over his turkeyed throat.

"Where'd you hide the horses?" asked one of them, their leader, his voice eerily clear in the predawn stillness. "The stables are empty."

The old man shivered and shook. A big globule of spittle gleamed on his mouth. He said nothing. An old barn slouched to the side of the cabin, black inside. Empty.

The leader took the loose end of rope, coiled it twice around his forearm, and pulled. The hemp tightened. The old man's bare feet went dainty, to the toes.

"The horses!"

The girl broke free for a moment. "They're gone!" she said. "The first lot of you goddamn bluecoats took 'em not two days back."

"And I'm supposed to believe you're telling the truth?"

"We had to shoot the ones they traded us for. They was jaded. Dead on legs. Bodies is out in the south pasture. That's the truth. You wanna go look?"

When she said *south,* the leader didn't look the right way.

So they were lost. A foraging party separated from the main column, trying to find their way back in the night.

The soldier looked down at his boots. He wiped his forehead with the back of his arm. "What about food, then? What have you to eat?"

"They took our whole store of sweet potatoes. That and the molasses, the corn. Our two hogs. Burned all our wood, too. Hell if I know how me and Granddaddy's supposed to last the winter."

The soldier let go of the rope. The old man crumpled to the ground. The soldier cocked his head and watched him writhe, as he might a worm on hot stone.

"Reckon you aren't," he said. He turned to the other men. "Boys, mount up. They got nothing for us."

The men turned and began shuffling toward their mules like sleepwalkers. The animals had their heads down, some hobbled at the front legs. One of them tried to hop away. Its forelegs collapsed; it plowed into the ground headfirst. Their mules were broke-down, dying, pushed too hard for too long.

"'Nother body walking," said one of the men, chuckling.

"Damn you," said a second, squatting down to cut the fallen animal's throat. He straightened up from the work and his head exploded, atomized in red mist. There rose the blood shriek of myriad voices, murder-tongued, and bolts of blue flame intersected the yard at all angles. Men clutched themselves and fell.

Callum knew that sound.

He reached over and pushed Ava flat to the ground. He dropped his own chin to the leaves. Riders, the Colonel's, catapulted themselves into the yard upon spines of horseflesh, shooting downward into the blue-coated soldiers. Smoke filled the clearing, and screams. The men on the ground threw up their hands in surrender. They were cut down where they stood. Empty-handed.

The sun was beginning to stab through the trees. The riders remounted and disappeared into the pinewood, as if in retreat from dawn. The one-armed man rode point. For a half hour, Callum and Ava lay unmoving, afraid to move, trying to calm their breath. Waiting. Callum tried not to look at what handiwork the Colonel's men had left beneath the dead oak, but he couldn't help himself. Ava was holding his upper arm with both hands. He could feel stripes of bruise blooming beneath her grip. Her eyes were wide open, toward the dead.

They led the horse out of the grove and down the embankment. The old man and his granddaughter sat huddled on the porch, whimpering, their faces shining with tears, snot, spittle. The fallen men of the foraging party had been raised vertical like marionettes. They ornamented the tree like some perverse work of art, a chandelier of the gut-shot, the disemboweled and disfigured. The branches of the oak wept slightly with the weight.

Callum led the horse amid the dangling feet, many unbooted. Some were missing pants, some coats or gloves. One a finger, a ring still gleaming on the bloody nub. The Colonel's men had left messages upon the bodies. Some by knife, some by paper and stake. Personal oaths against occupation. On one there was a scrap of parchment driven into the sternum. A message: HUNGRY NOW? The corpse's cheeks were swollen with viscera, his own or someone else's. Some of the corpses twisted eastward on their ropes, toward the dawning sun. Their eyes still open, shining with false life.

Callum stopped the horse before the porch.

The girl looked up at them, her face twisted to an angry rose. But the sound she made—it was not a cry of pain, as Callum had first thought. As he had expected. It was too harsh and cackling. And her eyes: They were full of light.

So strange. This girl, she was laughing.

Her grandfather, too, his slack-sided mouth leaking with the spasms. Wild, crazed laughs.

Beneath it all, Callum could hear the wind rustling the trophied oak, the scabbards and buckles clinking like wind charms. He turned his head toward Ava, keeping his eyes on the man and girl.

"Let's get on," he said, a whisper from the side of his mouth. He started to tug the reins.

Ava stayed his arm. "Wait," she said. Then she leaned out from the saddle, holding his shoulder. "Nothing seems awful funny right about now." She cocked a thumb behind her. "Not to them, not to me. Not to nobody."

The old man wiped his mouth, his eyes, and shook his head. "Fai—!" he said, his words slack-mouthed to a roar. "Fai— in Gaw!"

Faith.

"The Sorry Man say," he said. He nodded. "Foresay."

"The who?" asked Ava.

"The Seer Man," said the girl. "We heard tell of an army on the march. Went straight to him. He said to have faith. Said evil'd kill evil on our land, and then we'd last many a winter here, Granddaddy and me. But the army come once already, took everything. Nothing to stop them, not evil nor good. So we think, False prophesy, no hope. We think, We's walking dead. Then these-uns come through this morning." She jutted her chin toward the dangling corpses. "Get their comeuppins." She put her arm around her grandfather. "Now we know we'll live." She shrugged. "Somehow, anyhow. We will."

The old man hooked a crooked finger at them. "Fai—!" he said. "Fai— in Gaw!" He nodded vigorously at himself, his broken words.

Callum wondered if they were addled. How could they be so goddamn sure? He wanted to go, but Ava squeezed his arm again.

"This Seer Man," she said. "So he can read the future?"

The girl nodded. "Got him a direct conference with the Almighty," she said.

"So how do we find him?"

"Shit," said Callum.

Chapter 12

“I don’t want to go see him,” said Callum. He was digging at a root with a stick. It was dusk. “He could say something ugly’s gonna happen. Something we don’t want it to.”

Ava sat next to him, her hands clasped around her knees.

“Least then we’ll know,” she said. She looked around her, and Callum followed her eyes. The close-grown trees, the growing shadows, the empty spot where they made no fire despite the cold.

“I don’t know that I want to know. What if it’s the knowing that makes it happen? The believing. You ever thought of that?”

Ava nodded. “I thought of a lot of things,” she said. “Not least of them that we need help, bad. Especially when they could be anywhere now. Ahead of us, behind. And we don’t even know if there’ll be a place for us on the coast. If we’ll be taken in.”

Callum dug harder with the stick. He was thinking she

toted around a lot of crazy beliefs: monkeyed ancestors, sea monsters, soothsaying seer men. And, somehow, he found himself believing in much of what she did, these great unknowables that might explain a world he did not understand. And she was right. Their pursuers could be anywhere now. He scanned the dimming world of autumn, its deepening recesses and places to hide, and then he looked at Ava. Her cheeks were seamed with tears, her chin tucked tightly between her kneecaps. She was shaking, and he hadn't realized how sick she looked, how ghostly pale. He worried it was the thing inside her, consuming her strength, and them with so little to eat. So little peace.

He crept behind her and put his arms around her arms, his legs around her legs. She was rigid where he touched her. Slowly she softened against him. He could just barely stretch his chin over her shoulder. He set it there.

"You really think this man could talk to God?" he asked. "Could tell us something?"

Ava shrugged, her shoulder blades pushed up against his chest. "I'm tired of the not knowing," she said. "Tired of being afraid. Hoping there'll be a place for us somewhere." He felt her ribcage swell underneath him. "So what I say is he damn well better. I intend to get answers from him. Nothing but."

He pushed his cheek against her jawbone. She pushed back. He imagined the blades of his own shoulders stretching outward, enveloping them both.

It was noon. They looked upon not a cabin, but the skeletal remnant of one. A structure reduced to flame-licked framing beams and burned-out clapboard. There was too much light flaring beneath a roof that yawned inward over this ill-propped gape of a structure. The wind its probable enemy, the rain. The infinitesimal weight of a cricket or pallid squirt of a crow.

Callum halted the horse before the cabin. He could see clear inside the wind-lurched hulk. An old man sat beneath the imploded roof, the groaning beams. His boots, cherry red and well oiled, were propped upon the great desk behind which he sat, a claw-footed beast of carved oak filigree and lioned crests. A halo of hair ringed the bald dome of his head at ear level, and he had a chevron mustache. His hair was the brightest white. His eyes were yellow. A handsome man once, perhaps, his flesh now surrendered like something left out in the rain.

The old man cocked his head. He lifted his nose and eyed Callum up and down, up and down. His nose climbed higher and higher. His eyelids drooped. Callum felt somehow lacking.

"We're looking for the, uh, Seer Man," he said. "You him?"

The man pressed the fleshy notch of his upper lip with his thumb. His yellowed eyes were red-lipped, but the blue-black pupils were sharp, light-specked. He cocked his head. A tiny stone glimmered in the lobe of one ear.

"Infamy," he said, "is a small price to pay for immortality."

"So that's a yes."

"Young man, that does depend."

Callum scratched his chin.

"On what, exactly?"

The old man clasped his hands behind his head. "I cannot be asked to convene with the Almighty without the proper . . . *antifogmatic.*"

"The what?"

"A good drop of the strong stuff," he said. "That's what I need. Just to smooth up the revelating is all." He smiled politely.

Callum rolled his eyes at Ava. She shook her head at him, fetched the half jar of Lachlan's white liquor from the saddlebag. She handed it to him. They both dismounted. Callum walked toward the door frame bent crazy in midair, no walls to support it. He offered the jar slowly through the door.

The old man gestured for him to step inside. Callum looked at Ava, then at the man.

"No disrespect, sir," said Callum, "but it don't look real safe."

The man's face darkened. "You don't think I know when this old bitch'll come down?"

"I don't know what you know."

The man leaned back and dug his tongue into his cheek, almost smiling. "But you want to."

Callum hesitated. Ava nabbed the jar from his hand and stepped through the door. The floorboards groaned under her boots. Callum leapt in after her. The man took the jar.

"Much obliged," he said.

He unscrewed the lid and sniffed. He gave a big smile and sipped. He wiped his mouth with the back of his hand. "Goddamn," he said, snapping his fingers. "I mean God*damn*." His red tongue squirmed from his mouth to wick the bristles of his mustache.

Callum looked out at the white-columned main house standing down the drive. Only a portion of one wing was burned, and that not too badly.

"How come you don't put yourself up in the big house?"

The old man snorted and took another sip from the jar. He made a face. "My wife threw me out." He fluttered his hand. "She's a mad bitch. Always was. No tolerance for *eccentricity.*" He took another sip and worked his mustache around, as if cleaning his teeth with the inside of his mouth, then swallowed. "I have the cleanest mustache in Georgia," he told them. "Ask anybody."

Callum looked at Ava. She looked at the old man.

"So you can tell the future?" she asked.

He smiled at them and winked. Callum could see the drink going to work.

"How we know you ain't just spouting off any old shit comes to mind?" he said.

The old man bolted up straight in his seat and pointed at them with the jar. "I am a vessel of the Holy Ghost, goddammit." He leaned back in his chair and pursed his lips and fluttered one hand in the air. "Ask anybody."

Callum started to say something; Ava elbowed him in the ribs.

"Will you read us our future, then?" she asked. "Please?"

The old man looked over the jar's rim at her, at Callum. One big yellow eye summed them up, the rest of his face warped strangely inside the fluid reality of the jar. He had another pull, cringed, and snapped his head sideways. He put the jar down in front of him and laid out his hands on the desk, palms upward. He waved them to come nearer. "Give me your hands," he said. He belched quietly through the side of his mouth.

They walked forward slowly. The old man had his eyes closed now, his head on his chest, waiting. Ava gave the old man her hand. Callum looked down at the withered tracery of creases and swirls. The mapwork born upon a man's hand, the scars and scuffs the world overwrit. He placed his hand in the old man's. The skin was papery, dry as parchment.

"Kneel."

They did, upon a floor of charred miscellany. Fallen roofing and flat-spraddled books, a songbird cage with skewed wiring, its winged heart upturned black beneath an empty trapeze. The man put on an unctuous look, his eyes shut tight, his brow scrunched heavenward. Ash swirled in the shafts of light that punctured the roof.

"Close your eyes."

They did. Waited. The old man's nose had a kink near the bridge. It whistled. Callum twitched his nose around, impatient. He felt the old man's thumb begin to move along his pinkie finger, back and forth. Callum jerked his hand away.

"The hell?"

Ava cut her eyes at him, cross. The old man kept his eyes closed but smiled, his tongue bulging his cheek, as if at his own joke. He simply held out his open palm, waiting for Callum to put his hand back. Ava jerked her head toward the desk. Callum conceded, but he kept one eye open.

The old man was still now. His face looked up into the broken roof, the fractured sky. Time passed. There was a frozen clock on the wall. The shadows of the hands seemed to shift. Callum closed his eyes. He felt himself fading. Swooning kindly. This light-slashed darkness a place of sanctuary, hope.

The old man's eyes snapped open; his hands clamped closed. Callum's knuckles cracked.

"Ouch!"

Callum tried to yank his hand away. Ava, too. They couldn't. The old man was too strong. Their arms flailed like caught fishes would. The old man watched them fight. The blue of his eyes was cold now, the madness gone. The pupils yawned wide, black wells in which their crazings were reflected in twin and miniature. Tiny flailings, fleshings, played back at them in worlds their own.

The old man let go. They fell back onto their heels. Back into the room, the wreckage. The old man pushed the jar across the desk.

"Take it back," he said. "I can't read anything for you."

Callum stood quickly. "Thanks anyway," he said, reaching for the jar. "Appreciate it."

Ava stopped his arm. "No," she said. She stood and leaned toward the old man. She put her palms flat on the desk. Her eyes were smoldering, her voice fierce.

"Tell me," she said.

Chapter 13

The horse carried them down a road red-cut through pines that murmured in the dusk. Callum looked back into the dying light of the west, then ahead where broken lances of sun grew gradually longer, sharper, on the path before them.

He had the reins resting loosely in his lap. Ava squeezed his right hand. He didn't squeeze back. She had been trying to talk about it, what the old man had said, but he couldn't bring himself to do it.

He had wanted the old man to take it back, his vision. To renounce it. To say he was a liar. A charlatan. A man whose words carried no weight. For those words had struck him like a weapon, a stab in the gut. He had made the old man gag on his pistol before Ava could pull him away.

It hadn't helped. They haunted him, the old man's words, and the hidden darknesses between the trees seemed only to lend them credence. The cold sting in the air, the sharp-winged bats, the broken pack animals brained and discarded here and there on the side of the road. And Callum worried at what he was becoming. What might have slipped into him as he lay upon that sickbed months back. What curse. He worried that he no longer deserved to live, and yet that he would be the one who would. The only. He worried that most of all.

"One of you," the old man had said. "One of you will die before the year is out."

That night they bedded down in a dry ditch that fed a pair of dead fields. Weeds had grown man-high across the plots. Even the horse could hardly be seen. Callum wanted, needed, a fire. Some warmth and light. Around them the weeds whispered. He stared into the red core of the blaze. His heart felt like an alien thing in his chest, clutching and unclutching beyond his control. He felt it as real living flesh, the myth of forever stripped away, so it seemed the very points of his rib bones could puncture it. He looked up at Ava and saw a string of life tapping faintly beneath the skin of her neck. It made a shadow with each beat. He saw how skinny she was, how pale and weak. He felt like crying—it welled up in him too fast to stop. He drove his face into his hands, the sobs soon battering him, his fingers webbed with slime. He looked up.

"He could be wrong, couldn't he?"

Ava squeezed her temples with one hand and looked down between her legs. "Might could." Then she looked up and took a breath through her mouth and slid across the ground toward him. "Course he could," she said. "He's probably just some loon."

"But that he said it. Spoke it out there." He looked down into his hands. "I can't get it out my head."

Ava cradled his head, and he cried against her chest. He felt like the boy he was, the boy he wanted to be. But boys were too weak for the world outside this field of weeds, this fire. This girl.

"It can't happen," he said.

Ava pulled his face up to hers. "It won't."

"It can't."

"It won't. Not if you don't believe it, it won't."

He looked up at her. "I want it to be me," he said. "I just want it to be me."

Ava cupped his jawbones with her hands and thumbed the tears from below his eyes. She almost smiled. "I don't," she said. Then she kissed him, pulled her mouth away and looked at him. "Neither of us is gonna die, hear me? No matter what some seer says. He couldn't even tell us which one. I never should of taken us in there. I'm sorry. But it's done with now, and whatever comes, we've got to meet it standing up."

Callum nodded, trying hard to believe, trying not to see how sickly she looked, how purple the hollows of her eyes, how close to the edge of something he couldn't stop. Her end, or the end of the thing she carried.

"Look at me," she said. "Look."

He did.

"I love you."

"What?"

"I love you," she said again. "Goddammit."

Callum's mouth opened; his blood sprang. He drove himself into her arms, the two of them toppling to the ground in a tangle of limbs. There they lay, clutched so close they could hardly breathe. She clung to him, burying her face in his neck. He told her he loved her. He always would. Soon they were grappling and pawing, driving their bodies yet closer, as if each might claw a way into the very flesh of the other, as if their blood was some kind of home.

Callum woke once in the middle of the night and stirred. When he opened his eyes, there was Ava across from him, facing him. Her eyes were closed, her brow knit even in sleep. In the faint glow of the coals he could see pale scrawls in the ash and grit upon her cheeks. Tears. Her face glistened, and a little ways off he saw a little dried pool where she'd been sick sometime in the night. Callum made a decision then. The one he didn't want to make. It was hard inside him. Certain. He closed his eyes and went back to sleep.

The next morning they came upon a modest homestead. A cabin, a barn, a springhouse, a large pen for hogs. The place had been raided, but not too badly. Nothing burned. Two live hogs in the pen. A man and his wife were outside, on hands and knees, working with spades to mend their trampled garden. The man had one leg, a veteran. When Ava and Callum rode into the clearing, they smiled and waved. Callum knew he'd found the place.

The woman fried them each two eggs in a lake of crackling lard and gave them both a slab of fatback. She was fat-cheeked and big-boned, with kindness in her eyes. She couldn't quit saying how lucky she and her husband had been, that the Yanks hadn't done them worse, like they had so many others. The officer in charge of the foraging party had told his men to leave them their two prized Saddlebacks, big black hogs with white rings around their middles. They'd already slaughtered enough that day, he said.

Callum and Ava shoveled the fatback and eggs still steaming into their mouths. The couple sat on the other side of the table and watched, pleased, if a little astounded, at how fast the riders bolted their food. The husband, drinking his chicory coffee, said he'd been with the Cold Steel Guards of the Forty-ninth Georgia Infantry, and he'd lost his leg at Second Manassas back in '62. He had an iron-flecked beard and hard, clear eyes, and he said he'd been lucky that day, despite his leg. Callum liked him.

The food grew heavy after breakfast, after so many days of light stomachs, and Callum and Ava both felt a big sleep coming on. The older couple had a fire going in the hearth, and blankets, and the woman said they were welcome to them if they wanted. Ava fell asleep first, swaddled on the sofa in a big patchwork quilt, the fire coloring her face. Callum wanted to sleep, too, badly—it seemed that no one since Lachlan had been so kind, so warm and safe—but he asked for a cup of coffee instead. Then he sat at the table, across from the couple, and began telling them how he needed their help.

Chapter 14

She had not wanted him to leave. Had screamed and clawed at him, and he had been adamant, unbending, so much older of a sudden, this day, than before. He could feel it. He would send someone for her once he reached the coast, he said. And he told her he would make it. Promised he would. But he'd carved the name of his relations in a stripped piece of pine bark and slipped it into her coat pocket, in case. She'd screamed and clawed more at him; he would not be moved. He was the one they were after. The one with a bounty on his head. He told her she would be safe with these friendly hog raisers. He told her the riders would follow the trail of the horse on the road. He told her they would never know she'd stayed behind.

He told her he loved her.

He rode out on a farm road at dusk, heading east, and it was the hardest thing he'd ever done. But right, he told himself. Right. Because she was in peril every second she was with him. The older couple would keep her well and fed. They knew she carried a child, though it didn't show yet. They knew it was a thing conceived in outrage, and that she'd been sick and he worried for her health. All this he'd told them at firelight, as Ava slept. And they'd said they would take care of her until he could send help.

Still he felt his guts unspooling inside him as he rode, his insides tethered as surely to her as a rope or length of chain, and how she hurt going out of him, her presence, her hard and pretty edges tearing him up as they went. But he had done the right thing, he told himself. The only thing. For he feared the ride itself could kill her, if not the clutches of those who pursued him. They were his fate to bear, to outrun or not. He had gotten her out of the mountains with winter coming, when she could not have survived again on her own, not pregnant. But now he feared, against everything, that she was safer away from him—as far away as she could get. Let them come after him. Only him. And if they caught him, she couldn't be hurt.

He rode on into the eastern dark. The sun glared bloodred at his back, as if in anger at the world it saw. At him especially, perhaps, for taking so long to make this right.

The riders exploded from the trees, a flood of ashen horseflesh and pale faces. Their scream broke across the clearing, choral, echoing within the walls of the cabin, the empty barn, the little springhouse.

They dragged the hog raisers out of the house, a red-cheeked woman and her one-legged husband. They dragged him by the collar of his nightshirt. He hopped and hopped, then buckled before their leader. His wife knelt beside him, shaking, her hands clasped prayerlike before her chest. The one-armed man looked down at them. Something winked to life in his hand, metallic. Like a tiny star. And he took up the husband's hand. The first finger came off with a pop. It lay squirming on the ground like a large pale worm. Its owner screamed through his teeth, not opening his mouth. Not telling what he knew.

The one-armed man took up the hand again, then thought better of it. He began to unbutton the man's fly. The woman's mouth went crooked and black. She jabbed her finger toward the springhouse.

Callum caught the stench before he saw what was raising it. It was dawn and he'd been on the horse an hour, having slept but little. The smell slipped through the trees and turned his gut. He broke from the woods. There was a slate river, dark-rocked, the near bank leveed by flesh of every color and pattern, the bodies of horses and mules piled upon one another like so many bags of sand or meal. Hundreds of them. Beasts broken and no longer of use. Executed. A culling of the herd, of the lame and jaded. Those that could no longer serve the army, ridden nearly to death, needing only a bullet. Callum rode on amid their number. Heads twisted one way, legs struck another, rigor-limbed into the groins and mouths of their neighbors. They gaped at him. White horse teeth retched smiling in death. Black orbs unlooking at the reflection of boy and horse sliding warped through their orbit.

Callum looked down at himself, cut alien in their eyes. So unlike himself, a figure skeletal and pale, long-faced and concave under the dark oval of his hat. Some cavity yawned open inside him, cold as the morning without, and he knew something was terribly wrong. He knew it without thought, as sure as steel in the gut.

His face was hot, his insides cold. His stomach clenched on him, clenched, clenched, clenched, and then he heaved, a yellowish fluid ejaculated down the side of the horse. It glimmered in the sun. He had made a terrible mistake. He pulled the reins to one side and dug his heels into the horse. He buried his face into the mane and let him run.

A terrible mistake.

"Where is he?"

The girl wiped her mouth with the back of her hand.

"Where's who?"

Clayburn squatted down in front of her. He cocked his head to one side. "You like dogs?"

The men behind him chuckled, their chests quivering silently underneath their capes and coats. The fat man, Swinney, drove his beard into the crook of his thumb.

The girl looked at the two hounds. They looked back, their jowls grueled with desire.

Mean. Born or bred, no matter. Vicious.

The one-armed man had produced a coil of rope. He came toward her, smiling.

The big horse, slick with sweat, thundered through the trees. Callum's jaw was unhinged, the air cold in his mouth. He could not quit his chest from heaving. He should never have left her. Never. No matter the risk, the danger. He pushed a gloved hand out against the sky.

Trees finally broke: the clearing. Dark scores wrinkled

the bowl of light, a stitched ellipsis he squinted to see. He dropped down into the land of the hog raisers and found himself halfway across the field when the sight reared before his eyes. He hauled viciously on the reins. The black legs went rigid, the ground sliding torn beneath their hooves. Twenty white faces turned to look, half-blind, arms held high to block the risen sun. Then Clayburn, two hounds surging and snapping from the end of his arm like some evil appendage. Behind him a stake, a slump-tied creature naked but for a tattered shift. She was quivering.

Ava.

Beside Clayburn stood Swinney, looking. He took off his hat and held it against his chest. A round bald head, a round gray beard. Callum looked at him. The guns were coming out. The boy held his place and cocked his head. He was looking at Swinney. Only at him.

The old man looked back. His chin moved, at last, and he might have smiled, just one corner of his mouth. His face was sad, knowing.

Callum spurred the horse. They tore across the field, scattering the hobbled horses set to graze on the brown grass. The air crackled with gunfire. He looked over his shoulder and saw the men running and shooting, making for their horses. He saw old Swinney go toward the girl, his knife pulled. He cut her loose.

The air sang around Callum. He ducked low to Reiver's neck. Around them were the hobbled horses. These were not the ones the men had ridden out of the mountains. They were too new, too pretty, too little of something other. He drew down on a pretty bay and put a bullet in her haunches. She screamed and the others reared, spooked. He saw a second fall, shot by accident. Mania sprang upon them like contagion.

They went walleyed, spooked, and he was lost amid the stampeding flesh, the rearing and screaming. He kept low in the saddle. There was Ava, running toward the edge of the field, away. He wheeled the horse and raged toward her. Men jumped back from the crazed horses. They raised their hands against the sun, blinded, and tried to aim. They spewed fire and smoke. Ava turned to look as he rode upon her. She raised an arm. He leaned far out of the saddle and took her arm and slung her onto the back of the horse.

They were nearing the edge of the field when he looked back a final time. In the distance he saw big Swinney collapse, his head a corona of blood in the new sun. Behind him stood Clayburn, his pistol smoking. Callum blinked, his focus shifting to Ava's face. It was white. Ghost white. He looked down. Her shift was blossomed with blood, bright as life, and her arms were stringy and pale where she gripped his waist, hard. She drove her face against his cheek.

"Ride," she said.

Callum paced the horse a hair short of cruelty. No one could catch them across open country. They crossed an undamaged bridge upriver from the massacre of horseflesh and pushed onward. Whenever Callum would try and check Ava's bleeding, she would clamp her chin on his shoulder.

"Not yet," she'd say, her body cloaked now in his patchwork coat. "Not yet."

Daylight was a long blur. Come dark they topped a hill and looked down upon the campfires of Sherman's bivouacked army, a whole galaxy encamped beneath the starless sky.

Callum turned to look at Ava, his jaw open. She let him look this time. Her eyes were slits, her pupils huge and lightless save strange constellations of reflected firelight.

"Hurts," she said.

He looked down. Her thighs were trembling, blood so dark upon them it seemed some liquid nature of the horse itself had crept upward in dark jags upon her flesh. She let him open the coat. He did so gently, as if it held some object of great fragility.

The shift was fully darkened.

"Hurts," she said again.

He swallowed and looked down the hillside to the fires below. He looked back. "I know it does, honey. We're gonna get you help."

"No," she said.

"Yes."

Callum lowered himself from the saddle. He took up the reins and starting leading the horse down the slope. At the same time he began dropping each of the guns he carried, so as to be no threat to the sentries hidden in the darkness ahead. He dropped them in the dirt, all but one.

❧

Callum sat on the bare ground outside the surgeons' tent. Night was deepening overhead. Men in rancid uniform eyed the horse as they strode past, lusting. A boy maybe two years Callum's senior stood beside him, a musket hung from one shoulder. His guard. Callum watched the shadows of the two surgeons warp and swell against the irregular contours of the fabric, their silent blood labor illumined by a single lantern.

The pickets had seen her face and allowed them across the lines. Then the surgeons, into their tent. It didn't hurt that she was so pretty.

Callum had told them nothing of who he was, who he had been. What atrocities under what authority. He said bandits had shot her. Their home had been burned. She was his sister. One of the surgeons stepped from the tent. He wore gold spectacles, a butcher's apron, a graying mustache.

Callum stood quickly. "How is she?"

The man's eyes were pouched and fallen, like an old dog's.

"I won't lie to you, son. We were able to remove the bullet, but her condition is deteriorating rapidly. Where is the father?"

"The father?"

"She's with child. Surely you knew that."

"He's dead."

The man nodded. "And your parents, where are they?"

Callum sniffed. "I'm the only family she's got."

The man nodded slowly and squinted out at the many fires.

"You better come in and say your good-byes, then. I don't know she'll make it till morning."

The boy who emerged from the tent had nothing writ upon his face, a frozen mask the color of bone. Only his eyes spoke into the darkness, twin worlds of storm. He untethered the horse and led him toward the center of the encampment, where the fires were brightest. His guard knew what had transpired inside the hospital tent and followed him, silent.

She had given no sign of his presence, her eyes far off and unreachable, her body sunken and pale. Ghosted away into the world that comes, or doesn't. Into a history, a story, a fiction. Callum thought of the words of the seer, the weak and yellowing old man who presumed to speak their fate, words perhaps begetting a future otherwise unwritten. Just foul enough for the unknowable architecture of the world to cling to, to construct out of the vagaries of greed and hate, love and hunger, a fate to underpin the unfolding future. And Callum, with his one handhold on a bright world slipping away, found within himself a last faith. Nothing else but this. And he knew how to make of the world what he would. How to shape it to his will.

First he found men in dirty uniform, muddy boots and trousers. These were enlisted men. Infantry. He squatted near the fire of a certain group. Ohioans, they said, from the southern river valley of that state. He asked what they had heard of good Northern men, foragers, hanged by a dead tree in land to the west. Their bodies mutilated, messaged by knifepoint.

They knew of these men and others, droves of men gone missing when they separated from the main column. Their corpses found disfigured, cruel things to send home in a box. It was the work of rebel cutthroats, they said. *Guerrillas.* Their ire swelled over the talk, their eyes bright with hate.

The thing he needed.

He kept on, toward a fire encircled by horses and men with tassels upon their jackets, silver scabbards that held the reeling of flame like a liquid. Cavalrymen. They had thick dark beards and stared unspeaking into their fire, minds philosophic or vacuous. He didn't know which. Didn't care. He knew what way to summon them. He found an officer among them, a man of some power. He pulled him aside and told him of what things he'd done, what things he could still do. The man listened, and so did his compatriots. This intelligence began working its way through the ranks. Climbing.

The riders rose from the cold pallet of slumber, beds of molding leaves. White shafts of near-naked trees towered above them toward a blue sky. The morning was bright and cold, pure, like the Lord's Day always seemed to be. Limbs creaked, bone to bone, and they were thinking of food, coffee, hearth, blankets—other things they no longer possessed—when the eastern sentry stormed upon them at a gallop, his face red. He reeled his horse through the trees, the animal's teeth bared against the hard yank of the bit.

"He's in that field!"

"Who is?"

"Him!"

The sentry snapped his horse around and whipped its hindquarters and rode hard away. The others followed. They cut their hobbles and mounted their horses and gouged them onward, dropping out of the trees into a wide field flanked by a river, a covered bridge. There in the field was the boy on the black horse, alone, his hat tilting back on his head. The horsemen rode down upon him. Clayburn was first out of camp behind the sentry, reins in teeth, his pistol drawn. The boy sat his horse, unmoving. Watching. He wanted parley, perhaps.

He would have none.

Clayburn seemed to slow a moment, straightening, uncertain, until the other riders began to catch him and he redoubled his speed. The boy made a small gesture, a tip of the hat perhaps, and then he whirled on his horse, whipping the animal for speed. He lashed the rump one side and the other, again and again, making for the river. But the riders would catch him this time, no matter his horse.

Boy and horse disappeared into the covered bridge, and the riders followed close upon him, following the one-armed tracker high upon his horse like some double-goer of the Colonel. The horsemen became shadows of themselves beneath the rafters, the line of them hungry to end this. This boy, this chase, this war. The boy emerged from the far end of the bridge, and the riders were hard upon him, arched for glory, when the square of daylight before them erupted, the naked rafters of the bridge illuminated like a tunneled chapel, the world of their becoming undone in a fury of power and light.

The boy broke from the darkness of the bridge and drove the animal head-on into the belched awakening of flame, smoke, shot. Ambush. He had been told to cut for safety on the near side of the river, but he rode on instead to his own riddance, the violent certitude of which he had convinced himself. That if he ended here, she would be safe, his evils the better claimant to a prophecy that ended in the ground. No fate would let such as him out of this. He rode on into the artillery guns aiming down the throat of the bridge, the rifles exploding into the ruptured torrent of flesh within its walls. He waited to be cut down by the death shrieking invisibly through the forest. He waited until he had cleared the firing line, and the thunder had lapsed, and all you could hear were the moans of the stricken, the undead, echoing from the mouth of the bridge. He turned, sitting the horse. The roof of the bridge collapsed. Below, a red cloud churned slowly downstream.

A young cavalryman looked inside a small satchel he'd found on one of the bodies.

"Good Christ."

The captain stiffened. "Watch your mouth, Simpson. What did you find?"

The young man emptied the contents into his palm, a pile of white-pointed fragments. The captain plucked one from his hand and held it to the light.

"Bone," he said. "Finger joints, looks like."

"What kind of a sick son of a bitch—"

The captain snorted. "A dead one, like the rest of them." He flicked the bone away.

Callum stepped up to them. "Sir," he said, "I really got to be getting back to camp."

The captain had a long pointed beard, jet black, and an upturned mustache. He adjusted his navy slouch hat. "What you *got* to do is what you're told to."

"That wasn't my understanding of the deal."

The man looked at him like he was a dog, some nameless mongrel.

"You turn Judas on your own brothers and think it warrants immunity? Son, you're lucky you aren't swinging from a tree like the rest the guerrillas we've been rounding up."

"My sister, sir, she's dying."

The man snorted. He looked from the boy to the bridge and back again.

"And whose fault is that?"

Callum felt the blood rush to his face, hot, and the ground beneath him seemed to be slipping, a cold void where once he'd been standing. He could not get enough air. The whole world constricted on him, pinning him down, and he thought his heart might scream out of his chest, explode. He staggered to the horse, put a hand on his saddle. He felt sick, more than sick. That he was the sick thing, the sickness itself.

"Don't you mount that horse," said the captain. "You do, you'll be sorry."

The other cavalrymen turned from the gore of the bridge to watch this boy claw at the ropes and ties of his saddle. The captain slid his revolver from its holster and let it hang by his side. The boy struggled to set one foot in the near stirrup. He began to pull himself up. The captain raised his pistol along a straight arm. The young cavalryman closed his fist around the fleshless tarsals, watching the boy.

"Don't," he whispered.

Callum hugged Reiver's neck and slid his far leg over the horse's rump. The captain primed his hammer. Callum turned the horse down the road at a slow trot. The captain held the base of his skull beneath the barrel of his revolver a long moment.

"God favors a fool," he said. He dropped the gun back to his side and nodded at the young cavalryman. "Simpson, you and Brown go pull that son of a bitch off his horse. And bind his hands."

Callum rode within the parallel lines of blue-clad horsemen, his wrists bound uselessly behind his back. The sun was at its highest, the trees black and crack-limbed, the sky paler than a robin's egg. He could smell smoke but saw none on the horizon. The cavalry riders caught the rear guard of the army column along the dark wake of a churned-over road. The earth here was no longer red. It was black, how it got closer to the coast. The captain sent a courier toward the head of the column with news of ambush, victory. Callum searched the nearest faces for that of the surgeon. How he was to find him again in this sea of men, of hangdog faces thousands deep along the roads, and wagons that all looked the same, and ambulances and buckboards covered in mud and soot—he hadn't thought of that. He knew he couldn't do it with his hands tied behind his back.

The courier returned and spoke with the captain, who nodded and gestured toward the boy. The courier rode toward him. It was the man called Simpson. He cut the boy's horse out of the line. Reiver snorted but consented. Simpson slowly slid a knife from a sheath on his belt. Callum watched the round black eye of the horse track the blade as it neared them. He could feel the power swelling underneath him.

"Lemme see your hands," said Simpson.

Callum whispered to the horse. "Whoa," he said. "Whoa boy." He rotated on the saddle to give the man his hands. Simpson slid the knife between his wrists and cut the pigging string that bound them. "Somebody says you're free to go."

"The captain?"

The man shrugged. "Somebody up the line. Thought you deserved it, after what you done."

Callum massaged his wrists. "I got to find my sister. There was a surgeon that was helping her."

"What's his name?"

"I don't know."

"Company?"

Callum shook his head.

Simpson spit a bullet of black juice on the road. "Can't really help you, then. Wish I could. Reckon you just gonna have to go looking for him." He swept his hand ahead. The mud-covered parade of soldiers and carts and mules and horses receded far into the distance, what seemed a whole nation stretched out in file. The road wound them out of sight, then held them up again upon a distant hill, unbelievably far off. Callum took up the reins.

"Hold on," said Simpson.

He plugged his tongue into the corner of his mouth and cut his eyes left, right. The other cavalry riders had continued on. The two of them were alone on the road but for stragglers, ex-slaves following the march into some gloried future. Simpson turned on his saddle and dug under his bedroll. Out came the Walker Colt, butt-first. He held it out.

Callum hesitated a moment, his head cocked.

"Yours," said Simpson. "Don't go telling nobody I gave it back to you, huh?" He wiggled the butt. "Thought you might be needing it."

Callum took the gun. Turned it over in his hand.

"Appreciate it," he said. "Couldn't spare no extra powder and shot, could you?"

Simpson spat.

"Don't push your luck." He touched a couple of fingers to his hat brim. "I hope it goes well with your sister." He turned his horse back toward the column and rode off.

Callum stowed the gun beneath his own bedroll, hidden. His stomach was hollow and cold, his breath short. He glanced up at the sky a long moment. Searched its emptiness.

He took up the reins and rode off toward the procession, fast, as if in flight.

"You seen a surgeon with gold spectacles, gray mustache?"

The trudging soldiers looked up at him on the horse. White eyes in smoked faces. Some were hardly older than he was. Maybe a year. They shook their heads or shrugged, went back to their labor. Trudge, trudge, trudge. He continued up the line, asking for the surgeon.

They crossed a river by pontoon bridge. The water was black. Broad mangrove roots shouldered from the shallows. The guards let him pass on the horse. The road wound itself over a small rise on the other side, and he was asking, asking, when he heard moans and screams behind him. Everyone turned to look. The bridge had been cut loose on the far side, swinging toward the center of the river. Dark-skinned followers of the march wailed and splashed into the current, marooned on the far shore, their hands thrown skyward. Hysteria. Their bodies cut white daggers in the current, pointed downstream. Freedom's novitiates, newly unslaved, now abandoned. Some dove headlong into the waters, true believers, and others were forced in, screaming, as those behind them pushed for their chance. None made it. The waters here were too quick, too dark and cold.

"Goddamn niggers," said somebody. "Everybody knows they can't swim."

An officer galloped up the line, an arm straightened east.

"Move!" he yelled. "Keep moving!"

He gave the boy a hard look but kept riding the line.

By dark, Callum had ridden most of the column. No surgeon. Not that he had seen. The soldiers lit pine knots in the falling dark, red meteors that smoked above the road. He watched the burning snake of them, miles-long, wind and flare over the countryside, hell come on parade. The dark was cold, the flames almost welcome. His hands were bloodless underneath his gloves, and trembling. He hadn't eaten for two days.

The soldiers fanned out in an annex of fallow fields to make camp for the night. Callum wandered among the fires of strangers. Men soot-faced and strange from warring, addled and nervous with darting eyes. Others gone mean, eyes hunting the dark with a sliver of teeth, a squirming tongue. He gave no thought to the looks they gave him, his horse. He was dazed, mindless, hungry. He kept looking for her. Kept asking.

"Boy?"

Callum turned. He'd been squatting before a jumble of weak coals that had been abandoned, staring into them. Not thinking. Unable to think. Animated by want alone. When he saw who it was, he bolted upright and removed his hat.

"Doc?"

"Heard you been looking for me."

"How is she? Is she—"

The dog-faced man removed his wire spectacles.

"I don't know."

"Don't know?"

The surgeon wiped his forehead with the back of his hand. Dried blood grouted his cuticles and nails.

"I'm afraid she was in no condition to travel. We had to find somewhere to leave her this morning. Somebody to take her in." He held his hands in front of his chest, open, as if holding something the size of a man's skull. "I tried to find you. She was in terrible shape." The man waited for an answer. There was none. He closed his hands, clasping them before his chest. "I gave her to a foraging party."

"*Gave* her?"

The man nodded. "I told them to find a house that would take her in. I told them, though, told them if they touched her, I'd be liable to get real liberal with the capital saw should any of them come in with a minié ball before this war is out."

"Which foraging party?" asked Callum.

The man looked away. "I don't know. One that was going out."

Callum rolled the brim of his hat between his hands.

"God damn you."

"Well, where the hell were you? You were the one should of been here, finding a place to take her in. Where were you? Off killing, that's what I hear."

The boy halved the space between them in an instant.

"Maybe I ain't done."

The surgeon looked down at the boy, his eyes sad and round. No fear in them. They had welcomed too much for too long.

Callum took a step back, exhaled, his shoulders slumping. He shook his head.

"You don't understand."

The surgeon replaced his spectacles, hooking the curved wires behind his ears. The apron that hung from his neck was bow-tied at the rear, the front slashed and splattered darkly with the undoings of so many men. "You're right," he said. "I don't." He crossed his arms. "They went south off the road. That much I know. I'm sorry."

Callum just nodded, saying nothing. He turned and started west through the camp. He needed to backtrack along the road to the bivouac site of the previous night, then begin searching south.

It was full dark now. The stars were high and bright, the night black and cold. Wood smoke stung the air, and the hacking laughs of killers and thieves. They watched him pass, this vagrant ghost of a boy whose too-big boots shuffled stubbornly along, whose coat showed an amalgam of fabric bolts and scraps from the backs of dead men. A boy who trailed a saddled stallion that might fetch a year's wages at auction. Word had spread of such a rider that morning. A killer with a boy's face, a steed the color of night.

He heard the whispers.

He kept on, the lead slithering audibly through the grass behind him before arcing upward to the horse's bridle. He passed a circle of infantrymen circulating a bottle among their number. Their bayonets were fixed to their rifles, arranged into a wood-framed tepee of blades that flowered toward the sky. He heard them talking low as he passed. He paid them no heed, kept walking.

The lead burned out of his hand, yanked, a hot scoring even through the gloves he wore. He turned. There were three of them, infantrymen, the outer two with rifles, the center one with the limp end of the rope. The man had a heavy black beard and the navy kepi of an enlisted man.

"Keep walking," he said.

Callum hawked and spat. "Or what?"

"I think you know what." He grinned. "But don't worry, we'll take real good care of your horse for you. Looks like it could use some feeding anyway."

Reiver snorted and spasmed, as if to throw flies off his back. The massive cage of ribs corrugated his hide. Callum looked at him, then looked at the men. He raised his arms out to either side.

"Nothing like cold blood. Best use the sharp stuff, though. Don't want no officers to hear."

The man stepped closer.

"Don't think we won't."

"I'm right here. Hundred ten pounds, dripping. Just stick

me and get it done, because I ain't leaving without my horse. I got a girl to find, and you, you got a deep rung of hell to damn yourself to. Best get to it."

The black-bearded man stepped even closer, too close.

"Don't shit with me. Get smart and get walking."

Callum sighed. "If that's how you want it." He took a deep breath and threw down his arms and drove his right boot upward into soft tissue. The man's face twisted as he fell to his knees, clutching his groin. Callum snatched the lead and clanged a boot in the nearest stirrup, and he was out of range before either of the two riflemen could try to stop him. He raced across the camp at a gallop, dismaying many, slowing to a lope only as he crossed the outer perimeter, so as not to alarm the pickets standing guard.

He and the horse rode hours down the road, west, before turning off into the woods for a few hours of sleep. He still had his flint. He was cold but found himself afraid to build a fire, afraid of what creatures or men it might invite. It was an unexpected fear. He staked Reiver with a long lead of rope and huddled himself in the gnarled knees of a giant cypress, the empty pistol in hand. He knew the Colonel's men were gone, dead, and the slave hunter too, but the cold in his gut told him otherwise. With no one to chase him, hunt him, the world seemed wrong. Nameless fears hunted the peripheries of his knowing, echoes of the men who had been chasing him for all those weeks. Ghosts, he knew, real if only in your own head.

There was one redemption that shone in this darkness like a gate lamp of the world to be: to find her. He searched for her in his mind. Hunted her in every cabin he could imagine, every farmhouse. He found her in a thousand different ways, a hundred different places. He couldn't stop. Sleep finally came over him, a welcome opiate, but the world it offered was little better, corrupted by nightmare. He saw their faces. In the bridge. Lit with revelation. Saw their bodies exploding in red bursts, startlingly red, torn limbs ricocheting from ceiling and siding. And the horses screaming, their eyes and teeth white with fear. The innocents.

Before dawn he was on horseback, riding, hoping to be anywhere but where he was.

He found the field where the column had camped two nights ago—the night he had brought Ava bleeding to the surgeons. Pines in the east bit the first glow of a new day. In the dim minutes before daybreak, he saw the littered castoffs of an army twirling and fluttering across the field. Rolling papers and journal pages. A collapsed and abandoned tent, white, and rolling cans of purloined foodstuffs from neighboring farms. Libraries of stolen philosophy and tragedy and science lying flat-backed on the ground, their pages sailing in the wind like Oriental fans. Countless craters of dead ash, cold coals, and the yellow-hearted stumps of trees sawn off for a better night of sitting.

The buzzards were already in flight, spiraling.

He climbed down from the saddle and led the horse across the grounds, searching for something to eat. He passed a birdcage hanging from the limb of a dead tree, empty. More empty jars and cans. Thighbones from chickens and hogs, sucked clean and cracked for the marrow inside. Someone had already picked over the leavings. Locals, probably, eating the waste of their plundered storehouses before it turned queer and worm-ridden. Toward the center of the field there sat a makeshift dining table, an unhinged door laid over a whiskey barrel. The table was set. Porcelain dishes and saucers, a sterling silver serving dish and candlesticks. A place of feast.

He lifted the lid off the serving dish; a mash of beans and corn bread coated the edges. It was hard as stone. He scraped free a pile of shavings with one of the dinner knives and put them on a china plate painted with blue filigree and a scene of men on horseback. He pulled out a chair to eat. Reiver lowered his head over Callum's shoulder and snorted.

"I hear you, boy. I hear you."

Under a buckboard wagon, down with a smashed wheel, he found a wicker basket of spilled apples. He brought it back to the dining table. The apples were bruised and soft where they had rested against one another or the ground. He carved out the dark places of three apples and set them on a plate for the horse. He found three matches in the pocket of a discarded shirt and used them to light the dinner candles. When the ruddy yolk of sun overwhelmed the trees, it found boy and horse breakfasting by candlelight, the boy picking pale chunks of apple off the tip of his knife like hors d'oeuvres at a fancy dinner. Meanwhile, a yellow stab of feathers jetted from shadow to shadow around them. A songbird. A canary. It sang like a tiny alarm in all that ruin.

He thought of the world they might have, he and Ava, if only he could find her. The two of them working their own little plot of land on the Gosling plantation, having their own tin-roofed cabin beside one of those streams full of tadpoles and baitfish. He could see her on the porch already, rocking a baby to sleep, as he rode in from the fields at dusk. He could see a slim band of gold on her finger, her black hair dashed all upon her shoulders like something wild, her blue eyes glowing. They would sit on the porch and watch the lightning bugs hang like tiny lanterns in the coming dark. They would eat streak o' lean and buttery greens, johnny-cakes smothered in sorghum. They would know no matter how bad it got, how lean the times, they had seen worse. They would not have much, but it would be enough.

He was headed south before the sun had fully cleared the trees. There was a dark creek running through a deep fold in the ground, the current tripping and pulsing against the stones. Too steep for Reiver to negotiate. Callum slid down its banks and watered the horse from the upturned bowl of his hat. He lifted up the trembling clarity again and again, like an offering of some kind. He needed Reiver fast and strong and tireless. He needed to find her. If not today, tomorrow. Soon. He feared he wouldn't. Feared there would be nothing really to find. A slant-nailed crucifix, a mound of loose earth.

He tried not to think of that.

He rode a farm road that skated south between cotton fields. They were unharvested. Empty. The first quarter mile of split-rail fencing that bordered the road had been cannibalized for fuel by the army. Here or there lone timber rails littered the shoulder and road. Endless streaks scored the dirt where rails had been dragged by man or mule for burning.

Buzzards were up against the climbing sun. He cut east toward them along a lane double-rutted from wagon traffic. Cotton fields ended; an orchard began. It was scorched. He watched each straight-planted aisle of stunted apple trees fall away into an ornate tunneling of branches, the columned trees condensing into a long-off vanishing point, a tiny speck of light. Then a new tree would swing into the foreground. It went on like that for a long time. Tunnel after tunnel.

A white farmhouse appeared through the trees. It was sided with shiplapped heart pine and wore green storm shutters. The near side was stained black from the wind drift of a fired chicken coop.

In the yard a dead bird dog, a spaniel. It was liver and white, its hindquarters destroyed by a close-in shotgun blast. Callum turned away from the sight too late. He rode past and helloed the house from the saddle. No answer. He tied off the horse at a hitching post and started toward the front steps. The door was ajar. A spool of dried blood the color of molasses zigzagged up the porch steps and into the house. He knelt down and touched two knuckles to it. Day-old. Tiny black ants hovered motionless in the coagulant, entombed.

He gave the door a quick knock and helloed again. Nothing. He turned sideways and slipped through the partially opened door, no groan of hinges. A staircase took up one half of the foyer, a hallway the other. Closed doors to either side, windowed. He looked down. The blood trail wormed its way between his boots and turned right, skirting underneath one of the doors. He looked up and saw the twin-bore mouths bearing down on him. He hove onto his side as a torrent of crystalized glass blew sideways across the hallway behind him. He scrambled on all fours down the hallway and into the kitchen, his ears ringing. He looked for a back door, an escape from this room. There wasn't one.

"I'm unarmed! I don't mean no harm."

A woman's voice called out, rasp-throated with the gravel of age or wear. "I'm like to kill any little son-bitch comes sneaking in my house, harm-hunting or otherwise."

"Yes, ma'am."

"You looking to loot me, too, that it?"

"No, ma'am. I'm just looking for my girl is all."

"Your girl?"

"Yes, ma'am."

"Come to this doorway here with your hands up."

"You ain't gonna go and shoot me, are you?"

"Probably I'm not."

Callum got to his feet and walked slowly back to the shattered door frame. He had his hands up. The woman was sitting on a fainting couch tufted in red velvet. She had the white-swirled hair nest of a sophisticate, streaked crazy on one side, and a handsome fowling piece with twin barrels, one of them still smoking. In the lady's lap lay a bloodied spaniel, its ribs swelling and laxing too quickly, its breath ragged and audible. It was licking the louvered flesh at the inside of her elbow, slowly. It didn't look at him.

She did. Wetness came into her eyes like a dam breaking. "They shot my dogs," she said. Her face had begun to twitch, the sunken skin prodded by strange tics. "Why would they do that?"

"I don't rightly know, ma'am."

"Evil," she said. "Pure as pure."

Her eyes narrowed.

Callum shifted his weight from one foot to the other.

She jutted her chin at him.

"You one of them?"

He looked into the black bore of the twin barrels, shaped infinitylike. "I don't much know what I am," he said.

"Too bad," she said. "I'd have liked to shoot you."

"Yes, ma'am. I better be going."

"Don't."

He took a step back. "I got to. I got to find my girl."

The barrels began to shake. "I'll be your girl."

"Much obliged, ma'am. But—" He took another step back. "But I got to get on."

"Don't leave me," she said. "He's dying." She looked at the dog.

"I'm sorry," he said. "I'm sorry."

She wasn't going to shoot him. He was out of the door and down the steps and around the house and on the horse before she started screaming for him. She was still screaming when he passed the charred carcasses of hens that radiated from the fired coop into the far end of the yard, how far they'd gotten on flaming wings. Still screaming when the lane veered southward and the house was lost beyond the trees.

"I'm sorry," he said.

He haunted the roads the day long, a scarecrow rider on a horse that blended well with the land to which she was lost. He found nothing. Not her. No sightings, no rumors. Char-colored killings littered the land. Crazed minds. He was given incongruent accounts of raiding parties, none of them with a girl. He was given food and shelter in some instances, the barrel of a gun in others. He was given preaching on the Coming of God, the Leaving. Given safe passage by a band of Confederate cavalry riders, bearded and red-eyed, who said Sherman was advancing on Fort McAllister, near Savannah. They said if it was overcome, the city would surely fall. He was given shot and powder by a faceless man dead in a ditch, a case of the flux by a maggot-ridden turkey he stole from the buzzards.

He went fireless in the long nights and he feared what dreams would come. He did not want to close his eyes. The world had drawn down on him, the sky tattooed with death. Spiraling, spiraling. Everywhere a corpse. The cold sun cut him hard in the daytime, and the bite of smoke, and come sundown he just wanted the light. She was never out of his mind. When the nightmares came, the visions of men gone faceless, she was the good thing he knew existed. Knew. He was with her again. On the horse and in the beds they'd shared, wrapped up in the buffalo blanket for one of those long cold nights they'd spent on the ground, their limbs tangled for warmth. She was slapping him or kissing him, holding him tight, or him her. She was a thing torn out of him, which hurt a hundredfold worse than a saber or knife.

He found nothing. No hints, no clues. It was like she had vanished, winked away by some magician. Like she had never even existed. He began to call his own sanity into question. Whether her advent had been the work of his own imagining. Whether he was something more than a killer. Something less. A ghost that would wander the land forever, searching.

Then, on a cold morning somewhere west of Savannah, he happened upon a clan of negroes washing themselves in a roadside ditch. They had their few possessions wrapped in gingham bundles, scattered along the bank, and a fire going to warm themselves after their bath. The women were naked to the waist and they covered their breasts as he rode up. They said they were headed toward Savannah, to find the savior Sherman. To follow him north. They had seen a white family on the road east, a week ago, with a dark-haired girl in the bed of their wagon. They said she'd been alive.

Callum's heart surged. It had to be her. It had to. He rode east toward the coast, the land of their hope. He thought surely she was close. He was a week crossing and recrossing the army's path, searching, and she was around every bend in his mind, in every house and cabin, in every wagon he saw, and yet she wasn't. He didn't find her. No sign nor rumor. Nothing.

He reached Savannah. Occupied. Sherman's army had marched to the sea and captured the once-mighty city, presenting it like a gift to Lincoln. Bluecoats marched through the streets. There was broken glass and the reeling of drunken men, the periodic report of gunfire. Pistols mainly. Men dueling in the streets, too much peace, and people selling corn dodgers through their basement windows, afraid to come outside. He rode neatly squared streets shadowed by live oaks, down cobblestones to the brown river lined with flat-faced buildings whose windows echoed with laughter and screams, grunts and shrieks. He did not find her amid the riverfront taverns or the cotton warehouses or the shadowed monuments of square on square, the bronzed generals of more glorious wars, or in the green-tangled cemeteries with their ghostly statuary, their mossy oaks weeping in the breeze. He did not find her before the Customs House or the City Exchange or the State Arsenal, before any of the imposing buildings now draped in victors' flags, or in the churches or hospitals or colonies of poor in the gutters and alleys.

He rode Christmas the night through, and he thought out of some alignment of stars or winds or gods he would find her on this night, of all of them, and he rode the dark hours among men prostrated by whiskey and whoring and he was wrong. Nothing. Come daylight he rode south, out of the city.

He rode shell causeways between flooded rice fields full of empty sky, passing the quieted guns of Fort McAllister, the great earthwork fortifications still fronted by an abatis of felled trees, their snarled crowns sharpened to stakes. He'd heard it took Sherman's army only minutes to storm the place, charging through all the entanglements, the ditches and buried torpedoes, overrunning the men within. Old Glory now whipped from a flagpole in the center of the fort.

Callum rode on south, down the coast, toward that lost destiny of theirs, carrying the tiny hope that Ava had somehow made it that far. That she was waiting for him there, in a place as good as they'd ever dared imagine. A hope, he knew, as feeble now and ill-born as any he might allow. In time, the rice paddies gave way to salt marsh and swamp, a sea smell blown in on the wind. Dark arteries of brackish water spiraled and spread thin-fingered through marsh and sedge. Sharp white birds with S-curved necks stood one-footed among the browned sawgrass, watching him. Reiver reared once at a half-submerged length of timber in a creek that shouldered the trail they rode. Callum yelped when the log writhed and kicked itself into the water, an ancient reptile whose yellow eyes and armored snout veed through the current like an ironclad gunboat. Not since Louisiana had he seen one of those.

There was a beach. At dusk he would tie Reiver off on a piece of driftwood and strip naked, standing waist-deep in the cold embrace of the tide. So cold. These were his ablutions, a boy alone on the shore under falling darkness. He was weightless and numb in the water. Afterward he huddled close to a fire raised on the naked sands, trembling, the blood flushing back from the deep parts of him where it went to hide, once-white and cold-gone corners of him glowing, tingling like the return of a soul.

Strange creatures littered the beach, the remnants of

another world. Jellyfish like snow-blue snot and armored crabs the size of big tortoises with daggerlike tails. He lost track of days, weeks. He ate what he could. Turtles, ghost-colored crabs, fishes circumscribed in pools by an outgoing tide. After a time, the sands narrowed and he rode inland along a worn road of brown dirt.

Dawn. A healthy tree axed across the road.

Ambush.

Reiver sensed it—must have—surging toward the felled pine, leaping it just as smoke bellowed from the trees. Callum flinched, hearing balls zip through the branches all around them. He dropped close to Reiver's neck, feeling the sweat against his cheek as they thundered down the road, leaving the highwaymen behind them.

They rode a mile farther, hard, then slowed to a walk. Callum looked behind him. No one. He let out a breath, relieved, then reached for the beef bladder to take a drink. Reiver yawed suddenly sideways in the road, as if he'd lost his balance. Callum started to correct him, then didn't. Something wasn't right. The horse's gait seemed broken of a sudden, his shoulders and flanks firing all out of sequence, his legs jerked as if by vicious strings. His withers twitched, and he twisted his head as if to throw something off of it.

Callum slid from the saddle, his chest tightening. He removed his gloves and circled the big horse, his fingertips tracing the great dark swells that made him.

Please no. Please no.

There it was, just above his right leg. In his side. An angry red mouth, swollen and leaking in ribbons down his leg, bright against the towered black.

Callum could hardly breathe. He undid the cinch and pulled off the saddle and blanket. He dropped them on the side of the road and stripped off his coat and pushed it against the wound.

"You're okay, big man. You're okay."

Reiver turned his head out to the side to look back at him with one of those eyes that was round as the world and had no white in it. He knew Callum was lying. His breath was coming ragged now, loud and irregular, and Callum could see his teeth. His great ribbed sides flared hugely, like wings trying to break free from beneath a tautened hide. Callum's hand felt warm now. He looked at it. The blood had pushed through the coat. It wasn't going to stop.

This great machine that ran on blood, its hide not made of the armor that Callum once thought. Not invincible, as he had believed. As he had so badly needed to. How easily it had sprung a leak, the work of a tiny half-ounce ball of lead, the rich red stuff fleeing into the light. Callum could hear the animal's breath whistling through the wound. He stuck his thumb against the hole to plug it, but soon the big horse was coughing, his great lungs filling up, his teeth gone red.

Reiver's front legs gave first, buckling, and he crashed to his knees in the road, then to his chest, his muzzle clapping in the dirt before he rolled onto his side, his great belly coated in grit and leaves. Callum fell to his knees beside him. He touched the big horse on the head, gently between the eyes, then bent close to his ear, whispering to him. He told him how good he was, how good and how strong. He told him he was the king of all horses, the noblest thing God had made.

The handsomest. He told him they were brothers, the two of them. That he would never forget him. That he loved him. He loved him so much. And when he finished telling him, Reiver was dead.

Callum lay a long time in the road, holding him, his ear against the barrel chest. Hearing nothing shoot through it, no blood, the great heart stilled and cooling. He cried. He pushed his nose between the ribs and cried into the salty coat, the dried sweat and horse smell. He didn't care who might find him or what they might do. He didn't care for anything save the last bit of warmth leaving the big horse like a spirit. He wanted it so badly to stay.

It didn't.

He stood, finally, and wiped his eyes. He left Reiver there in the road. Had to. He left his coat on him to keep him warm. The one Ava had made. He slung the saddle wallets over his shoulder and started away on foot, looking back now and again as the dead horse grew smaller behind him, a shape mounded darkly in the road. Featureless now, a pile of coats or heap of coal. A thing grown smaller and smaller.

Gone.

He was two days walking. Clutching his own arms, shaking. He slept nearly in the fires he made, woken by cinders burning through his shirt. He needed a new coat if he was going to find her, and a horse. He couldn't find her if he was dead.

The coat came first, the morning of the second day. Callum found a black man dead in a ditch. He'd been shot in the throat. His eyes were still open, looking right down his nose, like he'd been trying to see the wound that killed him. He had a hatchet gripped in one hand. It looked like he'd meant to ambush someone—for their horse, perhaps—and chosen the wrong rider. Callum stared down at him.

What would he have done?

He knelt down next to the man. Those naked white eyes, staring, seeing nothing. He pushed down the lids. He pulled off the man's coat, a rancid wool-jean shell jacket with a six-button front, gray where it wasn't stained. There were at least two bullet holes in it, with patches of blood dried in the muslin lining. He put it on, wondering how many dead men had worn it before he did. He stuck the hatchet through his belt.

He dragged the man off the road, along a narrow game trail that led into the woods. He dragged him until the trees and palmetto cleared. Before them rose a dirt-speckled ring of shells, tall as a man's house. He'd heard tell of such shell rings but never seen one. They were built circling old Indian villages. Built of refuse. The pink sea meat scraped quivering from the shell, the leftovers cast off. Over generations the empty shells accrued into a rampart of sorts, nearly circular. There were no natives now, not here. Nor huts nor fires. He dragged the dead man into the center of the ring and let him go. The coal-dark limbs lay splayed over the ground, the palms colorless. Callum was going to bury him, proper, like Ava would have made him do. It was the least he could do, given the coat.

He knelt down and began digging with his hands, but it wasn't like he thought. It wasn't just dirt. The soil was full of broken shells, droves of them, sharp middens that didn't want to come out, that gnawed his fingertips until they were raw. He tried and tried, his fingers beginning to bleed. No use. It was like a wall just beneath the surface, trying to keep him out.

The man lay there, limbs askew, shells around him barnacled and broken. Callum sat beside him, his legs spread wide, spent. He had exhumed a huge bluish shell, spiraled, with a pointed base and spiked crown. He picked it up and shook the dirt out of it. He tried to look inside, but the inlet curved quickly into shadow, like the contorted innards of a trumpet. He shook it, then held the cool hollow place to his ear. Ocean surf sang into his ear canal. Startled, he dropped it. He drew up and fled from under the high walls of the place, all those sea skeletons that might speak to him in the same strange tongue. It frightened him and he didn't know why.

The next day he found himself in a citrus orchard, slim black trees heavy-hung with bright globes of fruit. Nearly ripe. He sat against a tree and skinned an orange on the blade of the dead man's hatchet. The sweet acid of the wedges swished around his mouth. The flies swirled around his sweetened fingers. He ate fruit after fruit, glutting himself on the sweetness. He sucked his fingers, one by one. They stung, raw from the day before, but he didn't care. He licked the tips, the knuckles, the webs that split them. His lids grew heavy.

"You kilt him?"

He opened his eyes to the voice, a woman's. He squinted at her, a slave woman with a wild streak of white in her hair. Other orchard slaves were gathered behind her, their faces coffee-colored, their picking baskets green. He'd fallen asleep underneath the tree.

"Killed who?" he asked. "What? I don't know what you're talking about."

"Like hell you don't," said the woman. "He was heading north. To Savannah. You got his hatchet."

He looked down at the bladed implement sitting in his lap, the edge glazed with juice.

"This? I—I just found him. I wasn't the one that killed him."

She grabbed the hatchet, and Callum, by instinct, yanked it away. The blade winked between the webbing of her fingers. An accident. Blood blossomed from her hand, into the sunlight. She grasped her hand bleeding to her chest, like a wounded animal.

"He was my son!" she screamed. "My son!"

Chapter 15

Callum peered through the palmettos at the big house. Beside it stood the stables, green-trimmed and cavernous. He crept slowly through the undergrowth, careful of twigs, his saddle wallets hanging over his shoulder.

He'd run from the slaves in the orchard. He hadn't known what else to do. The woman had fallen to her knees, wailing for her son. He hadn't meant to hurt her. Not any of them. He had only wanted to talk to them. To ask them where they were, and what day it was, and if they knew of the Gosling Plantation and if it was close. If they knew of a dark-haired girl, hurt, brought this way in a wagon. But he couldn't ask any of that, not after what he'd done. After delivering that kind of news. He'd just run.

He crept toward the stables now, pistol in hand. Stranger's stables. He needed a new horse. To find her, he did. He surveyed the grounds and saw no one moving, just the horses standing motionless through the open doors. He scampered out of the brush and into the barn. It had that familiar smell: alfalfa and manure and horse sweat, the tang of iron tools hanging on the walls. He tiptoed down the aisle, sizing the stock, running his palm over the swells that powered them. Some retreated in their stalls; others offered themselves for praise. He chose a big red roan and saddled her. It was an ancient Grimsley saddle with hair padding and beveled stirrups he found hanging in the tack room. He rigged his saddle wallets and mounted.

Just as he rode out of the stable doors, a white man rounded the corner. A boy. Thin, thin as he was, and Callum looked at him as if looking into the trembling mirror of a well, like a younger version of himself. So strange. The boy had a knife hanging from his belt, a shotgun cradled in the crook of his arm. Callum drew down on him with his revolver and primed the hammer and did not shoot.

Not this time.

Not again.

He wanted to say something, but the words caught in his throat.

He wheeled the horse onto the shell road and spurred it toward that future of tunneled oaks. But even as he gained velocity he knew this engine beneath him was not strong enough, was not his salvation. He could see already the noose hanging over him, the bleed-out of a slaughtered animal. He wanted a place to go but had none, no walls of centuries past. No ancestors, no progeny. No Ava. Only the road ever lengthening before him. He heard the hollering of a second man behind him and spurred the horse still harder. The shell road shone bone-white under the noon sun, the bleached backs of a thousandfold sea shields crackling underneath his hooves, protesting, as if he were something come newly wicked upon their prehistoric world. He wanted that sound to end, the crackling.

The first shot bellowed behind him. Shotgun. Then another. He was struck still stirruped from the horse, dragged, a red trail of himself scrawled across the armored path of ridges and spines. The horse stopped, stamping away from him. Callum lay there on the old shell road, his spirit spreading brightly beneath him. He heard the boots of men coming for him. The boy and another man.

"It ain't him, is it?" asked the boy.

"Nuh-uh. Look at that coat on him. Deserter is what he looks like."

Their boots. The shells. In his skull the dark crackling of broken backs took on weight and precedence, growing slowly into the thunder of far-off hooves, hard-riding. A big dark horse that would always run.

Their shadows cast him.

"You want to string him up?"

The man sniffed. "Best we can do for a horse thief."

Callum opened his eyes. Past the men, the noose. To the house. It rose like a great white arrow from the earth, as tall as it was wide, upon columns round as oaks. He saw a lone figure in a window. The second story. A girl. Black hair, white arms. A body motionless, alone, like a watching ghost.

Ava?

He blinked.

She was gone. The window black.

Shadows crisscrossed him. The tickle of rope. His chest was burning, his breath short. His eyes were open but barely. The outspill of his saddle wallets glittered on the road. He saw a jar. The jar. On its side. A babe, unborn. A seed. He looked up. Bare branches fissuring the blue sky. He closed his eyes. A naked white tree glowing in perfect darkness.

He felt the rope scratching his neck.

Tightening.

They'd tied the other end to the pommel of the saddled horse.

The boy squatted before him, his boots creaking as he did. "You got some last words?"

He looked past the boy, to the house. A figure came out the front door, black hair wild as she tromped down the steps, her white shift clinging tightly to her body. He felt her high in his throat. The most beautiful girl he had ever seen. Alive. Like a miracle from the house. He blinked, almost afraid to believe. His jaw hung slack, amazed. The boy said something, but Callum didn't hear him. Wasn't listening. His eyes only on her. He started to say it, the word that would save him—*Ava*—when the older man turned and slapped the horse's rump.

He was yanked skyward, shut-throated by the noose. His hands went to his neck, his feet kicking crazily beneath him. His head felt huge and red, ready to burst, and he couldn't breathe. He fought his eyes open. He had to see her. She was on the shell road now, running toward them, her arms swinging hugely, her cheeks glowing red. A vision that burned. He tried to reach for her, to point her out, but his arms would not obey him, thrashing the air like a man drowning. He tried to scream her name and couldn't. He saw her as if at the end of a darkening tunnel, her belly flat against the shift as she ran.

The baby, he thought. *The baby.* She should be showing by now. The loss boomed through him like a knell, a big echo of everything gone, and his heart swelled huge even as the darkness rushed in. A heart swelled big as a house, with chambers for them all. For the baby gone, and the horse, and the unborn brother in the jar. For these men even, who watched his spirit jerk from his body. For all of them, all over this land, who knew nothing of what they did. And for her most of all. A heart so huge and red, so full it could never die and yet. He tried to open his eyes a last time now, and the world was tiny, a pinhole of light in the great dark. Then gone.

A voice: "Cut him down! That's him! Cut him down!"

A snap. He slammed back to the ground, coughing and choking, and there were hands at his neck, fighting the rope. It loosened. He rolled onto his back, drinking air, and looked up. The darkness bled slowly from his vision, and out of it came those blue eyes, bright as whole worlds.

Epilogue

Spring

The sun was lowering in the west, coming in slantwise through the stable doors. Callum ran the curry comb along the great swells of the red roan. A mountain of flesh, red in her face and legs and mane, her barrel white-powdered as if with snow. In her right flank a sprinkling of solid red corn marks amid the mixed hairs. The places the shotgun pellets had gone in, where the hair had grown back only red, like some memory of the hurt. In Callum's own hip a mottled pattern of hard white welts, scars he sometimes thumbed through his shirt. He wiped down the roan's coat with a sheepskin mitt, polishing it to a sheen, then gathered up his grooming tools and walked into the tack room. Implements of iron and leather and hemp hung on the walls, telling him it was time to go home. He put away his brushes and combs, his rags and hoof picks, and walked out under the late sun.

The man and the boy were coming in from the fields, their horses' hooves crunching on the road. They were his distant cousins, Goslings, whose family had taken Ava in. The two of them were brothers. They stopped. The older one had lost three fingers with Clinch's cavalry at the Altamaha River in 1862. He spat off the far side of the horse from Callum, then leaned cross-armed on the pommel, the reins looped in one hand.

"Y'all eating up at the big house tonight?"

"Nuh-uh," said Callum. "Ava said one of those traps she made got a rabbit. Said she's making a stew."

The man eyed the faint rope scar at Callum's neck, like he usually did.

"Well," he said, "you know y'all are welcome to. Any night. You don't got to stay out in that nigger cabin ever night."

"I know," said Callum, "thank you."

The younger one's face was open as he looked at Callum, like he was looking at a ghost. He was twelve. The brothers nodded a last time and rode on toward the stables, dismounting to lead their horses into the stalls. Callum walked on down the road, too light of foot to break the bleached shells. They simply murmured beneath him, gossiping perhaps about this new stable groom. A ways down he took the footpath that ran along the creek. He stopped, as he always did, at the little bluff where the stone monuments loomed under the shadow of the oaks. Closest to the creek was the wooden cross Ava had fashioned herself of creosoted rail ties. Where one day, thought Callum, there would be a stone. He promised the tiny one in the ground, like he always did, that he would take good care of its mother. He told it there would be better times, surely, to come into the world. He made the sign of the cross, quickly, like a secret beneath the trees. It was the only time he would.

He moved on, following the path along the creek. The newspaper said Sherman had rent a wound across this state that would never heal. It said the people of Georgia were living on roots and game like the tribes of old. They were eating black-eyed peas, the stock feed Sherman's men had neglected to burn. Lee had surrendered the Army of Northern Virginia, and just five days later Lincoln had been shot by an actor from Maryland and killed. They said the world was coming apart.

The creek broke from the trees into the little clearing of slave cabins. Most of them were empty now, their residents fled north. The old negress with the streak of white in her hair sat on her porch, in from the field. She nodded to him. Hanging behind her, from a nail on the wall, was her son's hatchet, the one Callum had returned to her. He walked on, toward the cabin at the end of the row. The world was twilit, the windows floating yellow in the tabby. He could see shadows moving beyond the panes, wheeling against the firebright walls.

Ava.

The doctor had come to check on her six weeks ago. He said her womb was hurt from the horseman's bullet. He wasn't sure she would be able to conceive again. But, he said, there was no harm in them trying. They might, with work, overcome. That night, entwined under the covers, Ava had told him she wanted them to work at it. To work and to work and to work. Every day, as long as it took, and then some.

Callum stepped up onto the little porch, his heart drumming strong, and opened the door.

Acknowledgments

I'd like to thank my parents, first and foremost. You've always stood behind me, no matter how hard the path I took. You trusted I could walk it. They don't make words for how grateful I am.

I'd like to thank my agent, Christopher Rhodes, for loving this book so much. You have my eternal gratitude, buddy.

I'd like to thank Jesse Steele, whose thoughts, insights, and support were invaluable in the shaping of this book.

I'd like to thank Jason Frye for his editing prowess—look him up, you writers—and Wiley Cash for his generosity, and I'd like to thank everyone who's made Wilmington feel like home.

I'd like to thank my friend Blaine Capone, who taught me about horses. Here's to many more rides to come.

I'd like to thank Kevin Watson and Christine Norris of Press 53 for believing in my work early on, and Kevin for so much guidance and advice with my first book and beyond.

I'd like to thank Kristen. We had our own hard times in those mountains, but you always believed. I said I wouldn't forget that, and I haven't. And to a big brown bird dog named Waylon, who watched me write so much of this, who brought so much joy—thank you, buddy.

Last, I'd like to thank my editor at St. Martin's, George Witte, for making this book a reality, and Sara Thwaite for guiding me through the process. I hope to do you proud.

Reading Group Gold

FALLEN LAND

by Taylor Brown

About the Author

- A Conversation with Taylor Brown

Behind the Novel

- "From the Mountains to the Sea": An Original Essay by the Author

Keep on Reading

- Recommended Reading
- Reading Group Questions

Also available as an audiobook
from Macmillan Audio

For more reading group suggestions
visit www.readinggroupgold.com.

St. Martin's Griffin

A Conversation with Taylor Brown

Could you tell us a little bit about your background, and when you decided that you wanted to lead a literary life?

I was always making up stories as a child. My mother jokes that she sometimes had to lock herself in the bathroom just to get away from my incessant tale-telling, wherein I explained such profundities as why my toy triceratops sported rocket launchers or the reason why my GI Joes had tiny holes in their heels. (My parents are incredible and sometimes still field calls in which I go rambling down such storytelling paths.)

"All writers start as readers."

Then came school. I don't know what anybody else did in first grade, but in Mrs. Pruitt's class at St. Simons Elementary School, we wrote and illustrated a story every single day—at least that's how I remember it. I wrote a story about a spider who steals an RC car on Christmas morning, and it won a county contest, and I think that planted the seed.

What's more, I was born with a severe case of bilateral club feet, which has necessitated an array of reconstructive surgeries starting at a very young age and going all the way through high school. So I spent whole summers on the couch, recovering, and there wasn't much to do but read, read, read. I think that taught me the world of the mind at an early age, and a lot about pain and being alone, and of course all writers start as readers. So I'm grateful for those surgeries—they helped to form me as a writer.

Can you take a moment to tell us about your process. What challenges did you face, if at all? What does it feel like to hold a book that you've authored in your own two hands?

Oh, gosh—I think becoming (and being) a writer is a string of constant challenges. It would take a whole book to tell the story of getting to this point. *Fallen Land* was actually the third novel I wrote, and I spent years and years revising it.

I wrote in the margins of life while working at high-stress jobs. I wrote on nights and weekends and still do. I started and run a business. I got married and divorced and went through endless cycles of hope and doubt. I dealt with years and years of rejection. I lost friends and lovers and nearly my sanity a few times. But I kept going.

Persistence—I think that's the deciding factor. What did Calvin Coolidge say? *Persistence and determination alone are omnipotent.* I'm cautious to avoid melodrama when it comes to speaking of writing, especially as it relates to my own life, but it has been a hard road. Still is. You get knocked down again and again and again. I think you have to like the taste of blood in your mouth.

To hold a book I've authored in my own hands, it helps balance all of that pain and labor. But, in the end, I do this because I *have* to do it and I *love* to do it—and I'm very, very blessed to have a calling that is both of those things to me.

What was the inspiration for this novel?

The story was originally inspired by an old ballad, "When First Unto This Country," the first lines of which are found in Irish ballads nearly two centuries old! They are: "When first unto this country / A stranger I came."

The haunting, high lonesomeness of the song became my guiding force. At the time, I was living in Asheville, North Carolina, and I'd never lived a place where the leaves fired so brightly in the fall. It really affected me, the shortness of it, like the land was trying to tell me something, and so the season was very important to the book. This intersected with my interest in Sherman's March to the Sea—I'm from Georgia, after all—and my personal journey from a dark time in the mountains to a better time on the coast, and a book was born.

Did you do a lot of research for* Fallen Land*? And in so doing, what was the most interesting/surprising/shocking thing you learned?

The research was substantial. There were books on the Partisan Rangers of the Civil War and histories of Sherman's March, plus diaries and first-person accounts. There were nineteenth-century cavalry manuals and books on horses and horsemanship and firearms.

Some of the history was disturbing, for sure. The atrocity, the sheer savagery on both sides. But I find that's always the case when studying a war, no matter the setting or era. You find so much that's hard to wrap your mind around, to reconcile with what you want us, as a species, to be. That's the very nature of it, I guess.

What surprised me was how relevant, even contemporary, some of the history felt. When we think of the Civil War, we tend to think of these big, bilateral battles with gray and blue skirmish lines arrayed on the fields of Gettysburg or Chancellorsville. But here was the shadowy part of the war, with small units of irregulars operating much like modern-day commandos or special forces, engaging in ambush and sabotage, kidnapping and assassination—far from the big battlefields of the newspapers. Here were the fractured loyalties of the mountain communities, and people living under the oppression of outlaw gangs and night riders and guerrilla bands—common people stuck fatally between one side and the other.

Another thing that surprised me was the extent to which Sherman's March still impacts popular culture. For instance, many of us just ate black-eyed peas on New Year's Day for good luck. Well, some theorize that's because Sherman's army neglected to burn stores of black-eyed peas, regarding them only as stock feed, and the people of Georgia and South Carolina were able to subsist off of the unburned peas. That's how they became a good-luck tradition!

There was also the nonacademic, physical part of my research: learning horses. At the time, my good buddy

Blaine Capone (besotoro.com) was living on a land trust west of Asheville, in a very primitive manner: woodstove for heat, gravity-fed water, no cellular signal, and a road that was not always safe and open. He had two horses up there, and I would go up and help him chop wood or do other chores around the property, and he would teach me about horses. Some of the trails up there had only ever known boots and hooves, and it was a short leap to imagine the world of 150 years ago. I could never thank Blaine enough for what he taught me those days on the mountain.

Do you scrupulously adhere to historical fact in this novel, or did you take artistic liberties?

Fallen Land is by no means a history book, and I intentionally avoided the use of too many place-names and broader events because the characters themselves would be unaware of them. That said, I tried to capture the world as it was at the time, making the history an accurate substrate, leaving nuggets along the way for the knowledgeable reader. Many, if not most of the episodes in the Georgia section of the book are drawn from first-person accounts—Sherman's neckties, the lady with a goose on a leash, the former slaves living in abandoned boxcars, the pontoon bridge being cut away, and more.

Are you currently working on another book? And if so, what is it about?

My next novel is called *The River of Kings,* and it's set on the Altamaha River, also known as Georgia's "Little Amazon." The river, which I grew up paddling, is crossed by roads only five times in its 137-mile length, and the Nature Conservancy has named it one of the seventy-five "Last Great Places in the World." It's home to thousand-year-old virgin cypress, direct descendants of eighteenth-century Highland warriors, and a motley cast of rare and endangered species. It even has its own "river monster"—like a miniature version of Scotland's Nessie.

In the novel, brothers Hunter and Lawton Loggins set off to kayak the river, bearing their father's ashes toward the sea. Hunter is a college student, Lawson a Navy SEAL on leave; both young men were raised by an angry, enigmatic shrimper who loved the river, and whose death remains a mystery that his sons hope to resolve. As the brothers proceed downriver, their story is interwoven with that of Jacques Le Moyne, an artist who accompanied the 1564 expedition to found a French settlement at the river's mouth, which began as a search for riches and ended in a bloody confrontation with Spanish conquistadors and native tribes, leaving the fort in ruins and a few survivors fleeing for their lives.

Interested yet?

An Original Essay by the Author

Behind the Novel

"From the Mountains to the Sea" by Taylor Brown

Fallen Land is a journey from the mountains to the coast, and in many ways, *The River of Kings* picks up where *Fallen Land* leaves off. My fiction probably seems to exist far from my personal experience, as the characters and settings—often historical—bear scarce resemblance to my daily life. But I've realized—only recently, really—that there are some big, overarching, subconscious parallels. For instance, the journey from a hard time in the mountains to a better time on the coast closely parallels the narrative of my own life. I moved from the mountains of Asheville, North Carolina, to the coastal town of Wilmington during the writing of *Fallen Land,* and for some of the same reasons as my characters.

My ex and I moved to Asheville from San Francisco in 2009. We wanted to be closer to our families, closer to the landscape I write about, and we simply didn't feel at home in San Francisco. Neither of us had visited Asheville since we were kids, but we loaded up a trailer anyway with dog and motorcycle and IKEA furniture and took off for the other side of the country.

I think a lot about what Ron Rash says of landscape and geography: *I've always been fascinated with the idea of how the landscape that one grows up in affects his or her psychology or the perception of the world.* In discussions of *The Cove,* he talks about "landscape as destiny."

I remember driving up into the Blue Ridge Mountains around Asheville, hauling that trailer up the increasing grades, ears popping with altitude. It was summer, and there was this explosive green on every side, pushing itself into the road, and I thought, "Uh-oh." So did Kristen. I'm from the Georgia coast; she's from New Orleans. We were feeling the mountain landscape for really the first time, and we felt claustrophobic. I have friends from West Virginia and western North Carolina, and the mountains swaddle and comfort them. We felt closed in.

We moved into an old bungalow that had once been a "whorehouse"—so said the landlady. We thought she meant in the days of Thomas Wolfe, when such establishments were more commonplace. Not so. It was much more recent than that. I had nightmares about the place before we signed the lease, and I ignored them. All the drug deals in town seemed to go on in front of that house. I saw seven people arrested in the first two weeks—one person attacked with a length of drain pipe.

"My fiction probably seems to exist far from my personal experience."

There were mice in the house and ants and drafts and probably ghosts. There was a creepy basement that flooded when it rained, an even creepier attic with dark-stained carpet, and neighbors who hinted at poisoning our dog if he barked too much. We were accosted by bloody-faced men with "meth eyes," as we called them, and I kept a loaded 16-gauge just inside the front door. On good days, we sat in a blue plastic kiddie pool behind the chainlink and drank box wine while Waylon, our rescued bird-dog, patrolled for baby opossums and moles and a rumored groundhog.

I'd worked myself to the bone before the cross-country move and didn't know it. I had a very high-stress job at a business in San Francisco with a high turnover rate, and I'd been there for years, writing when I wasn't working. I quit that job to strike out on my own. Suddenly we had little money and fewer friends and fall came. I was twenty-seven years old. I was trying to write a novel and support a small family unit amid what felt like an unfriendly world. I was anxious, depressed, anxious again. It was a hard time.

A mouse ran across the floor during Thanksgiving dinner, and I thought my girlfriend's mother—a hard-barked member of old guard New Orleans—would split right down the middle. I'd brought her daughter *to this place?* Her boyfriend brought his Colt .45 to dinner. He'd heard about our neighborhood.

Still, the beauty of the place caught me in the throat. I'd never lived somewhere the leaves changed in the fall. It was beautiful—achingly so—and heartbreaking. Those leaves spoke so loudly to me of life—a bright flare before folding back into the earth.

My friend Blaine Capone—a painter and horse trainer—lived in a trailer on a land trust west of Asheville. His landlady was a Lakota-trained shaman. He had two horses up there—Greta and Badge—and I would go help him chop wood and he would teach me about horses. He and his girlfriend had no money. They had a five-gallon bucket of coconut oil—I saw them eat it with a spoon. The only heat was a woodstove. When the pipes froze, they melted snow for water. He was on the edge, too, but neither of us realized it. We weren't trying to prove anything. This is how life went.

My girlfriend and I found black mold in the bad house in Asheville—legal grounds for lease-breaking—and we moved into a smaller, unhaunted cottage in Black Mountain. The house was only seven hundred square feet, but it had a wraparound porch. The Russians on the corner were friendly and welcoming, what with their vodka and Ping-Pong table and giant German Shepherd, Zhivago. Our neighbors across the street were godsends. Tough mountain angels. Still, we worked and worked to make our way to the coast: Wilmington, North Carolina. Somehow, that seemed the answer to our problems.

In 2011, we moved. Of course, Wilmington was not the answer, but it was better. We got married—a golden week—then separated six months later. We'd been together seven years. I think we'd struggled so hard, so long, we hadn't really had time to wonder about our own relationship. Kristen and Waylon moved to Houston. I helped them load the U-Haul trailer, watched them drive away on a cold January morning in 2013.

I was alone in Wilmington. But I was on the coast now, and my parents and hometown buddies were within striking distance: five hours down I-95 into coastal Georgia. I was not home, but I was close. There were marshes, tidal creeks, wading birds. There were pelicans in their patterned flights and the white crash of waves. Here was a place that could be home.

I went down to Georgia. I went out on the Altamaha River with my buddies Whit and Ben. We motored around drinking beer and shooting at floating logs, and we talked about that strange shed we'd found on a paddling trip in college—the one with the tiny skulls dangling from fishing line and the gutted gar on the path in the woods.

Ah, here was another story. And on a river with its own mythology, complete with conquistadors and highlanders, sea monsters and Nazi submarines. A river crossed by roads only five times in its 137-mile length, harboring rare and endangered species of staggering variety. A river that had abetted the deforestation of the state, carrying timber rafts the size of basketball courts to the coastal sawmills. A river endangered itself by pulp mills and nuclear power plants. A river as beautiful and wild and savage as anything left on this earth.

Here was home, and it was calling me to write its story.

Recommended Reading

Southern Storm: Sherman's March to the Sea
by Noah Andre Trudeau

My Bible for the history of Sherman's March. Trudeau manages to capture the vast scope of the march as it fit into the greater narrative of the war, while also bringing the reader into intimate quarters with an array of individuals, from General Sherman himself to common infantryman, freed slaves, and landholders.

Sherman's March Through the South: With Sketches and Incidents of the Campaign
by Captain David Power Conyngham

This is an incredible bit of combat journalism, in which Conyngham—a New York reporter—was embedded with Sherman's army during their march through Georgia. The anecdotes he relates are alternately shocking and comic—I'm not sure any other book can bring you this close to the world of Georgia in the fall of 1864.

Woe to Live On
by Daniel Woodrell

My favorite Civil War novel, written by one of my favorite authors. The narrator, Jake Roedel, is a young German American who rides with a band of Confederate irregulars (bushwhackers), as they fight Union jayhawkers along the Kansas-Missouri border. Woodrell manages to balance the horrors of this guerrilla war with black comedy and memorable prose. The novel was made into the movie *Ride with the Devil,* directed by Ang Lee.

Partisan Life with Colonel John S. Mosby
by Major John Scott

Colonel John Singleton Mosby—also known as the "Gray Ghost"—is one of the best-known guerrilla commanders of the Civil War. Written by an officer from Mosby's band of Partisan Rangers, this book captures both the fearsome exploits and more mundane daily travails of life in "Mosby's Raiders."

Some Horses: Essays
by Thomas McGuane

Thomas McGuane is one of my favorite writers, and I'm not sure anyone captures the nature of the horse as well as he does. This collection of essays takes you deep into the mind and bones of the beast we love so much. I don't think I could have created Reiver without this book.

Red Cavalry
by Isaac Babel

I actually did not read this collection of stories until after I'd written *Fallen Land*. Isaac Babel—who has been called "the greatest prose writer of Russian Jewry"—was embedded with Budyonny's 1st Cavalry Army, consisting largely of (anti-Semitic) Cossacks, during the Polish-Soviet War of 1920. The great novelist Kent Wascom (*The Blood of Heaven, Secessia*) recommended this book to me. Babel's ability to capture man's brutality and grace in such close juxtaposition is simply staggering.

Reading Group Questions

1. What did you know about Sherman's March to the Sea before reading this novel? How, if at all, did *Fallen Land* inform you about, or change your impression of, this chapter in history?

2. To what extent do you think the author took artistic liberty with this work? What felt "real" to you—and what did not?

3. The main character, Callum, commits a string of violent acts throughout the novel. Do you find his actions justifiable? Are there any moments when you wish he'd acted differently?

4. The horse, Reiver, winds up becoming one of the main characters in the novel. He certainly has an interesting name. Why might the author have chosen to name him so?

5. Ava is a strong character in her own right—stronger than Callum in many ways. How do the couple's strengths balance one another? Do you think either could have survived alone?

6. The treatment of animals arises again and again in the novel. Do you find this distracting, or do you think the plight of animals is something we too often miss in stories of war?

7. Have you heard the song, "When First Unto This Country," which inspired the novel? Listen to a rendition of it on YouTube if you can. Can you hear the influence on the book? Do you think the writer captured the spirit of the song in the novel?

8. Did you think that Callum would die at the end of the novel? Would his death have changed your perspective of the book?

9. We are taught, as young readers, that every story has a "moral." Is there a moral to this novel? What can we learn about our world—and ourselves—from Callum and Ava's story?

10. Take a moment to talk about how you would describe *Fallen Land* to someone who hasn't yet read it. What adjectives would you use to detail your own reading experience? Would you recommend it—and to whom?

Turn the page for a sneak peek at Taylor Brown's next novel

THE RIVER OF KINGS

Available March 2017

Copyright © 2017 by Taylor Brown

1

Altamaha River, Day 1

The river, storm-swollen and heavy, gleams like a long dark muscle in the earth, a serpent sliding mindless through the yet-bare arcade of river birch and cypress that lines its banks. The two brothers stand motionless over the waters, silent, then haul their kayaks onto their shoulders, bearing them bloodred and blue down the old boat ramp, the concrete scarred beneath them like ancient stone. A pair of fractured gullies, parallel, mark the hard decades of boat trailers and trucks, and the traces shine wet and broken in the early light. The ramp runs like a dagger into the shallows, vanishing into the tea-dark current.

The brothers wear short-torso paddling vests, each with a silver dive knife affixed in an over-heart sheath. Their spray skirts hang from their waists like floppy tutus. They carry sufficient provisions for five nights on the river: canned beans and freeze-dried fruit, mixed nuts and combat rations and a flask of Kentucky bourbon. They carry eight gallons of fresh water stored in bottles and plastic bladders, along with sleeping bags and insect repellent and a tent they'll use only if it rains. On one of the boats, lashed aft of the cockpit, they carry five pounds of ash in a black nylon dry bag.

Their father.

Hunter, the younger, steps knee-deep into the current, and he can feel the weight of it pulling at his calves and ankles, the dark pull that is like an ambition. The spring rains charge down the dark swales of the Appalachian foothills, rumbling in wider and deeper confluence, birthing rivers that slither for the sea. Midway they tumble and crash over the Fall Line, the belt of shoals and waterfalls and hydroelectric dams that marks the lost edge of the continent, past which the state of Georgia was once the bottom of a prehistoric sea. The fossils of ancient corals and mollusks are found far up-country, and the land is full of sharks' teeth.

Hunter wears one on a string around his neck. It's the size of an arrowhead, with a jet-black root and blue-gray enamel, the edges slightly serrated. He found it digging for baitworms as a boy, several miles inland of the coast. It is from Megalodon, the fifty-ton shark of the Cenozoic era. He and his brother are putting in deep below the Fall Line, down in the ancient seabed of slash pine and cypress and gum, while above them roam heavy gray monsters of cloud.

Lawton sits erect in his boat, waiting.

"Boy, you planning to lollygag all day or what?"

Hunter looks down at him. His older brother has a bushy red beard, fire-hued, that he grew in-country. In some of his pictures, the other men have black ovals instead of faces, and the mountains and vehicles and buildings are of a color: sand.

"I'm coming," says Hunter. "Jesus, your horses run off?"

"I want to make the house before dark."

"So you said. You keep badgering me, you'll get an ass-whipping before we even get there."

Lawton, forty pounds heavier, grins. His eyes a vicious, merry blue.

"I'd like to see that."

"Keep it up, big boy, you'll have a front-row seat."

Hunter settles himself into the cockpit, checking the ashes are secure at his back. The eight-liter bag is waterproof, held down by crisscrosses of elastic deck rigging. He wanted to store the bag under one of the hatches for safekeeping, but Lawton wouldn't have it.

"The old man ought to see his last ride down the river, don't you think?"

Hunter hadn't said what he was thinking: the old man was long past seeing.

They push off, letting the river ease them out into its flow. The ramp retreats behind them, the pickups and trailers grown toylike, and the river stretches itself through the trees. They are outside the mill town of Jesup, Georgia, some fifty miles to the coast by crow flight, but their journey seaward will be twice that long, the river winding its way through the lowcountry before them, curling nearly back onto itself again and again, growing ever more brackish and tidal before it empties its mouth into the sea.

Half a mile downriver stands the old Doctortown Railroad Trestle, the iron trussworks red-rusting over pilings of wet stone. This is the Altamaha Bridge, where state militia armed with two cannon and a rail-mounted siege gun held off a brigade of Union cavalry—one of the only stumbles in Sherman's long march to the sea. Hunter squints, searching the woods for men on horseback, earthworks bristling with bayonets or gun barrels, purple plumes of gun smoke. The world alive from his history books. But the riverbanks are quiet, the ghosts asleep in the shade.

He looks to the bridge. Two boys who should be at school sit hunched on the edge of the tracks, bare feet dangling. They are watching wads of their spit swirl down into the current, comparing whose is fastest. One of them looks up, seeing the kayakers. He squints an eye, aiming, and shoots them the bird. Now he elbows his buddy, and soon they're both doing it, both-handed, grinning like fat-cheeked little devils.

Lawton's neck swells like a pony keg.

"Them little sons of bitches."

"Same as we would of done, that age."

Lawton isn't listening. He lays his paddle flat across his lap and gives them the bird in kind, pumping his arm up and down like a trucker on his air horn, his middle finger slightly bent from some old fistfight or doorjamb or car hood. On the belly of his forearm, there is a tattoo the size of a postage stamp, the tiny skeleton of a frog.

"Boy, get you some of *that*!" He slaps his arm for emphasis. "Get you some!"

"Bad idea."

They have to paddle hard for the cover of the bridge, passing through a hail of spittle and curse. They slide white-flecked into the shadowed hollows of the span, the pilings graffitied like cave art on either side of them. Above them the thump of bare feet, the enemy repositioning for a second barrage. Lawton lifts a hand from his paddle, two sharp chops.

"Spread out. Don't let them concentrate their fire."

His face bristles with flame. He shows his teeth to the coming light.

2

New France, June 1564

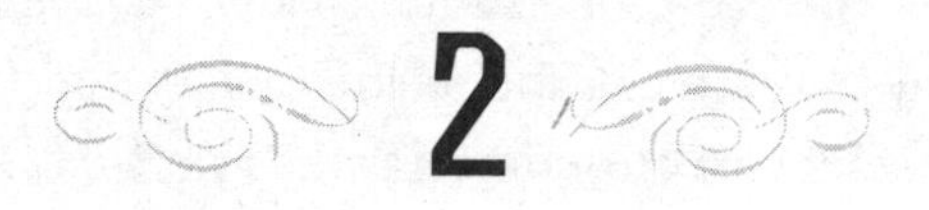

Jacques Le Moyne stands on the quarterdeck of the three-hundred-ton man-of-war, the *Ysabeau,* the hull timbers groaning beneath his boots. A pair of brigantines trail in the flagship's wake, their towering mainsails challenging the tall trees that line the riverbanks like sentinels of this new world. Le Moyne has his sketchbook out to capture them—*les cyprès*—before darkness falls. They are as tall as the top-masts, soaring giants with green ledges of leaves, their branches trailing gray mosses that sway in the wind like the long beards of indigents. Some stand from cutbanks white as sugar, the gray skeletons of their roots clutched for purchase, their lowest reaches blacked with tide.

He draws them.

They sailed from Le Havre on April 22, a three-ship fleet with three hundred colonists, Huguenots, mainly, soldiers and sailors and noblemen in flight from Catholic swords. A few musicians, with pipes and ditties to entertain the garrison, and one artist: he, Jacques Le Moyne de Morgue, commissioned by the King of France to map the coastline, the rivers and bays, and to catalogue the beasts and foliage that reveal themselves in this new land. The Spanish call the territory La Florida, but Le Moyne's king would have it La Nouvelle-France.

New France.

The expedition's leader, René de Laudonnière, stands near the helm. His hands are clasped behind his back, his chest swelled full. He was second-in-command during the disastrous expedition of 1562, which established the outpost of Charlesfort on one of the coastal islands to the north. Latrines were dug, walls raised, a twenty-five-man garrison left while the ships returned to France for supplies.

Only after accepting his commission did Le Moyne learn the fate of that settlement. Resupply was delayed, the men of the garrison soon starving and diseased. There was mutiny, the ranking officer murdered, and some of the men fled into the wilds to live like beasts among *les hommes sauvages*. Still others, desperate to escape, constructed a ship of their own, caulked with pine pitch and rigged with sails of stitched bedclothes, an open vessel in which they attempted to cross the ocean. They were picked up off the English coast, half-dead and sun-blistered like the victims of some new plague. A ship of lepers, they looked, cast out to sea. They had eaten their meager store of corn, their shoes and belts and own dry-burned skin. In the end they had subsisted on the blood and flesh of their own brothers, men sacrificed so that the rest might live. They had not simply eaten their dead. They had killed them first, by vote and dagger.

These stories, whispered after dark as the sea-wind skirled in the sails, became commonplace on the voyage across, the tellers bright-eyed with power, with the dread and fear they instilled. Le Moyne, try as he might, could not help but listen. He had been trained from an early age as a painter of flowers and fruits, tubers and leafy plants, the stuff of tamed gardens and somnolent drawing rooms. Now he was sailing to a land far over the edge of the earth, a savage Eden, to hear it told, where one could be eaten as easily by man as by beast.

There were the Carib Indians of the islands, rumored to have the heads of wild dogs, who butchered and ate the flesh of their own kind, and men of northern kingdoms with long wings and vests of golden fur. There were stories of headless tribes whose faces were embedded in their breasts, like some outward growth of the heart, and giantesses said to pleasure themselves with the stiffened bodies of the men they killed.

Some of these wonders had been rendered in ink or lead and distributed throughout the cities of Europe, though none by an artist who drew on more than hearsay. Le Moyne would be the first. During the long sea-nights of storytelling, when his heart raced like a rabbit in his chest, he recalled that he was chosen for this task, by God and by king. Over the long voyage, his hand itched for something to draw besides the men hauling at halyards and wielding marlinspikes, clinging spiderlike to ratlines as the ship rocked them through the endless troughs. He wanted only to begin.

In early June, there were cries and hurrahs from the men, the thunder of boots across the deck. Le Moyne scampered topside in time to see the whistling cloud of swallows that heralded land. La Florida hove into view. The coast was unlike any Le Moyne had seen. The sea penetrated the land in a maze of thrusting arms, inlets and sounds and rivers and creeks that shattered the coast into a multitude of sea islands, every spit of high ground protected by waving swords of marsh reeds. They sailed into a wide river furrowed by the gleaming backs of dolphins, and Le Moyne bent over the capstan with paper and stylus, trying to trace the coast as they'd taught him in the cartography school at Dieppe. He looked up to find figures swarming the riverbank like ants, the white blade of beach soon blacked with bonfires.

Laudonnière assembled a landing party. He looked at Le Moyne.

"You, Le Roux."

"Le Moyne, monsieur."

"Le Moyne. Can you handle a gun?"

Le Moyne could only nod. His uncle had insisted he learn firearms before going abroad.

They waded ashore to greet the natives, the iron barrels of their arquebuses arrayed like organ pipes, their swords banging against their legs. The surf exploding against their knees. The natives waited on the beach with round eyes, white as bone, and Le Moyne could smell them as he neared: an animal musk, smoky and wild. They surrounded the white men in twitching rings, their limbs long and powerful, their skin queered with inks and mazelike designs. They had long fingernails, sharpened into claws, their ears yoked with inflated fish bladders. Their eyes darted about, quick as baitfish. Like children they reached out, shyly, their brown fingers seeking the godlike torsos of the landing party's armor, the long black beards that pointed their chins.

All the time they chattered in their strange tongue, the words skittering too fleet to catch. Le Moyne could decipher only one word, said again and again like a chant: *Saturiwa*. Now there were more of the savages, a brown sea of flesh on the beach, and suddenly they parted. A chieftain strode forth through the throng. He was dark as stained wood, his body knotted, swelled with oaklike burls.

"Saturiwa," they said. "Saturiwa."

In the man's hand lay an ingot of silver, like a brick cut from the moon.

Le Moyne watched the eyes of his countrymen widen, spark.

The native bowed and presented the offering to Laudonnière—the French chief—and Laudonnière bowed in turn, drawing the ingot against his chest. The chieftain beckoned them: *Follow me into the woods.* His warriors mimicked the gesture.

This way, they gestured. *This way.*

Wary, the landing party followed the chieftain into a wood of sandy pine, the flesh of his warriors swimming through the trees on every side, shadowing them. Before long the pines broke onto a small clearing, and there Le Moyne saw the first scene he would record of this new land: a six-sided pillar of stone thrust white from the earth, one facet carved with the fleur-de-lis, the royal arms of France. The head of the stone was crowned in wreathes and flowers. At its foot lay baskets of fruit and roots, yellow gourds and discs of gleaming oil, quivers of arrows and scarred war clubs. Offerings, they looked, to some savage god. Natives lay crumpled before the idol, gape-mouthed, like grievers under the cross. This was the marker erected by the ill-fated expedition of 1562, pronouncing dominion over the land.

La Nouvelle-France.

The chieftain stood before the French. His black hair was knotted high atop his head, like the limbs of a trussed fowl, and from this topknot sprang a pair of banded tails that arched each to a side, bouncing on his shoulders. He was nearly naked, his manhood curled against a flap of animal skin that covered his loins. His nose and forehead were of a plane, flat as a ram's. He kept waving at the column with his claws, chattering in his unknown tongue. Laudonnière looked to their interpreter, one of the officers from the Charlesfort catastrophe.

"What does he say?"

"He says we are his brothers. His friends." The interpreter licked his lips. "He says you are brother to Soleil, the sun-god, sent to defeat his enemies."

Le Moyne nearly gasped—such idolatry. But Laudonnière stood unfazed, cradling the ingot of silver closer against his heart. He nodded, as if speaking the pillar's meaning.

"*Camarades. Frères.* Yes, tell him that."

They have come north since then, looking for a river deep enough to accommodate their fleet. Today it seems they have found it, sailing upstream into this unknown land. Le Moyne squints through the failing light. The sun is down, the river like polished black marble. It is the hour between the dog and the wolf, when the world grows smoky with night falling, when you cannot tell whether the beast from the woods is friend to you or enemy. Le Moyne sighs and closes his notebook on the tower of cypress he's been sketching. Beneath it, just visible, the ghostly outline of pillar and chief.

A cry goes up from the bow, now others, and men race toward the foredeck. Le Moyne dashes among them, elbowing his way to the rail. He looks past the bowsprit, seeing the reason for their cries, and the stick of charcoal slips from his hand, crushed underfoot as he staggers back from the rail.

"Serpent de mer!" cry the men.

"Monstre!"

It is thrice-humped from the water, this monster, its spine armored like the giant lizards that sun themselves on the riverbanks. But it makes newt of such creatures, a serpent the size of a cypress tree mounding its way through the water, a string of stony dark islands. For long seconds the creature swims upriver before their bow, as if leading them, only to slide beneath the surface, swallowed in black glass.

Le Moyne can hardly breathe, his heart sounding wildly against his ribs. He has been tasked on this journey to fill the white spaces on the map, the places that warn of dragons, and now it seems he must fill those oceans of white with blacker terrors still.